Stay, Girl

ANGELICA R. JACKSON

CROW & PITCHER PRESS, SHINGLE SPRINGS, CALIFORNIA

Crow & Pitcher Press
P.O. Box 1294
Shingle Springs, CA 95682
https://crowandpitcherpress.com

Publisher's Note: This is a work of fiction. Names, characters, places, and incidents are a product of the author's imagination. Locales and public names are sometimes used for atmospheric purposes. Any resemblance to actual people, living or dead, or to businesses, companies, events, institutions, or locales is completely coincidental.

Book Layout © 2017 BookDesignTemplates.com

Stay, Girl/ Angelica R. Jackson. -- 1st ed.
ISBN Paperback: 979-8-9862721-3-9
Ebook: 979-8-9862721-4-6

To all the dogs I've loved before

No dogs die in this book.

–ANGELICA R. JACKSON

Chapter One

May 1953
Sacramento

I lowered my binoculars and rubbed my eyes before stifling a yawn. Watching from above the card tables always gave me a headache, but thankfully my shift would end soon. This tiny booth, high on a wall behind one-way glass, was my refuge from the club's chaos. Even the other employees didn't bother me here. They all knew distracting me could cost my stepfather money, and he'd take it out of their paychecks—if not their hides.

The door opened behind me, letting in light from the hallway, and I hissed at Bruno to hurry and come in. He quickly shut the door, and the observation room dimmed once again; if it was brighter in here than the room below, anyone looking could see straight in. Smart money would bet that there was someone always watching the players—and staff—in any club, but no one had to know it was me.

"Anything to report?" Bruno asked, reaching for my radio. Hank Williams's voice cut off with a crackle and pop.

"Hey," I protested, "I was listening to that."

He grinned. "And now you're not. It's my shift and I work in silence. Aren't you supposed to be heading home?"

I nodded and stood up to stretch, stopping myself when I felt the fabric under my arms threaten to split. This old dress was on its last threads, but the frills and ribbons still did their job of making me look young and harmless. None of the card players gave me a second look when I roamed among the tables, not guessing that I was my stepfather's secret weapon. It fooled some of them enough that they asked why I wasn't in school or outside running with other kids. I felt bad for the guys who worried about me, instead of themselves and the trouble they could get into at the card tables.

I realized I hadn't answered Bruno's question yet, so I picked up my logbook and read aloud. "Some card counting earlier, and a really clumsy attempt at trying to mark corners. I sent word to open new decks, and that took care of it. The guy in the pinstripes on table five is good, though—I barely spotted him dropping a card into his lap and pulling one from his sleeve. I was just about to call it in. Felix might even want to recruit him."

"I'll call down," Bruno said. "You get your stuff together and get out of here. I know you want to get home to your mother."

I yawned again and grabbed my logbook, ready to hit the locker room to change back into my regular clothes. Instead, I nearly ran into someone as I came out into the hallway.

The sharp scent of cologne and cigars hit me, and I instinctively reeled back from my stepfather.

"There she is," Felix said brightly. "Tony, this is my daughter. Bet, we're setting up an exhibition game for you at his club in San Francisco."

The man had already reached out to shake my hand, but his smile wobbled and then he frowned. "What is this, Felix? She's a little kid. You're out here peddling an infant? No way." His accent told me he'd spent more years in New Jersey than San Francisco.

Felix laughed, though it sounded phony and loud in the hallway. "She's older than she looks. My wife always says she's thirteen going on thirty! But seriously, this girl is talented. Dress her up a little, put her in some makeup, and the poor saps will never know how old she is. Everybody bets against her, and then it's a big payout for us."

Tony was shaking his head before Felix even finished. "Look, Felix, even I have a line I won't cross. Call me up when I don't have to worry if she's working on a school night."

Felix called after Tony as he walked away, cajoling, but the other man waved him off. My stepfather's smile dropped as he glared at me. "Why are you still wearing that dress, instead of the new one I had made for you? I'm trying to get your career started, and you're defying me at every turn."

Never mind that I hadn't said a defiant word to Tony or Felix, my stepfather would be punishing me later for ruining his plans. I didn't bother defending myself and said simply, "I was on my way out. Mama is expecting me."

He sneered, but he let me pass. "You go straight home. No stops."

"I know," I answered wearily. Where would I go anyway? He made sure I didn't have friends who I could blab his business to.

In the women's locker room, the cocktail waitresses and cigarette girls were also changing shifts. They jockeyed for space as they each tried to put on, or take off, their makeup and outfits. Their dresses—uniforms—showed off generous cleavage and long stretches of leg under the short skirts.

My stepfather had ordered a uniform in my size, with added ruffles to look like I had curves and budding cleavage. My new dress still hung in my locker and swayed as I pulled open the door. I pushed it aside and reached for the pedal pushers and blouse I'd arrived in earlier that day. As I changed, one of the newer girls, Trudy, came to sit by me on the bench.

"That blouse is so cute on you," she gushed. "Makes you look so much more grownup. Why do you wear that dress at work? It looks like you're going to your Confirmation."

"That's why I wear it. It means fewer bruises on my rear after I've been working on the floor."

She laughed and then launched into the real reason she'd come over.

"Are you having supper with your daddy tonight?" Trudy asked sweetly. "I'd love to come along if you are. Wouldn't that be fun, just us two friends and the boss?"

I didn't have friends at the club, mainly because Trudy wasn't the first girl who had tried to get on the boss's good side through me. If I tried to act like a real friend and warn them off Felix, they just thought I was jealous and found some other way to get his attention. If they succeeded, they hid the black eyes and bruises under makeup and pretended it was all worth the presents he threw their way.

"I said, wouldn't that be fun?" Trudy slung an arm around my shoulders and gave me a squeeze.

I suddenly felt older than her nineteen years and envied how bright and hopeful she seemed. I'd grown too cautious of making mistakes, and too tired from juggling all my responsibilities. Thank goodness school had just ended for the year, so now I only had to split my time between the club and Mama.

"Sorry, I'm eating at home with my mother tonight," I said. "Why don't you see what Jerome is doing? I think he's sweet on you, and he's a good man."

She frowned. "Jerome, the bouncer? Sure, he's good looking, but I can do better."

I shrugged; if the reminder that Felix had a wife hadn't put Trudy off him, none of my warnings or matchmaking would either. I nodded when she said, "maybe another time" and left me alone. I finished getting dressed and headed to the kitchen.

"Did the pinstripes on table five order anything?" I asked a passing waiter.

He checked the tickets and said, "Yeah, a steak dinner, with baked potato. Why? Is he not going to need it?"

"Yeah, I caught him cheating, but Felix might want to see him before they chuck him out. Either way, he won't be eating that steak, so you can pack it up for me. But can I get mashed potatoes instead of baked?"

"Of course, anything for the boss's daughter," he said with a wink.

"Actually, it's better if Felix doesn't know I'm taking food home," I confided. "I'll owe you a favor if you keep this between us."

He didn't ask any questions, just handed me the foil-wrapped dinner and got back to work. But I knew he'd call in that favor someday, if he worked here long enough.

Stepping out the back door of the club and into the heat of the alley was a shock. I rushed through the gloomy stink to the sunlight on the street. The poker club always felt like midnight inside, no matter what time of day it was, and the bustling daylight crowds swept me up. I turned down J Street, walking until I could hop the bus to take me near Broadway. Then I still had to walk a few blocks to our house, and I entered through the alley gate since we only had the bottom floor of the old Victorian.

Felix wasn't there to scold me for acting common, so I hollered, "Mama, I'm home," as I came through the back door and into the kitchen. There was no answer, but she was probably still sleeping. I hummed as I plated up my steak and vegetables, and spooned the mashed potatoes into a bowl. Then I added a scarlet nasturtium flower I'd picked on the way home to brighten up the white goo.

I carried it all to Mama's room on a tray, and she stirred a little in bed as I sat in the bedside chair and chattered about my day. I left space for her to chime in, but she didn't, of course. Even though I always tried to be cheerful for her, sometimes it was hard to maintain in the face of her dying. My voice petered out, and I swallowed a bite of steak around a lump in my throat. Only the sound of her hands rustling against the sheets broke the silence.

When the doctor had told us she was dying a few months ago, I was so caught up in the thought of losing her, I didn't think about how hard it was going to be watching her lose herself. And how long it might take.

Hollywood films had fooled me into thinking these final moments would be a peaceful time: Mama looking pale but hauntingly beautiful, drifting into a gentle passing as I held her hand. A tranquil choir in the background singing her on her way. Instead, Mama's rosy cheeks gave way to a yellow wasting, and now her hands, brittle as butterfly wings, rarely settled long enough to hold on to. You'd think a body so worn out would have given up sooner.

For weeks, my mother had been floating in her bed, carried on a current of morphine provided by Felix. I could no longer tell if my stepfather was trying to keep Mama alive because he couldn't bear losing her, or if it was a punishment—to himself, to Mama, or even to me. But it was like she was cursed with an unending death, and I was caught in the curse too.

I finished eating, chewing without tasting anything, and stood to take my dishes into the kitchen. I left the congealing potatoes on Mama's bedside table, like an offering, and tidied the house as I listened to the radio. It was a few hours before I switched off the music, and I paused as I thought I heard a faint voice.

"Bet!" it called again. "My potatoes are cold. Bring me an egg sandwich, would you?"

I ran to Mama's room and my jaw dropped at the sight of her propped up in bed, poking her bowl of mashed potatoes with a suspicious spoon. She smiled at me and new, bleeding cracks opened on her lips.

"Where have you been, girl?" She asked. "Are you going to make me a sandwich?"

I hadn't moved from the doorway, afraid this was some kind of mirage. "I would, but there's no bread in the house. No eggs either. We might have mayo, but nothing to put it on."

She nodded. "Ah, he's up to his old tricks again, is he? What'd you do to rile him up this time?"

And then I knew this was real. If this had been some fantasy of mine, some miraculous event, Mama would never have taken Felix's side. But in reality, she blamed me for his mistreatment. Just like he did.

"Don't look at me like that," she said. "Come sit next to me and tell me about your day."

I didn't know how long this clarity would last, so I did as she asked. She laughed when I hammed it up and made all the boring parts of my workday sound funny, but she shook her head when I told her about Tony.

"You've been training for things like an exhibition game your whole life. That was a missed opportunity, Bet. Your father is only looking out for you."

She'd said things like this before, too, and I couldn't help shooting back my usual response. "Felix is not my father. He's the Devil."

Mama waved away my protest. "The Devil you know is always better odds. You just gotta learn to play him."

My lips thinned at her glib answer, but then I thought about how just an hour ago I would have given anything to have a conversation with her again. I had no way of knowing whether this was the "terminal lucidity" the doctor had mentioned could happen in the hours or days before death, but I didn't want our last words to be bitter.

"Yes, Mama." I took her hand.

But her eyes narrowed. "You can't fool me. I taught you that poker face, child. I know you're thinking of leaving your father, but twelve is too young to be on your own."

"I'm thirteen now, Mama."

Her brow knitted before she squeezed my hand. "Never mind that. This is important. Have I ever told you I have a brother?"

She had told me about him during other clear-headed moments. But I shook my head, so she'd keep talking.

"Promise me that if you leave your daddy like you're planning, you'll go to your uncle Earl's. He's up in Amber-fields, last I heard. You should tell him in person I've cashed in my chips. Stay with him. Promise, now."

I linked our pinkies and said, "I promise I'll go to Uncle Earl's."

My words seemed to lift some weight from her, and she sagged back into her mattress. I sang a few lines of "Keep on the Sunny Side" to distract her from noticing I hadn't promised to *stay* at her brother's. She drifted back to sleep and looking at her now, I would never have known she'd been able to sit up and talk, however briefly. My sniffles brought her awake again, and she looked at me with some tenderness.

"Have I done right by you, little Lizabet?" she rasped. "I've tried so hard to make you into a strong woman, so you'd have an easier time in the world than I did. I should have remembered you need to be a girl first."

A flash of anger rolled over me, and I wanted to blurt, "*Now* you think of that? When it's maybe too late?"

But Mama's breathing was interrupted by a rattling noise, and then it *was* like in a Hollywood movie. Her face turned away and her fluttering hands stilled on the sheets. I called her, but she was gone. I sat with her empty shell until the sun went down, crying so much that I was empty, too.

Chapter Two

I made the call to the poker club, leaving a message for Felix with the news. He didn't come home himself, but after a while, a pair of his flunkies came to collect the body. My mute self at the bedside, sitting in the dim wash of moonlight through the window, gave them a start. They took off their hats and stood for a few moments with us. But when I stayed silent, they switched on the light and bundled my mother's slight form into the sheets.

One man returned and pressed some coins into my hand. "For flowers," he whispered. "A girl shouldn't have to bury her mother so young."

Whether or not it should have happened, a few days later I found myself wearing a borrowed dress at Mama's graveside as a barely sober Reverend Green said a few words. It was hot and sunny for May and a rivulet of sweat ran down my back, making me want to squirm. Felix kept me close to his side, but it felt more like he was staking a claim than offering comfort. I knew better than to cause a scene in front of his cronies, so I kept my eyes on the marble stone engraved with "Lizabet Carter—Beloved Wife of Felix." No mention of her daughter, beloved or otherwise.

I stayed after everyone else wandered away from the fresh mound of earth. Pulling a nail from a nearby picket fence, I scratched out "Wife of Felix" and wrote "Mother" above it. On my way home, I peered into the windows of the corner bar to make sure Felix was already deep in a glass of whiskey. His friends would keep him in drinks all night, in honor of the departed, if I was lucky.

Hurrying now, I flew home to change out of the horrible black dress and to fetch a sack of belongings from my room. I left nearly all my clothes behind, so Felix would think I'd just holed up nearby to grieve, instead of actually running. Next, I climbed into the garage rafters to empty the old clay jug where Felix kept his emergency cash. I would be long gone before he realized I'd replaced the fold of bills with strips of newspaper and a five-dollar bill facing out.

While Felix was still drinking around the corner, I made my escape. My reason to stay in Sacramento had departed with Mama's soul. Now I fled too, with a bag slung over my shoulder and dust puffing under my worn shoes. I followed the railroad tracks north, staying out of sight of other people as much as possible.

Hopefully, if anyone looked for me (and only one person might), no witnesses could point him in the right direction. I didn't want to risk someone remembering me in a store or diner, so I ate only a handful of nuts somebody had set out in their yard for the squirrels. Then I washed them down with a gulp of water from a garden hose left stretched under some rosebushes. My bed that night was in a sycamore tree, with my knees braced in a crotch of branches to keep from tumbling onto the summer-dry thistles below.

After over a day of traveling, I heaved a grateful sigh to see "Amberfields, pop 581" on a sign at the town's border. The farmland, with neat rows of green crops or fruit trees, gave way to houses and businesses. Waves of heat rose from the asphalt and concrete, and a sprinkler on someone's lawn called to me. But the sooner I got to my destination, the sooner I could leave again.

Just in case she would let it slip to Felix, I'd never told Mama I had a plan already. I wasn't just running from my stepfather, I was running to someone. After I'd done my duty at Uncle Earl's, I would be joining my friend Nina at a lumber camp in Oregon. Nina had left months ago and begged me to come along then, since Nina's Aunt Kaja needed two girls to help her cook for the men. At sixteen, Nina would be "cookie" and assist her aunt, and I would be the "chore boy" while I learned to do more.

But the weeks-old letter now crumpled in my pocket had delivered the bad news from Nina: Aunt Kaja couldn't wait any longer and had hired someone else. Nina had tried to delay it as long as possible, since surely my mother couldn't last long in her state, but they'd needed help to keep the big camp running smoothly. She'd told me to come anyway when I could, and I agreed it was worth trying. Even if I just worked for meals, it would be better than the future Felix had in mind for me.

My feet were dragging by the time I turned down the driveway to Uncle Earl's place. It seemed like the midday heat had stifled even the sounds from the air, until a staccato of hoarse barks made me hesitate. I'd always liked dogs, but hadn't spent much time around them. Some dogs took their job of guarding too seriously. Was this one going to come after me? When the barking didn't come any closer, I traced the sound to a makeshift pen in the shabby stable beside the house. In the dim recesses, it was hard to see much more than a pair of hanging ears and sad eyes. The smell was easier to sort out: sickness and neglect, so much like Mama's last days that I fell back a few steps.

I nearly tripped over a pail, its depths as dry and dusty as the yard itself, lying outside the wire fence where the dog would never reach it. A pump handle beckoned in the shade of a shivering cottonwood tree; I doused my head in cold water first and gasped as the welcome shock cleared some of the hunger-fog. The nearby house lay undisturbed, even with the barking and the sound of the creaking water pump, so Uncle Earl must be away.

His dog raised its head when I deposited the half-full pail over the side of the pen, but it didn't get up until I put some distance between myself and the offering. I nodded to show I recognized the wisdom of not falling for wheedling words when grabbing hands were in reach, and it seemed it nodded back.

My narrowed eyes turned to my uncle's house, with its well-worn chair and spindle table on the porch, handy for taking a meal outside while his dog suffered just yards away. I was tempted to find a piece of rope and see if the dog would come with me; we could be gone before my uncle even knew I'd been by.

But too many things could go wrong with that plan: it could be too much for the dog, and then I'd have killed it, or Uncle Earl might send the law after me, or I would run through money faster feeding myself and a sick dog. Instead, I took a perch in an oak's prickly branches, ready to see how my uncle treated his dog when he thought no one was looking. The warm, dim space soon had me dozing, though.

When his dusty steps came up the long drive, the dog in the stables greeted him with a hoarse song of delight that woke me with a start. Two other hounds, sleek and dark as wet otters, bounded ahead to the porch and its shade. As he let the first dog out of its pen, Uncle Earl waved a bottle above his head.

"Whoa, Girl, I got your vitamins here. Don't you break this bottle, or Doc'll have to make up another one."

The skinny dog did her best to frisk around his feet all the way onto the porch and into his lap, proving his hands were not the ones she'd learned to fear. And maybe not hands for me to fear either—if such things were real in the world. If I was closer, maybe I could see if there was any of my mother in his face. Glimpsed through the oak leaves, he was just a tall man with dark hair and a big belly.

The dog laid her head in his lap and Uncle Earl crooned, "You'll be all healed in no time," as he dribbled dark liquid into the side of her mouth. He scratched the patchy fur on her body and head, raising a cloud of dead skin and hair. The stink wafted to where I hid and I struggled not to sneeze. I'd thought the other dogs were sound asleep, but as I shifted minutely on my branch, their heads came up. A low rumble started in their chests and throats, and Uncle Earl peered into the greenery.

They all startled as I dropped from the tree and announced, "I'm Liza's girl. Mama sent me."

"You were smaller last time I saw you." Uncle Earl studied me for a moment before waving a hand at his dogs to quiet them. "Is she finally going to leave him, then? And she sent you on ahead?"

I wanted to ask Uncle Earl when he'd seen me before, since I hadn't known he existed until Mama made me promise to tell him in person that she'd passed. Too bad she didn't tell me how I should deliver the news; he was waiting for an answer, and I didn't know what to say.

"She's gone," I blurted. "She's left this world." The raw edge of anger creeping into my words surprised me. Where did that come from, bleeding through the sadness I usually felt for Mama? Hadn't I only been mad at Felix before?

Bowing his head, Uncle Earl's voice thickened as he said, "I knew that man would kill her someday, but nobody could tell her different."

No sense in telling him it was the drink and drugs that got her in the end, since you couldn't really separate them from that devil, anyway. But I should have broken the news kinder—I should have kept in mind it was his sister who had died, and not just my mother.

Thinking he might be embarrassed by his tears falling, I took the conversation in another direction. "Why is your dog so sick? Those other two look fine."

He took a moment to collect himself before he answered, "She's only been with me a short while. A local man had too many dogs causing trouble, and the county went and took some. There was talk of putting this one down—they said she was too sick and too shy, but she got lucky and came to stay with us."

"Us?" Mama hadn't said that Uncle Earl had other family.

"Me and Nap and Josie here." The black dogs' tails thumped at their names.

Uncle Earl continued, "All these beagles were living on garbage and what they could hunt up, including the neighbor's chickens. This poor girl must have took one too many birds and ended up with a body full of shot. Then, getting chased with a net didn't help her opinion of people, I'm sure. They only caught her once she was too sick from an infection to get away."

The red-and-white dog must have known we were talking about her; she raised her head and turned those old-soul eyes to me and then Uncle Earl. Her gaze stayed fixed on his face as he scratched the whiskery beard on her chin. The contented sigh she gave made Nap nudge Uncle Earl's shoulder for attention.

I collapsed on a lower step and petted Josie when she scooched over. When I riffled her fur the wrong way, brindle stripes showed among the dark coat, and Josie shook off my hand. My eyes were on the smaller hound as I asked, "Are you keeping her? That man isn't going to try to get her back, is he?"

"We'll have to see whether the charges against him stick. Officially, I'm nursing her back to health while the county decides what to do with all the dogs. Doc Marsh—he's the vet in town—he knows I'm good with animals, so he vouched for me. He helped me with these two sorry cases after I found them floating down the creek in a burlap sack. Just unwanted pups with their cords still shriveling on their bellies."

I looked at Josie, plump and warm under my hand; mischief danced in the dog's eyes, with no sign of leftover worry from her rough start. Maybe Uncle Earl could do the same for the sick dog.

"Does she have a name? The new one?" I asked.

"You don't want to know what Mr. Bindle called her. I've been calling her Girl. You have something in mind?"

"Penny," I said. "Her name is Penny."

Uncle Earl stood and brushed off his pants, like it was settled. "Penny's a good name for a copper-colored hound. And what do you want me to call you?"

"I'm Bet."

"Of course you are. Named for your mama, Lizabet." He shook his head ruefully. "She kept the Liza and gave you the Bet part."

That wasn't Felix's version of how I had got my name—he always joked her daughter was the worst bet Liza ever made. She would have been better off making a Buck, or even a Bill, than a girl who talked back so much. Momentarily feeling lost in the tangled-stomach feeling that memory gave me, I started when Uncle Earl cleared his throat.

"Well, if you're staying, we'd best set you up a bed. And feed you."

I hadn't said anything about staying, but at the prospect of a meal, Nap, Josie, Penny, and I dogged his heels into the house.

Chapter Three

I assumed Uncle Earl would cook up a can of beans or something simple. That would have been fine with me—food was food, and I'd be grateful to eat anything. But after Uncle Earl pointed me to the table, he went over to the fridge and pulled out a paper sack and a bowl of eggs. A cool breeze wafted over me, and I scooted closer to the appliance.

Uncle Earl shot me a grin over his shoulder. "Feels good, doesn't it? Nap would lie with his head in it all day if I let him."

My growling stomach hoped the small talk wouldn't delay the food too much. Fortunately, Uncle Earl turned and deposited a plate in front of me. Two thick slices of bread held a slab of meatloaf, slathered with ketchup, and pickle chips hanging over the edge. I wasn't sure if I could open wide enough to eat it, but I was hungry enough to make it work. After chewing and swallowing two massive bites, I looked up and realized Uncle Earl was at the stove.

"You're not having a sandwich?"

Uncle Earl whisked some eggs in a bowl. The fat in the skillet sizzled as he poured them in before answering the question. "Nah, I don't always have time to eat at the diner if we get real busy, so sometimes I pack a sandwich for home. Was so tired last night after my shift that I didn't eat it. I would've had it before I go in today, but you eat up that sandwich and I'll cook these eggs for myself while I feed the dogs."

I asked around another mouthful, "You work at a diner? You the cook?"

"Yep, I learned cooking in the Navy. I made that meatloaf myself."

"It's good. Are you sure you don't want the other half back?"

He laughed and slapped his bulging belly. "Does it look like I'm starving, girl? You definitely need it more than me. Besides, my eggs are done now."

He scraped them onto a plate and pulled some old pie tins off a shelf. From another paper bag in the fridge, he pulled out a few takeout boxes and scraped the congealed contents into the tins. A cascade of mashed potatoes, bread chunks, bites of meatloaf, chicken skin, and other things I didn't quite catch. It looked like all the leftover food from a dozen plates, and since Uncle Earl worked in a diner, I guessed that's exactly what it was. A thick meatloaf sandwich was much better.

Nap and Josie dug right in, but Penny ate like the delicate lady she was. Her tongue swept up tiny bites to savor, with her eyes closed in bliss. The bigger dogs had already cleaned their tins and switched places to clean them again. Then they watched Penny's slow progress, with strings of drool oozing from their jowls. Nap's whining sounded like a balloon with a slow leak, and when Penny glanced his way, his tail went berserk. Josie tried to hold her dignity a little longer, but she also started whinging.

"Penny needs to hurry before the other two lose control," I said, worried they would fight.

"Nah, she puts them in their place when they get too pushy. You wanna know what Penny needs?" Uncle Earl asked. When I shrugged, he said, "She needs someone to take a special interest in her. Someone who has the time to sit with her until she knows she can trust them. Every time I have to leave her behind, I think the sorrow sets her two steps back."

He wasn't looking at me when he mentioned Penny needing attention, but I figured he meant me. Did he think I was a little kid who would fall for a sly word? Maybe he was trying to pawn an inconvenient dog off on me, but then again, he didn't have to take Penny in. He didn't have to give her medicine, or to bring her in the house even though she smelled awful.

"Why was she locked up in the pen before?" I asked, testing to see how he really felt about the dog. Was she somehow lesser in his eyes, compared to his own dogs?

He shot a rueful glance at Penny. "Because she tries to follow me when I go into town, and she shouldn't be walking like that. She's not strong enough yet. I don't have to pen her up when I'm home, but if I go somewhere—like to work, or to get her medicine—she's got to be locked up. Breaks my heart to do it, but it's better than her dropping dead for my sake."

I hadn't realized the dog was that sick, but then I only knew what sick people looked like. "So, if I stayed with her while you're at work, she wouldn't have to be locked up?"

"Hmm, she'd probably have to get to know you some first, but I expect she would stick by you then."

This time he winked at me, acknowledging he wasn't being so very sly with trying to get me to take on Penny as a special project. I looked again to where Penny lay digesting her meal, her eyes barely open and her itchy skin twitching.

I wasn't so confident I could save this dog—after all, I hadn't even been able to save my own mother. Or I wasn't enough to make Mama want to save herself, but it came to the same ending. The thing was, it had become obvious a long time ago that Mama was her own worst enemy, but I had kept trying anyways. Mainly because if I had a choice to help someone who was suffering or to ignore that suffering, like so many of my mother's "friends" had done, I would always want to be on the side of helping.

Maybe it was just stubbornness, maybe it was trying to prove to myself that love was worthwhile, but I was inclined to try with Penny. So I lowered myself to the floor near the spotty red hound, not close enough to spook her, and with my back towards her. All the while, Uncle Earl and I continued to make small talk as if Penny hadn't started shaking like she was going to get a beating.

My backside was getting numb from the hard floorboards, and Uncle Earl was finishing the washing up, before I felt a dry nose in the gap where my shirt had ridden up. I let Penny sniff me and then casually moved my hand back to lean on it. This time I felt the tentative swipe of a tongue on my fingers, so ghostly I could have imagined it.

When I turned towards Penny a little, she got up and lay on the other side of the two dark hounds. I raised up in a squat and duck-walked over to her, holding out one hand, only to have Penny slink away and escape out the screen door. Apparently, just wanting to be her friend wasn't going to win Penny over.

"I'll try again later," I said with a sigh, and Uncle Earl started a pot of coffee. My special project came back in to watch us with wary eyes.

Chapter Four

Uncle Earl needed to get ready for work, so he excused himself to the bathroom. Balsam-scented steam crept out into the hallway, and I could suddenly feel the grime coating my skin. I probably didn't smell much better than his dogs, but my uncle had been too polite to say. I slumped in the kitchen chair, too afraid to sit in the living room and smudge the chair upholstery while I waited.

When Uncle Earl came out into the living room again, he said, "Now then, let's get you a bed set up. For now, you can sleep in my chair, or the pantry is big enough to lay a pallet on the floor. Just don't eat all the food at once."

While he guffawed at his own joke, I peered around the corner to look at the pantry. It had a door, but no window. Still, being able to close a door was good, and I might find something heavy in there to wedge it shut.

"Pantry, please," I replied. He brought a stack of blankets and a pillow, along with a sizeable piece of cardboard, to lay on the floor. I made a nest and laid on it to try it out, but I already knew it was better than the times I'd spent locked in the shed with nothing.

"We can figure out something better later, if that's okay," Uncle Earl said. "I'll have the whole day off on Tuesday, and we'll find a way to make you feel at home."

Would I still be here on Tuesday, or was three days long enough at Uncle Earl's that Mama's ghost couldn't accuse me of going back on my promise? No sense in cluing Uncle Earl in on my plans, so I answered, "No lie, I'm tired enough to sleep anywhere, after walking all this way."

Reminded of that dusty walk, I asked, "Uncle Earl, is it all right if I take a bath while you're at work?"

He nodded. "That's a good idea. Take those dogs in with you, in case you gave them fleas!"

He said it so earnestly that I couldn't help laughing. The jokes might have hurt coming from someone else, but he softened his teasing with a wink, making it clear it was all in good fun. It wasn't too much of a stretch to think Uncle Earl and his sister shared a similar sense of humor, and Mama loved it best when I shot back with a quip of my own. Still, I decided to hold back on my barbs until I felt sure how he'd react.

Meanwhile, I fidgeted at the table while Uncle Earl gathered up his hat and put on his shoes. With my mind set on taking a hot bath, I couldn't focus on anything else. But Uncle Earl had something on his mind, too.

He turned at the door and asked, "Bet, I've got to ask something—it won't mean you can't stay, but it might mean some paperwork. Does Felix know you're here? Did Liza leave a will or paperwork saying she wanted you to live with me?"

My breath caught before I answered, "Not exactly. She told me to come, though, more than once. She made me promise."

"All those years and she refused to hear a bad word about Felix. What changed her mind?"

How much should I tell him? Trying to tell other people before hadn't gotten me any help—only false promises and pity. And a reputation as a liar, since Felix could charm his way out of anything. The bruises lurking under my clothes served as a reminder that our family didn't share secrets with outsiders. Uncle Earl was family, so did that rule still apply?

Better to stick to a simple truth. "I think it was my uniform that decided her. Felix got an outfit made in my size to look like one of the women at his poker club. So I could work more hours there and earn my keep."

"More hours? You mean you already been working there?"

I shifted uncomfortably in my chair. "Yeah, not officially, but since I was little. I started out signaling what cards the other players had. Once I got good enough at spotting the cheaters, I took that over."

Uncle Earl turned and looked outside for a minute, like he was enjoying the view. But the way he crushed his hat in his hands told me he was angry. As quietly as I could, I slipped out of the chair and sidled towards the back door. He turned to say something, but noticed me poised to flee, and he deflated.

"I'm not mad at you, Bet. You don't ever have to worry about that with me. I wish I didn't have to go to work this minute, but ... will you be here when I get back?"

I bit my lip, but remembered Uncle Earl's dogs trusted him, and supposedly dogs were excellent judges of a person's character. Plus, I had Felix's money, and I could run whenever I wanted. I nodded, and added, "I'll be here," to show I really meant it.

He smiled in relief. "I'll be back around midnight, though I suppose you'll be asleep by then. Do you want to try leaving Penny in the house with you, or should I put her in the pen?"

I called Penny and snapped my fingers to see what she would do. The dog darted a glance at me, but went and leaned against Uncle Earl's leg. Her eyes clearly begged him not to leave, and he patted her on the head.

"The pen it is, then." He opened the door, and the dogs all tried to get over the threshold at once. "Nap and Josie will walk me to the road, and then they should come back on their own. If you get nervous here by yourself, bring them in the house with you, and they'll let you know if anyone comes around."

I watched Uncle Earl take Penny to her pen, and the little despairing howl she gave almost made me say she could stay in the house instead. But if she was to bust out of the house on my watch, Penny would probably try to go after Uncle Earl, and like he said, she wasn't well enough for that. So instead, I waited for Nap and Josie to leap back onto the porch and brought them inside.

Giving it a good half hour before going into the bathroom, in case Uncle Earl had forgotten something and came back, I filled the bath with water so steaming hot I could barely stand it. All the scrapes and scratches from my travels stung as I sank into the tub, which probably meant it was good for them. I had just heaved a sigh and relaxed when the door bumped open a few inches. I nearly sucked in a lungful of water as I gasped and sank mostly below the surface, but it was only Nap who stuck his head in the room.

"Get outta here, or I'll do like Uncle Earl said and give you a bath too!"

He gave a look of grave offense before withdrawing and leaving me to a quiet bath. The water had turned a coffee-colored tint by the time I got out, but better in the tub than on me. After I dried off, I changed into my only other outfit. I was regretting I hadn't at least brought more underwear; in my haste, I had grabbed just one pair. I spent a few minutes dunking the dirty clothes in clean, soapy bathwater. Then I wrung them out and headed to the clothesline in the yard.

Josie and Nap followed me outside for a happy snuffle in a patch of blackberries, going so deep into the brambles all I could see was a pair of tail tips cutting through the leaves like shark fins. I looked up in time to catch the sun kissing the horizon, and the chorus of chirps and buzzes from the night bugs swelled in the trees.

Settling into the chair on the porch, I watched as the stars spread across the sky in a milky track. It felt wilder and lonelier here than in the city, although I already knew it was possible to feel alone even in a place bustling with other people. This place bustled with life in a completely different way, and the longer I sat and watched, the more I felt a part of it. With Josie and Nap at my feet, I could almost pretend I belonged.

Mama would like it here. I slumped at the weight of the thought that my mother wouldn't get to see it—or anything—ever again. Tears prickled at the back of my eyes at the unfairness of it. I tried to think of happy times with her—like trying on ugly hats at the department store, or dancing to "Ac-Cent-Tchu-Ate The Positive" on the kitchen radio while the skillet sizzled—but Felix poisoned even her memory. He'd pushed himself into our lives, with his oily smile and his shiny suits, and the laughter and singing had shriveled up and died in his house.

Then, a few months ago, he nearly killed Mama with a beating. When he kneeled beside her, begging her not to die, I wasn't even sure she could hear him. I'd huddled in the corner, hand over my mouth to prevent my own whimpers from catching Felix's attention. After he fled the house, Mama couldn't—or wouldn't—answer as I begged her to leave. So I stayed too, and laid a damp washcloth on her forehead and prayed it would be enough to save her.

Later that night, Felix brought something home from work for Mama—something he kept neatly in a pouch with a syringe like it came from a doctor. But I had seen these pouches around Felix's poker club and knew no doctor was behind this. It helped with the pain and kept my mother from dying, but then she kept taking it—taking the "medicine" and taking the beatings when they started up again.

That was the start of the long slide for her. Then I only saw the Mama I remembered in those short times when she tried to kick the booze or morphine, but they never lasted. It was like that beating really did kill her—it just took its time. I turned thirteen waiting for things to change, but Felix was still the same, so how could anything change?

As if he had been waiting for a break in my thoughts, Nap jumped half in my lap and swiped his tongue across my salty cheeks. Then I was fighting Josie off too, and it was impossible to keep from laughing when surrounded by such exuberance and wagging tails. The grief didn't go away, but maybe the world had some pockets of joy alongside comforting memories of my mother, if I could let myself look for them.

Chapter Five

When Nap and Josie took off after a rabbit, who was foolish enough to poke its head out of the brush, I checked on Penny to see if she would follow me to the gate. But the hound stayed wary in the shadows of the pen, so I sat nearby for a bit to let her get used to my presence. As long as I didn't stare at her, Penny relaxed onto her pile of rags.

Nap and Josie followed me inside the house; when I came out of the bathroom, Nap met me with a mischievous sparkle in his eyes and a man's dark sock dangling from his mouth. He gave it a shake, like he was killing a rat.

"I don't think you're supposed to have that. Give it here."

Instead, he danced away from my grabbing hand, and Josie snagged the other end. Their growls sounded like they were savaging prey instead of a poor, helpless sock. Intent on their tugging match, they still managed to stay out of my reach. By the time I tackled Nap and crawled up his body to pull the sock away, it was three times its original length, and we were all joyful and panting. I looked at the soggy footwear, limp in my hand, and quirked an eyebrow at the dogs.

I held onto the middle as a dog lunged at each end, and they took me skating across the polished floorboards. They only dropped it when Josie stopped for a drink of water, and Nap decided drinking with her was more pressing than continuing the game. They drank the bowl dry and waited as I refilled it. I was just as grateful for the chance to rest, as I was that the dogs had pulled me out of my low spirits.

Then my responsible side reared its head, and I wondered where the sock had come from. A basket in the bathroom had a few shirtsleeves flopping over the edge, so I went to drop the sock inside. I laughed all over again when I saw its mate in there, also stretched out and tattered like a shed snakeskin. Obviously, Uncle Earl knew about his hounds' taste for mischief and socks, so at least I wouldn't have to figure out a way to tell him.

The play session with the dogs had left me happy but tired, so I went around turning off the lights, leaving on only the lamp next to Uncle Earl's threadbare reading chair. That way he could see when he got home, and the house wouldn't look so strange to me while I fell asleep.

But after crawling into the makeshift bed in the pantry, I couldn't settle down. Drained as I was, the dusty smell of the cornmeal sack on the floor next to me reminded me I wasn't in my room at home. Indistinct shapes huddled on the shelves, stacks of cans and sacks of sugar made sinister in the dark. The sounds here were different too, with some kind of night bird calling mournfully in the yard.

In the pantry's dimness, it started to feel like the walls were only inches away from my shoulders. It was too dark to tell, but had the ceiling lowered? My quickened breaths seemed to bounce off a surface only a palm's width away from my face. Stop it, you're being silly. There's nothing here to be scared of.

Maybe it would feel less confined to have the door open after all. I relaxed a bit after that—until something cold and moist bumped the sole of my foot and I let out a strangled shriek. All the fears of monsters under the bed, which I thought I had outgrown, had me scrabbling away from the open doorway. The beast framed in it made a curious "whuff" sound and I sagged in relief. Just those mischievous dogs again, giving me a poke on the foot.

"Nap?" I whispered, because he seemed to be the instigator. In answer, he pushed his way into the pantry and flopped onto the blankets. Before I could get settled around him, Josie came and took the rest of my bed. Since I was still sitting up from my scare, I only had the pillow and they had claimed the rest. I nudged Josie and Nap in turn with my foot, but they each seemed to have magically increased their gravity and weren't budging. One of them even let out an audible snore.

"Why don't you go sleep in Uncle Earl's bed? Or his chair?" I griped.

Nap cracked one eye open and gave me a look like "Why don't you? And be quiet so I can sleep while you're at it."

With a sigh, I grabbed a pillow and went into the front room. Uncle Earl's chair didn't look too comfortable for sleeping, but maybe there was a breath of air on the porch. The rickety chair and table out there, pushed together, made a platform just the right size for me. With a pillow and a throw blanket, it wasn't really that bad. That feeling of belonging seeped into me again. I was dozing off when I heard an inquisitive sniffing at the screen door. Nap and Josie must have realized I'd moved out here and now they wanted to see what I was up to.

"You can stay in there, you old so-and-sos," I muttered. Nap muttered back at me, and I fell asleep with a smile on my face.

I woke to a hand shaking me. "What're you doing out here, girl?"

The question had me waking up and ready to say a pair of pushy dogs pushed me out, but when I opened my eyes, I froze at the dark shape looming over me. The reek of old liquor on his breath enveloped me, and with a gasping cry, I scrambled out of the chair. How did he find me already?

His reaching hands only made me more desperate, and I flailed in the throw blanket, trying to untangle myself. One of my wild kicks connected, and he stumbled backwards long enough that I could squeeze past. Vaulting the porch rail, I raced across the dirt yard and clambered up a sturdy oak tree. Shinnied up the trunk and into the safety of the branches before he could start after me.

"What in the world? Has the Devil gotten into you, Bet?"

A small part of my brain recognized Uncle Earl's voice, but in the main part of my mind he was still the dark shape smelling of booze and meanness, so when he took a few steps towards my tree I hollered, "Stay away!"

"Just come down so I can see what's wrong—" But as he took a few more steps, I scrambled higher.

A branch snapped under my foot, sounding gunshot-loud in the yard. I whimpered before finding a knot to curl my toes around. When I looked down, the ground seemed a long ways away, but at least the Devil had stopped chasing me.

In fact, he'd retreated to the porch, and a smaller shape huddled behind him. Suddenly, it clicked in my whole brain that they were Penny and Uncle Earl, and I was here at his house. Not back with the Devil and Mama and the night.

"Uncle Earl?" On my perch, my voice was weak as a baby bird's, but he must have heard me.

"I'm here, girl. Me and the dogs and nobody else. Are you still here?"

I gave an odd laugh, because it was a silly question, but at the same time it fit. "Yeah, I'm here now. But … I'm not sure I can get down."

Now that the initial shock was over, my limbs trembled, making it even harder to keep my grip. "Or, maybe I'm going to come down all at once."

"Wait a sec." Uncle Earl switched on the porch light and went inside; Nap and Josie squeezed out as he opened the screen door and they watched me from the foot of the tree. Their wide-open grins showed they thought this was all some midnight lark.

"It's not funny," I said. "This is kind of your fault, Nap."

At his name, he did a jaunty, prancing dance. Josie spun in delight, barking her head off like I was the best squirrel they'd ever treed. In spite of myself, I laughed. But after the shot of terror, it was too fine a line between laughing and crying, and soon I was clinging to the tree with my tears wetting the bark.

A vibration through the trunk meant Uncle Earl had stood a ladder against the tree a few feet below me. He pushed on it to make sure it was secure and then took a few steps back.

"Now, I'm going to let you come down in your own time, but I'll be here to catch you if you need me," Uncle Earl said. "Do you think you can make it?"

Through a coating of mucus in my throat, I said, "You must think I'm crazy."

He shook his head. "I've seen something like this before. My ship blew up in the war, and I landed in the hospital. They put me in a ward with shell-shocked men, and I'd hear them foundering in the dark, battling their nightmares. Have you been through a war too, girl?"

I wiped my nose on my arm without answering and shakily started down the ladder. I nearly made it all the way before I stumbled, and Uncle Earl reached out to catch me. I held myself stiffly away for a moment, and then trusted him with my burden. As he enfolded me in his arms, I looked over his shoulder—Penny's eyes met mine and this time, the dog didn't look away.

Chapter Six

After coming back inside and washing up *again*, I was plain exhausted from the roller coaster of emotions in the last few days. Or months, really. Uncle Earl rousted Nap and Josie out of my blankets, where they'd made themselves at home *again*, and I crawled into bed. Just as my body sank into sleep, I felt a warm weight settle on my feet and I sighed as I let go of the day's troubles.

When I woke, an aged-cheese smell told me the dog at the foot of my bed was Penny. I carefully lifted only my head so I could look down at the dog; Penny shifted to look back, but her gaze wasn't particularly anxious. In fact, there might have been curiosity in her eyes. Had she realized how pathetic I was last night? Or was I less of a threat when I was lying down? When I sat up, Penny skittered away into the kitchen.

I followed her and found Uncle Earl quietly reading the newspaper, a plate of jelly donuts in front of him. I lingered around the corner, embarrassed of how I'd acted the night before. Felix would have scolded me for losing control; you had to be unflappable in a poker game or on a con. But Uncle Earl just nodded to the pile of powdered-sugar-and-raspberry delights without a word and I dug in. He pushed a pot of coffee and carton of milk my way, again saying nothing.

It reminded me of how he'd set down Penny's dinner the night before, gently so as not to spook her. Next, he'd be patting me on the head—if I didn't bite his hand. He already called me *girl*, like he did with Penny before I named her. Maybe he was waiting to take his lead from me, and whether I wanted to talk about last night? I acted like it had never happened, hoping he would, too. A new start for both of us.

"Penny slept with me last night," I said, with a puff of donut sugar on the exhalation. "Have you ever tried to give her a bath so she doesn't smell?"

He set his paper down and topped off his coffee. "Yeah, I got some tar and sulfur shampoo from the vet. Penny got one whiff of it and took off. I have to say it didn't smell much better than she does now, so I don't blame her."

As I laughed, a blob of jelly squirted on my shirt and I tried to wipe it off. It smeared more, so I offered the fabric to Nap, and he licked it clean.

Uncle Earl shook his head and laughed. "While I admire your ingenuity, I don't think that will clean your shirt long term. I was planning on dropping off some laundry today. Do you want me to take your clothes too?"

"I don't have any others. Just what I'm wearing and the overalls I washed last night."

He frowned. "That won't do. You can keep what you have to play in, but you'll need to look civilized on occasion. I can't afford much, but I'll do what I can to set you up."

I brightened. "I have a little money." He was right, I might need a dress at some point; I preferred pants, but even my overalls were sad and worn. They had been the perfect disguise while I was on the road, though, making me look like a boy living rough. Not worth paying attention to as long as I kept moving.

"Tell you what," Uncle Earl said, "if you want to go shopping in town with me today, we can stop at the neighbor's on the way and see what she recommends for Penny's bath. If that dog is going to sleep with you, we can't have you smelling half-rotten like she does."

"Deal," I said, and ran to the pantry. I dug the sock full of cash from my bag and peeled off some bills before hiding the rest behind a dusty jar of preserved peppers. It didn't look like the jar had ever been touched, so the money should be safe there until I found someplace better to hide it.

"Oh, Uncle Earl," I said as I emerged from the pantry, "about your socks…"

"I'm well aware of Nap's fixation with my footwear," he said with a roll of his eyes. "I leave old ones out as decoys and he hasn't found my stash of good socks lately. He likes them best fresh off the foot, so watch out for yours."

Uncle Earl had two canvas bags of soiled laundry gathered up and took them out to an old wheelbarrow. I washed the jelly Nap had missed from my face and hands, and we were ready to go. Uncle Earl had already fed the dogs while

I slept, so Penny went into her pen (with only a half-hearted whimper) and we headed down the driveway.

The iron-rimmed wheel on the front of the barrow squeaked like a weathervane in the wind and Uncle Earl whistled a jazzy tune to match it. I alternated trotting beside him and darting off to cool my feet in the ditch before running to catch up again. When I came alongside, my battered shoes made a squelching sound and we both laughed.

"Seems like you might need some shoes, too."

"Nah, those can wait until school starts," I said.

He nodded. "Your mama and I didn't own a pair of shoes until we were eight and ten years old. The soles of our feet were as cracked and ridged as an elephant's."

I side-eyed him. "When did you get close enough to an elephant to see its foot?"

"Why, in India, of course. When I worked for a maharajah."

He laughed when my skeptical expression didn't change. "All right, I see I can't fool you. As a boy, I snuck around the circus tents when it came to town. In one, I found an elephant chained up, and it was calling and carrying on—just young and lonely, I think.

"Once it had some company, it blew bubbles in the water with its trunk. Then it offered its foot, like a dog wanting to shake hands. I touched the sole with my palm, and it felt all over ridges and calluses. Amazing how all that weight rested on those four pads, even if they were each the size of a tire off a Model A."

"Did you take the poor elephant home, like you do with dogs and nieces?" I asked, only half-joking.

He laughed. "Don't think I didn't consider it! My mama would have drawn the line at elephants; she barely tolerated my broken-winged birds and one-eyed cats. No, the elephant handler ran me off, and when I tried to go back the next day, they had pulled up stakes. I dream of that elephant sometimes though, and how he looked at me with those eyes, just wanting some sympathetic company."

We were both silent for a moment as we thought of deep elephant eyes and loneliness. "How come you didn't end up working with animals somehow, instead of in the Navy and at a diner?" I asked.

His shrug raised the wheelbarrow handles up and down. "I always manage to find critters wherever I am, or they find me. We had a ship's cat, and some fellas bought birds or little monkeys for their families back home. There's a whole family of raccoons who come to the diner for their supper—but don't tell my boss because he made me promise to stop feeding them."

"Of course I wouldn't tell! You'll let me feed them sometime, right?"

"Oh, I don't feed them directly. I put scraps out for them. Raccoons lose their fear of humans way too easily, and they need suspicion to survive."

Now that I could understand. The poor schlubs who came into the poker club with big smiles usually left with empty pockets. "Which neighbor lady knows about dog baths?" I asked.

"We're almost there—see the yard a few doors up on the right? The one all full of plants belongs to Fae."

It was obvious which one he meant. The other yards we had passed were nothing but dirt this time of year, with maybe a tree to shade the house or some pots of geraniums on the porch. Some homes also had a tidy vegetable patch, lined up in strict rows in the side yard.

Fae seemed like the perfect name for a woman who lived at the heart of a secret garden. Her place was a riot of leaves and vines, with greenery crawling along the ground and hanging from the trees. Insects and birds called from the dark tangle, like it was a different time of day—or time of year—from the rest of the world. When we came even with a gate, a graveled path wound its way towards a shadowed porch.

A woman a little younger than my mother called out to Uncle Earl from behind the screen door. I could see she was balancing a toddler on her hip, and somehow this happy picture hurt me more than if she had run over and slapped me for no reason. It was too much for my raw feelings, and I hung back.

"I'll stay here with the laundry," I said when Uncle Earl creaked his way through the gate.

He cajoled, "Fae won't bite, and this is your chance to ask questions about helping Penny get better."

I shook my head. "You know what to ask. Go ahead."

He turned and made his way up the path, stopping to smell a cluster of honeysuckle on the way to the rickety porch. The shadows swallowed him up and I felt bereft—but not enough to follow him.

Chapter Seven

I sat on the edge of a flower border, pulling gravel from my shoes while I waited. The quiet heat of the sidewalk made me wish for some lemonade, and Uncle Earl was probably drinking a tall glass of it right now. But it would be better for me to keep to myself and Uncle Earl, instead of making friends in a place I wasn't planning to stay. And I'd already learned that getting close with your neighbors was only a setup for disappointment, since they could leave whenever they wanted.

The gate squeaked as Uncle Earl came out. "Fae asked about you. Wanted to see if you'd come inside for some lemonade." When I only shrugged, he handed me a napkin folded over a piece of cornbread.

"Hey, there's a bite taken out of this." I turned away slightly from my uncle as he grinned, showing no guilt.

"I don't pass up a chance to eat Fae's cooking. You'll have to come inside next time if you want a whole piece to your-self."

As he picked up the wheelbarrow, I fell into step beside him.

"So, what did she say?" I asked finally, in between bites of cornbread. "Do I have to buy some pricey soap?"

"You're in luck. She said you should soak Penny in tea."

"Do you have a teacup big enough?"

He guffawed. "I wish I'd thought to ask her that. No, she said to make a big pot of tea and sponge it onto Penny, and to let it dry. That should do the trick."

"How is that lucky? I'll still have to buy tea."

"It's lucky because she said used tea bags would work fine, and I can bring them home from the diner. Won't cost us a dime." He winked as he turned down an alley smelling of steam and harsh soap.

"How come you don't do your own laundry, if you're so thrifty? Is it because you don't have a wife to do it for you?"

"It's true I've been on my own for housework for a while now, but I got used to doing chores on the ships. Now that I'm a civilian, I'm willing to spend a little money when it saves me from drudgery. But now that you mention it, you'll be at my place now—are you going to take over the laundry?"

My stomach dropped and I kicked at a loose cobblestone. "I will if you'll show me how you want it done. I've been keeping house while Mama was sick, so I can cook, clean, and sew a little—"

"Bet," he interrupted, and waited for me to look at him. "I was only teasing. I'll keep you if you never lift a finger around the house—you're not here to be my maid. Why don't you concentrate on being young this summer?"

I nodded because it seemed to be what he wanted, and of course Mama had said something similar in our last conversation. But what if I was already too old to have a childhood? I might look thirteen on the outside, but I'd been parenting my mother for as long as I could remember.

The smell of soap got stronger, and Uncle Earl turned on his charm as we came into a yard behind one of the brick houses. Two girls a bit older than me, their faces red and steamed, came to give him hugs. Their mother came out and she waved to see Uncle Earl. They all seemed almost as happy to see him as his dogs did, so maybe he was kind to people, too? Will wonders never cease?

Uncle Earl reached out to pull me in for an introduction, but I sidled away from his arm as I said, "Nice to meet you, Mrs. Grant."

Uncle Earl said, "Now Missus, this girl needs some new clothes. Would you have anything to fit her?"

Thinking he was begging on my behalf, my face colored. "No, that's okay, I can buy some in town."

Mrs. Grant smiled kindly. "It's all right, Bet, I trade in secondhand clothes too. I won't have everything you need if you're starting from scratch, but I can fix you up with most of a wardrobe. Why don't you come inside?"

A rope, stretching along the back wall of her enclosed porch, held hanging clothes of different sizes and vintages. Mrs. Grant started riffling through them and it looked like shuffling a deck of flowered cards. "Now, I think I have some dresses that ought to fit you."

Felix preferred me to wear dresses at the poker club—those childish, frilly things. But I realized I could pick anything I wanted, so I declared, "I'd rather have pants or overalls, please. I'm not much for dresses."

Mrs. Grant eyed my current outfit of well-worn and patched boy's bib overalls, plus a shirt all the color had washed out of long ago. To my relief, Mrs. Grant winked at me instead of arguing. She dug out a pair of men's overalls that were only a little long on me, plus some jeans that fit with the cuffs rolled up, and we picked out some blouses together. As much as I preferred sturdy pants, I was a sucker for a brightly printed top and chose four of those.

"I'm afraid if you want any girl's overalls, you'll need to buy those in town, or wait for me to sew some for you. Most girls your age have moved on to skirts or shorts from overalls. Are you sure you don't want even one dress? You'll need some for school."

Pretty dresses wouldn't do me any good at a lumber camp—plus, they might draw the wrong kind of attention from the workers. My brow furrowed; how could I put this woman off without giving away my plan to leave soon? "I'm still growing, so don't you think it would be better to wait until closer to September for a dress? Some pedal pushers might be better."

"You can wait for a dress, or you can get something now and if you grow much in the meantime, we can add a band of fabric to the length." At my shrug, Mrs. Grant continued, "Now, how are you fixed for underthings?"

I didn't want to tell her I only had the one extra pair of underpants, and when I washed those, I wouldn't have any until they both dried.

When I just shrugged again, Mrs. Grant laughed, "Are you always this quiet? I wish my girls took a moment to breathe like you. They even talk in their sleep if you'd believe it! Now, what about up top?"

"Pardon?" I had lost the thread of her speech. Seemed like her daughters got their habit of talking from their mother.

"Are you wearing a brassiere yet? Or a bandeau?"

Rendered speechless again, I shook my head and hoped that would be the end of it. No such luck with this determined woman.

"You could buy new undergarments at the store," she said. "Or I can sew you some drawers from sack cloth and make you a simple bandeau. You look to be my Ella's size, but it's probably best to take measurements. Now, where did I leave my tape?"

Face flaming, I began edging towards the door. "No thank you, Mrs. Grant."

She looked up, startled by the pitch of my panicked voice. "No to the underclothes, or no to the measuring?"

I stopped, swaying in the doorway. I needed new drawers, and my top half was liable to jiggle uncomfortably when I ran anywhere. It would be good to arrive at the lumber camp with my own things and not have to impose on Nina by borrowing unmentionables. "No thank you to the measuring."

Mrs. Grant took the sweaty dollar bills I offered her and packed the clothes I'd chosen in a canvas sack. "The rest should be ready by the time your uncle comes again next week. I hope you'll come again, too."

"Thank you," I mumbled, and scooted back outside before she could ask any more questions.

A truck pulled into the yard and Uncle Earl stepped up to talk to the driver, a man with red hair like Mrs. Grant's daughters. After more introductions and small talk, Uncle Earl got permission to leave his wheelbarrow to pick up on the way back, so I dropped my sack of clothes into it, too.

"Where to now?" I asked.

"Figured we could introduce you around the diner. It's nearly lunchtime, but you'll have to make do with Rufus's cooking since I'm not on shift yet."

Before I could answer, my stomach rumbled loudly. We both laughed and Uncle Earl said, "Sounds like you agree."

Chapter Eight

Once we left the shaded alley behind and turned onto the main street, the temperature jumped about ten degrees higher. The noon sunshine blazed off the glass and chrome on the cars parked along the curb. Only the awnings jutting from the shop fronts offered relief, leaving pedestrians scurrying from one rectangle of shade to another.

Most people nodded and smiled as they passed, with some greeting Uncle Earl by name. But between the heat and our hunger, Uncle Earl didn't linger as he led me purposefully to the red awning with *The Mercury* in flowing script. Underneath the name, the list of offerings got my mouth watering: burgers, pancakes, sandwiches, hot soup, pies, milkshakes. And the most beautiful words of all: Air Conditioned.

A bell jangled as Uncle Earl pulled open the door and I breathed in the tantalizing food smells and the promised, cool air. Glad cries met us, and two men leaving gave Uncle Earl a friendly clap on the shoulder. I could see him puff up a little under the attention.

"Where do you want to sit?" Uncle Earl asked.

The setup was pretty typical of other diners I had been in: a long counter (with most of the stools already taken), booths along the windows, and space for a few tables scattered along the checkered floor tiles. A row of windows shaped like portholes above the kitchen pass-through gave the place a nautical flair. One booth in the corner looked like it would let me watch the other customers without being stared at so much like I was now, so I picked there.

The vinyl of the seat squeaked as I slid into the booth, but Uncle Earl didn't join me right away.

"Let me talk to a few folks and I'll be right back," he said. "I was going to order me a patty melt, since they're the only thing Rufus does halfway decent."

He raised his voice for the last part, and right on cue, a cry of "I heard that! Don't be badmouthing my food" came from the kitchen. Uncle Earl just laughed.

"A patty melt would be good, thanks," I answered. "Can I have a menu anyway, though?"

The menu did double duty—it gave me a look at The Mercury's list of pies and other desserts, plus it gave me something to peer around at the other customers. I caught a few glances my way, so I wasn't the only curious one sneaking a peek. The faces were friendly enough, except for a sour old lady whose lace dress was nearly as ancient as she was.

Uncle Earl stopped to top up the coffee for a couple of older men at the counter and when he pointed my direction, they all turned to look at me and I ducked behind the menu. When I looked again, they were nodding along to something Uncle Earl had said. He shook their hands and then moved on to another group of men seated in a booth, and the same scene unfolded.

I wasn't sure I liked that Uncle Earl was so obviously talking about me—he had said he would introduce me around, but this was more like gossiping. Unless he was just laying the groundwork? Or maybe he was waiting for me to join him? With Felix, I would have known what was expected of me, but I wasn't sure about Uncle Earl yet.

Before I could decide what to do, a waitress headed my way. She arched one dark eyebrow playfully at me and took out an order pad.

"You seem to be spending a lot of time on the desserts page. Is there something I can get you?" the waitress asked.

I shook my head. "My uncle put in an order for us, I think. He works here? Earl?"

The waitress laughed, not unkindly. "You don't sound too sure. Anyway, he probably ordered you patty melts and fries and didn't even think about a milkshake. But you look like a strawberry girl to me."

I smiled shyly. "How'd you know?"

"I've been doing this for a while now. Ain't no mistaking a favorite milkshake flavor, or a girl who needs one. So, one strawberry milkshake coming up."

I thanked her and looked for Uncle Earl, who was coming out of the kitchen.

"Did you see those fellas I was talking to?" he said as he took a seat in our booth. "They're going to come out on Tuesday and help me close up the back porch, so you'll have a room of your own. It won't be fancy, but it will be a space all to yourself."

My finger traced along a scratch in the tabletop as I tried to think of a polite way to put off Uncle Earl's plans. Now would be the time to let Uncle Earl know I wouldn't be staying long enough to need a room, but it felt rude to throw his welcome back in his face.

I mumbled, "Thanks, but I wouldn't want to put you to any trouble. I don't mind the pantry floor, really."

"Nonsense! What happens when you get so tall your feet stick out into the living room? We can't have that."

But I didn't join his laughter and said again, "Really, I don't mind. Don't go to the trouble on my account."

Uncle Earl got serious. "Well, if you won't accept it on your own account, will you accept it on your mama's? I tried to help her lots of time and she wouldn't let me—Liza was pure stubbornness all her life. Won't you let me help her daughter? You said yourself she wanted you to come stay with me."

I wondered if he really had tried to help. My mother hadn't even mentioned she had a brother until she'd started pushing me to go find him. It wasn't like he had ever come to visit, not even for Christmases. So, what did I really owe him? Maybe it would be better to let him know I already had a plan in place, with a job and a friend waiting for me.

Uncle Earl must have been a mind reader, because I jumped when he said in a low voice, "I understand coming to stay with me might not be what you wanted. You're almost the same age I was when I ran away to join the Navy—I had to lie about my age for them to take me, but it was better than staying at home. Your mama and I didn't have an easy time growing up in Philly, and I'm thinking you haven't either.

"But I'm older now and I've discovered if you start the habit of running, it's hard to know when to stop. It took me years to find a home. You've just lost your mama, and you might—you might not be thinking straight. People can make wrong decisions when they're grieving. I'd ask you to stay at my place until you've healed some, at least."

I didn't answer, taking the time to think before I whispered, "Will I heal, though? I don't know if I can get over ..."

When I trailed off without specifying what I needed to get over, Uncle Earl said, "I can't promise you'll never miss Liza, or you'll have a perfect and happy life if you stay. But I can say your odds are much better if you are in a place of love and safety. I can offer you those things—and a room of your own as of Tuesday—if you want to try."

I mulled over his offer. I couldn't deny he seemed sincere—plus, it sounded like his own regrets talking, and not just empty wisdom from a sermon or something. Mama would never admit there was anything wrong in our house, and here was Uncle Earl, not only acknowledging the hurt but also reassuring me there was a better way to live. Like my wounded heart was a garden to be tended, if I only stayed put long enough to see it through to the harvest.

I was reluctant to change my plans and I also felt a pang of guilt. I'd been lumping my uncle in with Felix and the bullies he ran with, but now I could see Uncle Earl might be different. And I might regret getting to know him before I moved on. Maybe my mother sending me here was not for more of the same kind of life, but a chance for me to have the sanctuary Mama had never found.

"Okay," I said, nodding slowly. "I'll stay for now. But if anything changes—"

"If anything changes, I hope you'll talk to me instead of disappearing," Uncle Earl interrupted. Then he did a gleeful drumroll on the table, changing up the mood. "Now, it looks like our food is up, and just in time, before I waste away."

The waitress, whose name tag said she was Rita, rolled her eyes at his complaining as she expertly laid our plates down. We thanked her and Rita ruffled Uncle Earl's hair, making him swat her hand away. While the grownups teased each other like kids, I turned my attention to lunch.

I could almost hear the onions still sizzling, and the cheese bubbling, since the patty melt had come straight from the grill. I closed my eyes to appreciate the savory scent, and opened them in time to catch Uncle Earl stealing a few of my fries.

"Hey! You have your own right there!" I squawked.

He winked at me as he stuffed them in his mouth, and he didn't look one bit sorry.

I curled over my plate like a dog protecting a bone and growled at him, "Don't mess with my food, lessin you wanna get bit."

He laughed and shook his head. "No wonder the dogs like you. You're a kindred spirit. I won't try it again."

"I wouldn't worry about this one. She can hold her own," Rita said as she turned away. She was right—if I could hold onto myself under Felix's rule all these years, there was hope for me yet.

Uncle Earl and I ate in silence, but it was because we were both chewing too much to talk, not because we hadn't yet found a level of comfort together. His playful response to me defending my fries went further to soothing my doubts than all his kind words had done—Felix was the type to spout charming words, but then backhand you when no one else was looking. I was beginning to believe Uncle Earl was a bona fide gentle man.

Just to be sure, I asked, "Is that the vet clinic?" and pointed out the window to a storefront across the street with frolicking animals painted on the awning. When Uncle Earl turned to look, I nabbed the pickle spear from his plate.

"Yeah, that's Doc March's place," he answered, facing me across the table again. His eyes narrowed as he glanced from the pickle I was munching on and down to the empty space on his plate.

"Touché," was all he said.

I smiled, smug around the crunch of the last bite of pickle.

"It looks like your strawberry milkshake is about ready," Uncle Earl said. "If you really want to make Rita's day, you could fetch it yourself and save her poor feet. You might even get a few extra cherries on top for your trouble."

I nodded and got up, but before I had taken more than a few steps, I turned back. I counted my remaining French fries aloud and gave Uncle Earl a stern look that made him give a snappy salute. Rita was indeed happy to have been saved even the short trip to our booth and finished off the milkshake with an extra swirl of whipped cream. Then, as Uncle Earl had predicted, she winked and pushed *three* cherries into the tower of cream.

Anyone else might have had trouble with the lofty whipped cream, but I'd been waiting tables at the club since I was old enough to see over the tray. As I carried the milkshake back to our booth, some instinct made me veer away from another customer as I passed. A slashing cane just missed my toes, and I couldn't help letting one cherry roll off and splat on the tile. Only after it nosed against a polished shoe did I look up. It was the older lady who had been sitting by herself, and she had definitely done it on purpose.

"What are you wearing, child?" the old woman barked.

"What?" I asked, looking down at my clothes. Sure, my overalls and blouse were faded and worn, but they had been clean before the milkshake splashed onto them. Nonetheless, I ducked my head and my cheeks felt redder than the cherries on the floor.

"You look like one of those men who ride the train cars," the old woman continued. "Who are your people, letting a young girl run around dressed like that? And if you did not hear me, you say 'excuse me, ma'am' instead of blurting out another question."

I wanted to answer back in the same tone, but this was Uncle Earl's place of business and I didn't know how much sass I could get away with. I looked for Uncle Earl, but he was leaning over the back of their booth and chatting with someone else and hadn't noticed my predicament. People at nearby tables had noticed, but were wearing expressions that showed they weren't likely to interfere. I recognized the look from the times Mama yelled at me at the poker club, and everyone pretended they couldn't hear the awful things she said.

"You have yet to answer my question. I am waiting," the old woman called me back to the present.

I opened my mouth to answer, but a boy my age swung off his stool and sauntered the few steps to stand by me.

"Don't you know clothes when you see them, Mrs. Ridgeway? Or is your eyesight as bad as your manners?"

The old woman sputtered in outrage. "You watch your tongue, you little miscreant! I should have known this was a friend of yours, Georgia Wood!"

So, not a boy then, if this was a Georgia. The girl said, "She's not my friend yet, but I hope she will be. And I might be a miscreant, but even I know trying to break someone's neck with a cane is not a polite way to welcome them to town."

I only realized how sticky my hand was when Georgia grasped it and gave a firm handshake. The mischief in the other girl's eyes showed she had expected the stickiness, but I felt my face heat up just the same.

"How do you do?" Georgia said in a snooty voice, much like Mrs. Ridgeway's. "I am Georgia Wood, of the Yellow-house Woods, don't you know. Whom might you be, and which important people do you know?"

I stifled a laugh before replying gravely, "Why, I am Liza-bet Carter, and I breakfasted with the very elegant Napoleon and Josephine only this morning. And the Earl of Meatloaf Sandwich is my uncle, of course."

Georgia bowed over my hand and we giggled, but Mrs. Ridgeway drew our attention again by banging her cane on the floor.

"Do not ignore me, you pair of urchins," cried the old woman, "or I will give you worse with my cane."

A firm hand stopped the waving weapon. Uncle Earl had finally noticed what was happening.

"You and Georgie butt heads a lot, Mrs. Ridgeway, but I know you didn't call my niece an ugly word and threaten her. Especially since you've only just been allowed back into the diner after your two-month ban."

The old woman glared up at him but did not deny it. She pulled her cane from Uncle Earl's grasp and stood; with nothing more than a sour pursing of her lips, she strode out the door.

Uncle Earl's gentle hand guided me to our booth. "We'll get you some more cherries, Bet, and would you mind cleaning up the mess?" He said the last part over his shoulder to Georgia, who nodded and went behind the counter like she worked there.

When I sat down and tried to lift a spoonful of milkshake to my lips, my hand trembled. I dropped my hands into my lap and blinked at the table, trying not to let the tears fall. Just when I had started to hope things could be different in Amberfields, a snake slithered across my path.

"She's a bitter old woman," Uncle Earl said softly. "I'm sorry she upset you."

I hissed, "I'm not upset, I'm mad. Why'd she have to go and ruin things? I was—and she was—she's just mean!" Not my most scathing insult, but at least it came from the heart.

Georgia set a small bowl of cherries down for me. "Yeah, and who is she to talk about clothes? Maybe if she wasn't so tightly laced into that ancient dress and corset, she wouldn't be so mean."

Uncle Earl barked a laugh, and then tried to cover it up with a cough and a stern expression. "That was unkind, Georgie."

Georgia winked and said, "But it was true. And too funny not to say it out loud."

The saucy comment made me chuckle, and Georgia snatched a cherry from the bowl before sauntering out the front door.

"Who is Georgia? Or is it Georgie?" I demanded.

"She's Fae's oldest, and she definitely prefers Georgie. I'm sure you'll be seeing more of her if you can get up the courage to visit Fae yourself."

I smiled. Maybe it was worth making friends with the neighbors if one of them was Georgie. "I just might do that."

We reached for the bowl of cherries at the same time, and I let my uncle grab a few before I pulled it away.

Chapter Nine

Once we'd finished eating, Uncle Earl said, "You've already met the town grump and our resident troublemaker, so it can only get better from here. You still want me to introduce you around?"

Since his friends were pitching in to build me a room, I thought the least I could do was to meet them. To my relief, they proved to be kind and full of laughter over Georgie's antics earlier. By the time Uncle Earl and I left, I was feeling properly welcomed to town, but so tired that I decided to finish my shopping another day.

We walked home in the heat, with each of us swinging a bag from the diner. Uncle Earl's held my spaghetti dinner for later, since he had to be back at work again at four. Mine had the first collection of used tea bags for Penny's skin. After we stopped by the laundry again, we went back to our earlier pattern: Uncle Earl pushing the squeaking wheelbarrow, and me darting in and out of the roadside ditch.

The red-and-white hound pranced around both of us when we let her out of the pen, but she still kept a safe distance from me, only giving a touch on my ankle with her cool nose. The nose-poke still held suspicion, but maybe a little friendly curiosity, too.

Uncle Earl stowed the spaghetti in the icebox and slapped his thighs. "Give me a minute to change into my work clothes and we can see what all we have in the stable to use for your room."

"Guess I'd better get out of my good clothes, too," I teased. "Or at least get the strawberry malt off them."

All three dogs followed us out to the stable, but Penny slinked a little farther back, probably worried she was going to be locked up again. The well-organized workshop in the intact part of the stable surprised me, with its tools hung on pegs and saw blades stacked on a rack. Uncle Earl seemed to know right where everything was, and it got me wondering about why Penny's pen was so messy.

"Uncle Earl, why don't you pen Penny up in this part of the stable, since it's so much nicer? Or maybe fix up her part?"

"Well, that part was pretty much empty when I fenced it in for her. But she didn't like being so exposed. At least that's what I guessed by how she would huddle there shaking. Once I piled up some rags and threw more junk in there, she felt right at home. It's probably closer to the conditions she grew up in, and she's been through a lot of changes, so I think it was a comfort to her."

"I didn't know what to think when I first got here and saw her locked up," I confessed. "I filled her water bucket."

"Oh, she has plenty of water. Come see."

We went into Penny's pen and Uncle Earl showed me how he'd rigged up a barrel of water to flow into a metal bowl. "It's got a float valve in there, so it doesn't overflow, but when the water goes down in the bowl, it refills itself from the barrel."

I kneeled to examine it, splashing the water out so I could watch it refill. "Wow, you made that, Uncle Earl? That's really clever."

His grin turned shy. "Well, I didn't think it up, but I built this setup. I may have been a cook in the Navy, but there were times I had to turn my hand to some other tasks, so I learned to be handy, har har."

When I laughed dutifully, he clapped his hands together and said, "We should have grabbed gloves on the way out the house. Can you fetch them? They're hanging on nails on the back porch—soon to be your quarters, I guess, so I'll have to find a new place for them."

I ran back to the house as directed and also looked closer at the rear porch. It obviously wasn't meant to be a sitting porch like the one out front, since the floor and the roof were smaller. Just enough shelter to let you get through the door and not bring the rainstorm in with you. There was no window on that corner of the house, so we shouldn't have to close one over while making it into a room. If we left the back door from the kitchen in place, it would be my access to the rest of the house, but a bolt would give me some privacy. Maybe we could add a window or door to the outside, so it didn't feel so confined.

Satisfied that it would make a pleasant sanctuary for however long I stayed there, I started looking for the gloves. There was a row of nails next to the door, but only a single glove hung there. I peered around in case the others had fallen, but saw only dusty boards. With a shrug, I returned with my prize to the stable.

"This is all there was, Uncle Earl," I called.

He stopped trying to push the reluctant door at the back of the stable open wider and turned to see what I had. As I waved the glove, Nap sprang from nowhere and snatched it in his teeth. He was gone with it before I even realized what had happened.

Uncle Earl's aggravated sigh chased Nap's disappearing backside. "Now we really will get dirty, I'm afraid. But it's about time I check on his dragon hoard again, and make sure he doesn't have anything dangerous. Follow me, Bet."

I trotted after him, wanting to know what "dragon hoard" Uncle Earl was talking about. Maybe Nap's favorite chew bones? Josie and Penny came along too, and Uncle Earl stopped at a big patch of blackberry bushes. When he bent to look closer, Nap shot out and blocked the front of the greenery. He wagged his tail apologetically as Uncle Earl tried to call him away, but the dog stood fast.

Finally, Uncle Earl picked up Nap's thrashing form and wheezed, "You'll have to go in. I'll hold him as long as I can."

I crouched to look, and Nap had carved himself a little den beneath the thorny, arched branches. I ducked my head and crawled in, feeling a soft nest under my hands and knees. The smell of green leaves helped cut the strong smell of dog. Enough light filtered through to tell most of the fabric pieces lining the nest were from socks Nap had torn up, plus some remnants of undershirts. Maybe scraps of blankets too, and, of course, the gloves—I gathered those up and left the rest.

Once I was back in the sunlight, I held the gloves high over my head as Nap squirmed out of Uncle Earl's hold. The indignant dog went into his hidey-hole with a peeved huff and we left him to it.

"I found five gloves in there, but none of them are from the same pair. And all but one are lefties."

We spread them out on the workbench and found two that were somewhat smaller for me, and two that would fit Uncle Earl. Oddly, the fifth was actually a very dirty, lacey evening glove. Since the work gloves were big on me anyway, Uncle Earl helped me turn one over so it would fit my right hand. We looked at our mismatched mitts and doubled over with laughter.

"We only need them for when we're moving the wood, so they should do fine," Uncle Earl said finally. "No splinters or spider bites will get through."

Uncle Earl sorted out pieces of wood he thought would work, and I dragged them to a spot beside the back porch. A few boards looked so old they could have been hand-sawed, and most had nails studding the wood, but they felt sound where I gripped them through the gloves. Sweat and dirt covered me by the time I'd made the fifth trip, and I hoped we had enough.

"Come look at this," Uncle Earl called from deeper in the stable. "I have just the thing."

I followed his voice and saw him wrestling with a metal hip bath, trying to pull it into the afternoon light for a better look.

"Is that for me?" I asked. "Are you going to build me a bath house too?"

He shook his head, panting out a laugh. "No! I thought it would be just the thing for you to bathe Penny in. With the tea? Help me drag it into the yard."

Together, we walked it out on its base, and I could see he was right. The tub was not too deep for me to reach into, but the walls were high enough to discourage a dog Penny's size from jumping out. Nap and Josie would be a different story, with their longer legs. But then, I figured Nap and Josie didn't stay still long enough for something like a bath—unless you could wash them in their sleep.

"Where did this tub come from? Did you and Mama use it when you were kids?" I asked.

Uncle Earl shook his head. "Oh, we didn't grow up in this house. I got it a few years after the war ended. The whole place was nearly as shabby as Penny's pen, after the previous owners gave up on farming and walked away. I paid the back taxes and then I was the proud owner of this vast estate, along with whatever they left in the house and stable."

"Mama didn't talk about where she grew up, or even her parents—your parents—really. I think you mentioned Philly before?" I fished again for some stories about when my mother was younger.

But Uncle Earl didn't take the bait, only saying, "I don't imagine she wanted to talk about it."

I shrugged, since it was obvious Uncle Earl didn't want to talk about it either, and slapped my gloves together to get the dust off them. "Should we see if Penny will get in it?"

"Maybe tomorrow. I need a bath myself, and then maybe I can manage a quick nap before I leave for work."

I felt at a loss for what I could do while Uncle Earl was busy. It was true the Devil could find work for idle hands, because Felix couldn't abide seeing anyone relaxed when they could be making him money. I always had a list of chores at home, and even at the club.

But now I was overwhelmed by choices: should I go to Fae's and see if Georgie was there? Go through Uncle Earl's books and see if there was something good to read? Try to get Penny in the bath on my own? I needed to channel my nervous energy into being useful. In the end, I made up a pail of soapy water and attacked the dusty back porch; I didn't want my room to be full of cobwebs and grime.

A freshly bathed Uncle Earl came to check on my progress before he laid down for his nap, and he smiled in approval. "Might be some furniture we can use out in the stable too, if you want to poke around and check. I don't even know what all is in there. I put the gloves on top of the china cabinet, where Nap can't reach, if you need 'em."

I nodded. "Also, I was wondering, do you have any books I would like? I thought maybe if I read something to Penny, it would help her get used to me, and the sound of my voice, I mean."

Uncle Earl made a thinking, humming noise and went back into the house. I followed him to his overflowing bookcases lining the living room wall. Stacks of books tottered next to his chair and filled random corners, too.

"A lot of these might not be, um, right for a girl your age. Too many gunfights and corpses," he muttered to himself. But then he straightened and plucked a book off a higher shelf. "Have you read this one?"

I turned it over to read the title. "*Black Beauty*. I got it from the library once, but it's sad, isn't it?"

"It is sad in parts, but if you've read it before, you can always pick the parts you want to share with Penny. It's got lots of hopeful parts too, and an understanding of animals."

That last detail must be why it made the cut in his library, in spite of it not having any gunfights. Or at least, not any I could remember. "This one should work," I said.

Uncle Earl went to his room for his nap, and I finished my cleaning. Soon enough, I'd have a room of my own to nap in if I wanted to—but my excitement faded when I remembered I wasn't supposed to be happy about it. Not if I wanted to make a clean break and be on my way.

Then I remembered how Mrs. Nowak said her time in Poland during the war had taught her to enjoy the good times while they were happening. Bright moments could become treasured memories to think on in dark times—even the literal dark times I spent locked in a shed. If I could relax, a few weeks with Uncle Earl might just turn into a treasured memory.

After I came back in the house, I saw Penny lying in front of Uncle Earl's bedroom door. He had locked out Nap and Josie, along with their hijinks, so the bigger hounds were dark puddles on the shady front porch. Only Penny was in the house, keeping watch on her person. I felt a pang at the sight and knew I wanted to be Penny's person.

I dragged a pillow from the couch and sat on the floor near enough where Penny could hear me, but not so near as to spook the dog. Penny raised her head enquiringly, and I took that as a signal to start reading in a soft voice.

"Chapter one: The first place that I can well remember was a large pleasant meadow with a pond of clear water in it. Some shady trees leaned over it, and rushes and water lilies grew at the deep end..."

Chapter Ten

I stirred briefly in my pantry bed as Uncle Earl came home around midnight, and the joyous sound of dog nails tapping on the floor accompanied a laughing whisper. "Shh! Settle down, you mongrels, you'll wake the girl!" But I went back to sleep and didn't wake again until my nose caught delicious smells seeping under my door.

When I stepped out of the pantry, the scent of yeast and baking hit me full force. I marveled at the trays and pans spread around the kitchen: golden rolls with sausages peeking out the ends, muffins dotted with blueberries, half a dozen peach pies, a towering stack of cooked bacon, and an entire sheet pan of scrambled eggs. As I watched, Uncle Earl pulled another tray out of the oven—bread pudding with raisins.

"What is all this, Uncle Earl? Didn't you get any sleep last night?"

"Everyone will be here any minute, and they'll be wanting breakfast before they set to work. Some folks dropped off food at the diner last night, so I only had to make the bacon, eggs, and bread pudding this morning. Won't be sur-prised if they bring even more food with them."

A caravan of trucks and cars pulled into the yard, and more people (and dogs) than I could count boiled out of them. The neighbor ladies set up trestle tables covered with checked cloths, and soon had them loaded with even more food. The younger children circled the platters like sharks, angling for a bite, and Nap and Josie ran wild underfoot with the visiting dogs. Penny had slinked off to the stable at the first sign of commotion.

I walked to the tables and started helping the ladies, but I couldn't quite get into the rhythm of their work. I was in their way as often as not, though they seemed happy enough to see me. Finally, one of the aproned aunties pulled me aside.

"Wouldn't you rather be playing? We've got this han-dled."

I looked to the kids, who were playing tag and running races. Some of the boys—and Georgie—had marked off a small baseball diamond and were already well into a game. It seemed like theater to me, like some Norman Rockwell painting. Before I had to decide, it was time to eat.

"Come eat!" one of the ladies hollered. "Working bodies go first, so if I see you at the front of the line, I better see you working after."

A few dejected kids headed to the back of the line at her words, but Georgie marched to the front. She beckoned me to join her, and we took our brimming plates to a spot on the front porch.

"I didn't know you were going to be here today," I said. "You weren't helping us set up the tables."

Georgie made a face. "I had to do some chores at home first, but I'm here to help with the building. Most of the men can't get away from their jobs on a Tuesday, so it's down to boys and old fellas to get the job done." Her tone made it clear what she thought of their skills.

"So, where does that leave me? Should I be wearing a frilly apron or a tool belt?"

With a snort, Georgie replied, "You won't catch me in a frilly apron, but do what you want. I'll be helping build you a room after we eat breakfast and unload the trucks."

"What's on the trucks? More wood? I thought Uncle Earl already had enough on hand."

"Most everyone pitched in something: a window, an old door, a bed frame to fit the mattress somebody else brought, a dresser, a couple rag rugs, plus a little table you can pull up next to your bed. You should be all set before the day is over."

My eyes widened at the thought that so many people were willing to pitch in, but then narrowed as I suspected there might be a catch. "They're doing all that for me? But they don't even know me."

"But they know Earl, and he's always the first person to lend a hand, or to give his time when someone else needs it. Now it's our turn to repay the favor with whatever we have to spare."

"That's not repaying Uncle Earl, though; it's my room."

Georgie shook her head. "Don't you know, if it makes you happy, then Earl will be happy too. You're his family."

I didn't know what to say. Felix's moods and needs always came first, and it was exhausting trying to anticipate what would make him happy—and when that failed, Mama and I had better get out of his way fast. There wasn't much energy or will left over to do a good deed for anyone else, let alone ourselves.

"Earl brought out another tray of those sausage roll things. Do you want me to grab a couple for you?"

Georgie's question brought me out of my thoughts.

"I'll come with you," I answered.

We ran to the back porch, rolls in hand, and watched the baseball game as we ate. The game paused as a dog ran through with sausages trailing from its mouth, and most of the kids gave chase. A pack of dogs was close behind and I could hardly believe how much racket they were all making, and not one adult yelled at them. In fact, many of the grownups were roaring with laughter and joining in the pursuit. It was like some kind of circus skit. Or a toddler's birthday party where everyone had too much cake.

"Is Amberfields always like this?" I asked, trying to keep the judgment from my voice. After all, it wasn't even my voice in my head saying how undignified they were behaving—the voice sounded just like Felix's.

Georgie laughed, unoffended. "Like what, fun? School just got out last week, so we're all wild with freedom. Give 'em a few weeks, and most of these kids'll be dull slugs waiting for school to start again."

Someone finally tackled the thieving dog, but he had already eaten his spoils. The baseball game started up again, and people wandered back to the food and drink. I shook my head, wondering if they were ever going to start building my room.

Then, Uncle Earl gathered everyone at the back of the house, calling, "Let's get this room built!"

And despite how many of the grownups juggled bottles or cans of beer while they worked, they put together the new space in record time. I watched in awe as the floor area expanded, the walls raised up, and the roof extended over the addition. The new outer door hung true in its frame, just like the window, which cranked open. The old porch light was now a wall sconce. It should have looked hodge-podge, but instead the effect was charming and homey.

A few ladies dressed in coveralls and kerchiefs, like aging Rosie the Riveters, tacked down the shingles so expertly it was like they were still on the assembly line. Then the paintbrushes and buckets came out and, in the blink of an eye, the recent addition looked like it had always been there. Georgie surprised me by painting some vining red roses around the window, but they were a sweet accent.

A line of friends and neighbors moved the furniture in before I even got a look inside, and when I finally poked my head through the doorway, it was a bedroom. A bedframe in one corner, the mattress made up with striped sheets and a quilt with Noah's Ark animals romping across it. The quilt was far too young for me, but complaining about a gift wasn't exactly a way to prove I was more mature than that. Besides, it came with a bunch of animal-shaped pillows so I could lounge luxuriously.

A curiously fancy lamp, with its base shaped like a pineapple and its shade trimmed in silk leaves, waited on the bedside table. And rag rugs: one for beside the bed so my toes could land on it in the morning, and smaller ones inside of each doorway so nobody tracked dirt into my space. I tested the drawers in the tall chest, lined with flowered paper and ready for my things. Last, I ran my fingers along the spines of a stack of well-worn books brightening up the little desk near the window.

My room in Sacramento was not a safe place, but this one felt like it would be. For one thing, the locks were on the *inside* of the doors. I fought tears of happiness, glad I'd waited to leave for Oregon. A throat clearing behind me announced Uncle Earl, where he hovered in the doorway. I hugged him tight, whispering my gratitude.

"I'm glad you like it," he said, "but people are fixing to leave, and I thought you'd want to say thank you."

I ran outside and went around to everyone, thanking them in person. One lady whispered her mother-in-law gave her that bizarre pineapple lamp, and she was glad to pass it on to me. With one last wish that they hoped I would feel at home, the cars drove away in a cloud of dust. Uncle Earl got another hug and I skipped back to my room.

Nap and Josie came running out as I ran in, and I skidded to a stop when I found all my pillows on the floor. Those dogs! I would definitely need to keep my doors closed. As I picked the pillows up, I frowned: hadn't there been more of them? I knew there had been a big round pillow with a smiley lion's face, and then smaller ones with maybe a zebra, a giraffe, an elephant, and...a monkey? Only the giraffe and elephant rested with the lion now.

With a sigh, I made sure the door closed behind me and went to check Nap's hidden nest. The dog hung his head and wagged his tail as I climbed under the blackberries with him. My pillows weren't there, but it looked like he'd added a few handkerchiefs to his hoard. I slapped the dust from my knees after I crawled back out. Where else would he hide pillows?

I went back to the house, calling through the screen door, "Uncle Earl, does Nap have another stash somewhere? Some of my new pillows are already missing."

He pushed the screen open and motioned for me to come in. "Not that I know of. Did you see him in your room?"

"Yeah, he and Josie were both in there."

"What about Penny? Did you see her?"

Come to think of it, I hadn't seen Penny with the other dogs, or out in the yard anywhere. I looked around the living room and didn't see her in the house either. "No Penny, but my doors are shut now."

Uncle Earl and I opened the door off the kitchen and looked into my bedroom. There were all my new things, but no dog.

Except...

"Hey, now the elephant pillow is gone too! It was just here."

Uncle Earl looked around, hands on hips, before kneeling beside the bed and peering beneath it. "Yep, I'm afraid you have a monster lurking under your bed."

I gave a soft laugh when I took a peek and saw two shiny eyes staring back, with the pillows cuddled around her.

But then I felt bad for laughing when Uncle Earl said, "She had puppies when they captured her, you know. They were about five months old and nearly as big as her, but then she's on the small side for a hunting hound. I would have taken the four pups too, while the courts decided, but they were so pretty people were lining up to give them a home. And of course, Penny had surgery right away, so she was separated from them before she knew what was happening."

"So she didn't even get to say goodbye? Do you know who has them now?"

"Oh, they're mostly local folk, but scattered around. They come into the diner sometimes."

"Maybe they could bring the puppies by so she could see them all again."

"That'd be nice. In the meantime, do you want your pillows back?"

I shook my head and stood to grab the giraffe pillow, too. I crawled far enough under the bed for Penny to take it gently from my hand. A stuttering thump sounded.

"Did you hear, Uncle Earl?" I whispered. "She wagged her tail, I think."

Chapter Eleven

We left Penny in her hiding place, with both bedroom doors cracked open, and went to see what treasures the depths of the stable held. The neighbors had fitted out my room so well I didn't need much, but I wanted to see what was on offer. Stacked like toy blocks, furniture filled the entire back wall, shrouded in old sheets and covers. We selected a comfortably worn chair for the living room so I could have my own place to sit and read, plus we found a mirror to go over my desk so it could do double duty as a vanity.

We had gotten dusty again, so we figured we may as well give Penny her first bath. I had left the old tea bags soaking in the hip bath and the water was now the same reddish brown as the soil. It was less dark once we added warm water to the hip bath too, but it smelled enough like tea that I commented, "Now all we need is a plate of iced lemon cookies."

What we actually needed was some cold ham from the fridge to lure Penny into the hip bath. As long as Uncle Earl fed her tidbits of meat, she didn't seem to notice when I trickled the tea over her fur. I gave Penny's shoulder an experimental swirl with the sponge and the dog turned her head to investigate; after she touched her tongue to the tea-infused sponge, Penny went back to the tastier ham shreds. I applied the tea more confidently, and the white patches on the little beagle were soon a chestnut color.

Once the ham was gone, Uncle Earl joined in with massaging the tea into Penny's skin and fur. Then Uncle Earl carried her to a sunny patch on the front porch to dry off. Penny was so relaxed she fell into a doze immediately, while I fluffed her drying fur with my fingers. I could see a shaved patch on her belly growing back out, the fur slightly darker.

It wasn't until a curious Josie licked Penny's face that the smaller dog awoke. I froze in place as the usually skittish dog caught me out, but Penny thumped her tail and went right back to sleep. I exchanged delighted glances with Uncle Earl, who left us to our grooming session. He told me when he checked on us later, I had curled up in the late afternoon sun too and I looked like one more puppy in the pile of sleeping dogs.

But in spite of what looked a lot like progress, once we were all awake and moving around again, Penny kept her distance from me. The little dog didn't quite seem so anxious about it, but our nap obviously didn't prompt a miraculous transformation in our relationship. When Uncle Earl got dressed to go out after dinner, it was plain he would still have to put Penny in her pen.

"Or would you rather close her up in your room with you?" he asked me.

I thought before answering, "No, if she got too scared, she'd probably never go into my room again. And that's where 'her' pillows are."

"Well, I won't be too long. I'm meeting some friends for drinks, and maybe to play some poker."

"Maybe I'll walk with you part way. Do you think it would be okay for me to drop by the Woods's?"

"Georgie would be glad to see you, and Fae will be, too." But as he was reaching for his hat, his hand stalled. "In fact, I wouldn't want to send you over there empty-handed. Georgie can be so generous with the gifts she sends me, but doesn't like it when I pay her back. If I give you something, will you say it's from you?"

"Sure. Is it leftover food?"

"Yes, I'll send some of that with you, and then something special for Georgie."

And that was how I found myself carrying a bag of foil-wrapped packages, plus a tin of fancy butter cookies. Uncle Earl watched me walk up to the door, and Fae waved to him as she welcomed me inside.

"Uncle Earl wanted me to give you this food, Mrs. Wood, and something special for Georgie." I whispered, "Except, I wasn't supposed to say he sent the cookies. He didn't want me to feel like I was coming empty-handed."

"Please, call me Fae. All my friends do." She gave a secret smile and added, "Your uncle knows exactly what Georgie likes, so I'm sure those cookies are perfect."

What sounded like a hundred soldiers' footsteps rattled down the stairs behind Mrs. Woods—behind Fae—and Georgie jumped to the tile floor. "I thought I heard a knock. Hey, Bet."

"Hey, Georgie."

"Wanna see my room?" Georgie asked.

"Yes, please," I answered, grinning.

Fae walked away with the bag, and I called, "Oh, can I have—"

"Of course." Fae pulled out the tin of cookies and handed it to me. She smiled again as Georgie and I charged back up the stairs, chattering away.

Georgie showed me around her room, pulling out treasures like the shed skin of a lizard and the almost-complete skeleton of an opossum. And instead of socks in her top drawer, Georgie had bundles of colorful feathers identified with handwritten tags. Well-worn copies of guides from the Boy Scouts sat on her bedside table.

I cocked my head. "So, you're in the Boy Scouts?"

"Nah, I traded Will from up the street some marbles for his old books. I was in the Girl Scouts, but I didn't want to make friendship bracelets and earn badges for being kind to old ladies forever. They made us go to Mrs. Ridgeway's house to help her garden! Plants I don't mind—obviously, since I live in the middle of Mom's wild garden—but Mrs. Ridgeway tried to kill a toad with a shovel. Right in front of me."

Georgie pulled up the leg of her jeans and showed a white scar on her shin. "She got me with the shovel instead, and nobody would believe that it wasn't an accident. She did it because I let the toad escape—she probably wanted to use it in a spell."

"I believe you. She's awful," I commented.

Georgie nodded. "I'll get us something to drink if you want to wait here."

It wasn't until I really looked around that I noticed how many wood carvings there were in Georgie's room: chess pieces lined the windowsill, with the horses and figures looking almost like they could move on their own. A flotilla of brightly painted water bird decoys swam on shelves hugging the ceiling. In a basket on the dresser, a dozen wooden whistles nestled under scraps of sandpaper. Even the bedside table held some tools and lumps of wood with carvings started. I ran a finger along the snout of a sly fox emerging from the swirling grain.

Georgie noticed what I held and said, "I only started the fox last night. I'm still trying to decide what to enter at the county fair. Oh, don't tell my mom I have tools in here, though. I'm supposed to lock them up in my workshop, so Cami doesn't cut herself."

"Did you do all these? Even the ducks?" I wasn't skeptical, just admiring.

"Mom does the painting for the ducks because I don't have the patience. And the chess set, our—my grandpa carved those. He taught me how."

I wasn't sure why Georgie had hesitated before mentioning her grandfather, but I didn't ask. If anyone knew families could be complicated, it was me. Instead, I handed Georgie the tin of cookies.

"Want to eat these with your lemonade?"

Georgie's eyes lit up. "Those are my favorite. Let's dig in!"

We sat on Georgie's bed and Georgie carefully broke the seal on the tin. But as soon as she lifted the lid, a mass of many-legged black things poured out. We both screeched and scrambled away, until I was brave enough to look again.

"Wait! It's just—just black thread knotted up to look like spiders. How did they get in there?"

Looking closer at the tin, I moved the spiders aside and saw a layer of cotton batting. When I pushed on it, it compressed flat and sprang back again when I let go. I was going to show Georgie how it worked, but she was still lying facedown in the pillows, her shoulders shaking.

"Are you okay?" I asked. Maybe Georgie enjoyed carving critters, but not the real thing.

Finally, Georgie sat up, her face red and cheeks wet. I was worried for her until Georgie's laughter rang out without a pillow to muffle it.

"That was great!" she wheezed.

Fae stuck her head in the room, asking, "What was that screaming? Don't wake Cami if you can help it."

Georgie gestured to her bedspread, where it still looked like a plague of spiders had emerged from the cookie tin.

Fae nodded knowingly and said, "Ah, I see. Well, I'm making a batch of caramel apples for the kids at Sunday school, if you two want to help."

Georgie sat up, grinning as she said, "Oh, we'll help. Will there be a few left over? We wouldn't want to send Bet home without a treat for Earl."

Still confused, I followed Fae and Georgie downstairs. Fae set up an assembly line with the apples and wooden sticks for us, while she started on the caramel mixture at the stove.

"I don't get it," I said. "What happened with those *spiders*?"

Fae chuckled. "Georgie here and your uncle have had a prank war going for a few years, almost since we moved here."

"Yeah," Georgie piped up, "but my jokes were stupid when I was little. Things like jumping out from behind a tree to scare him. It's better now that we're equals. If I'd known those cookies were from him, I would have suspected something was up."

"So he used me?" I squawked indignantly.

Georgie grinned. "That he did. But don't worry, I'm planning on using you to pay him back."

She slid out of her chair and disappeared into the pantry. She reemerged with two onions, holding them up like they were evidence before the court. Evidence of a crime about to happen. I watched as Georgie peeled the onions and then used a knife to shape them more like apples.

I had a sneaking suspicion I knew where this was going, so when Georgie handed me a prepared onion, I stuck a wooden stick in it with a shake of my head. Georgie lavishly coated them in caramel, laughing like a Disney villain.

"Once they're chilled, you won't be able to smell the onion," Georgie explained as she put the pair of deceptive treats into the refrigerator.

As we all got to work on the real apple treats, I asked, "Who's Cami, anyways? You've both mentioned her."

Georgie snorted and said, "My bratty little sister, Camellia—or Fidget, as I call her. She's three and a half."

Fae tutted. "She's not a brat all the time."

"True," Georgie said with a wicked grin. "I like her when she's quietly sleeping. Less fidgeting."

Fae laughed along with her older daughter, but I furrowed my brow and asked, "Wait, isn't your last name Wood? So, you're Fae Wood, Georgia Wood, and Camellia Wood? Was your dad's name Sher Wood?"

The pair of Woods chuckled, and Fae replied, "That's a good one. I'll add it to the family names. But no, Georgia and Camellia's father was Red Wood. His family embraced the Wood name and they have all sorts of funny combinations in the family tree: Leif Wood, Rowan Wood, North Wood …"

"Aspen Wood, Barry Wood, Long Wood," Georgie chanted, then rolled her eyes. "You can always tell when people catch onto the ridiculousness, and when they're afraid it would be rude to laugh. But how could you not laugh?"

We went back to making the rest of the apples, with Georgie sneaking blobs of caramel when she could. Cami woke up before I left, and the sleepy-eyed toddler seemed sweet enough from her perch in Fae's lap. She sucked on one of her fingers as she watched me with wide brown eyes. The little girl was the picture of innocence in her lacey nighty—until a rumbly staccato of flatulence sounded from beneath it, interrupting the conversation.

Fae made a show of shoving Cami away from her in disgust, and the little girl shrieked with laughter as she tried to climb back in her mother's lap. Fae sent her to Georgie, who leaped up and ran away from her sister—slowly enough that Cami could catch her. Then Georgie swung her into her arms and blew raspberries on her neck.

"No more black-eyed peas for you!" Georgie scolded. "You stink, Fidget!"

"No, you stink!" Cami yelled back, trying to blow a raspberry too, but mostly wetting Georgie's face. Georgie whispered something in Cami's ear and the look they turned my way was pure mischief.

"What are you two planning?" I asked, arms crossed in suspicion.

"Whatever it is will have to wait until tomorrow," Fae said. "It's getting late, and Bet should head home. And Cami should be back in bed."

Fae carried Cami's protesting form upstairs while Georgie got the caramel "apples" she'd made for Uncle Earl out of the refrigerator. Then she grabbed another paper-wrapped package and handed it to me with a grimace.

"What is this?"

"Chicken livers. You were asking Mom what foods might tempt Penny to let you get close, and she mentioned liver is one treat a dog can't resist."

"But she didn't buy this for me. Isn't this for your supper or something?"

Georgie shuddered. "That's exactly why I'm giving them to you. Mom buys them even though she knows I think they're disgusting. It's like eating fried slugs."

I had previously liked chicken livers, breaded and fried in bacon grease, but I doubted I'd ever be able to think of them as anything but fried slugs now. "You have a way with words, Georgie. I'll take them for Penny, but won't you go without supper tomorrow?"

"Don't worry about it. You already brought all those leftovers, and we can make a good meal with those. Just make sure you tell Penny there might be more of those coming after Mom goes shopping again."

I shrugged and added the chicken livers packet to the bag of treats for Uncle Earl. Frogs serenaded me from the ditch as I walked home, and I skipped a little since there was no one to see me. I stopped to say hi to Penny and the dog thumped her tail, but she didn't get up from her nest in the stable yard.

At the house, Nap and Josie were delighted to see me, and even more interested in the bag I carried. I had to lift it high above my head so they would stop crowding me long enough to get through the door. Uncle Earl wasn't home yet, so I left him a note on the table: *Fae makes the best homemade caramel! Georgie sent you some caramel apples so you don't miss out. In the fridge. See you in the morning.*

Chapter Twelve

When I woke up the next morning, I lay in bed and reveled again in having my own private space. The curtains, made from striped bedsheets, cast a muted pattern of light and dark into the room. Quiet enveloped me, and I wondered what time it was, since I didn't have a clock in my room. As I sat up, the bedframe creaked and squeaked under me.

The noises didn't go unnoticed by Nap and Josie in the main part of the house. Snuffling sounded beneath the door, and the wood panel rattled in its frame. I expected to hear Uncle Earl calling them away, but only heard the dogs as I changed into my clothes. I was about to pull the door open when I remembered the caramel onions I had left for Uncle Earl in the fridge. Would he retaliate?

I opened the door slowly and Nap and Josie shoved their heads in so they could greet me. After I got them to calm down a little, I stepped into the kitchen. No Uncle Earl, and no traps I could see. A piece of paper caught my eye on the table.

Gone to pick up my laundry. Will pick up any of your clothes that are ready and be back for a bite of lunch before I go into work.–UE

Hmm, maybe he was saving the "treats" for later? I cautiously opened the icebox and saw one of the caramel onions had a slice cut off, exposing the deceit. Another note rested on the plate: *Nice try. It begs the question: are you going to side with your own blood or some upstart new friend? Make up your mind which side you're on, girl.*

I couldn't tell from the note whether Uncle Earl was genuinely mad about the prank, or if he was only pretending to be stern. My instincts told me it was the latter, especially since he and Georgie had already been playing tricks on each other for a while. If I was dealing with Felix, there would have been no doubt which meaning held true—but then, I wouldn't have dared to joke with him like that.

I decided the best thing to do was to jump in the bath while the tub was free, and then take my cue on how to act from Uncle Earl when he got home. I was curled up in my chair, adding slips of paper between the pages of Black Beauty to mark sections to read aloud to Penny, when Uncle Earl got home. In an encore of my arrival the night before, he had to hold a bag out of Nap and Josie's reach as he made his way to the kitchen.

"You want something to eat?" Uncle Earl asked. "Is this breakfast time or lunchtime for you, sleepyhead?"

"Both! Haven't you heard of brunch before?"

"Who do you think you're talking to? Of course, a cook has heard of brunch."

I chuckled as I helped him unload the groceries. "What should we make? Maybe a meatloaf so we can eat a whole pan ourselves?"

"Eat the whole pan yourself, you mean, while I'm at work. I was thinking about egg sandwiches. Do you like those?"

Uncle Earl turned to look at me when I didn't answer right away. I stood frozen. When I was little, my mama had made the best egg sandwiches on toast, with nearly too much mayonnaise. But later on, I had pretended not to like egg sandwiches anymore because she burned the egg as often as not, or dropped cigarette ashes into it, or didn't notice the fur of mold on the bread. Another memory which should have been pleasant had turned to rot.

Uncle Earl was waiting for an answer, so I asked, "Do you make them like Mama did?"

"There's a good chance of it," he answered gently, "since I taught her how to cook them."

I brightened. "Let's have those, then. Maybe you can teach me, too."

"I can teach you all my specialties. As long as you're not gunning for my job at the diner, that is." He snorted a laugh.

I wasn't after his job, but knowing how to cook other things might help me at the lumber camp. I pictured cracking and frying individual eggs for forty men, and I shuddered. Maybe I could ask Uncle Earl later what kinds of meals he fed the sailors in the Navy.

Uncle Earl walked me through the steps as he cooked the eggs and toasted the bread, spreading the slices with a generous dab of homemade mayo instead of the jarred kind. I took a bite and it was perfection, somehow exactly like the kind my mother made, but also a little better. With enough of these in me, I could forget about those disastrous sandwiches.

As our drooling dog audience begged for bites, Uncle Earl polished off half of his sandwich and said, "Oh, I forgot the lemonade in the fridge. I made it before I left so it would be cold for lunch."

I got up and fetched the pitcher, pouring a drink for myself and one for Uncle Earl. The glass was already sweating in my hand as I raised it and took a big gulp—only to choke and sputter on it. Tears sprang to my eyes as Uncle Earl pounded me on the back. The dogs barked as they circled, simultaneously worried and excited by the commotion.

Finally, I gasped, "So sour! It tasted like straight lemon juice."

"I must have forgot the sugar. Silly me." Uncle Earl was all innocence.

I glared at him through still-watering eyes. "Or was it payback for the caramel onions?"

He shrugged as he reached for the sugar bowl and took a generous spoonful. "Maybe so, maybe not."

I slumped in the chair with my arms crossed and a pugnacious scowl. The sugar dissolved into his lemonade and Uncle Earl smugly raised his glass to take a drink—and also gagged.

"Salt!" he choked out as he pointed an accusing finger at me.

I leaned towards him gleefully. "I didn't really think you'd fall for the caramel onions so close to when you tricked Georgie, so I filled the sugar bowl with salt as a backup plan. You didn't expect a prank war on two fronts."

Uncle Earl shook his head ruefully and got a drink of water. Then he rummaged in a drawer until he found a pencil and a scrap of paper.

"All right, if it's war you want, we need to set basic rules, like I did with Georgie."

He wrote some lines and pushed the paper over to me. It said:

Remember, this is a prank war, not an actual war. No truly dangerous tricks, only silly ones. Extra points awarded for cleverness or style (these extra points to be awarded by the victim for outstanding work). Limited to one prank a day, and three a month. If you specifically say something isn't a prank, it better not be a prank. Any time one of us wants to stop, they should say "rutabaga" and it will stop.

"Anything to add?" Uncle Earl asked.

"What's on the dangerous list?"

He ticked them off with his fingers as he answered, "Fire. Moving a ladder when somebody's on a roof. Greasing the floor. Putting something in food which will make you truly sick. Scaring somebody while he's cutting things up with a knife."

I thought about his list with narrowed eyes. "Which one of those did Georgie do that made you set rules?"

"She greased the floor, and I went down like a giraffe on ice skates. My hip still hurts some on rainy days. I bet it was hilarious to watch, though."

"Yeah, I bet it was." I stifled a grin and wrote something on the paper. Then made a few more marks before sliding it back to Uncle Earl.

No scare pranks at night. Bedrooms are a safe space.

Uncle Earl read it and nodded. "You're right, and since we both met our prank quota for the day, we can relax again."

So we went back to our egg sandwiches in companionable silence. I wondered if it would be too greedy to ask for another sandwich when I finished mine, but then decided I could always make one for myself now that I knew how.

I asked, "Uncle Earl, do you have any good paper for writing letters? Or bigger scraps than this?"

"Yeah, I think so. Check that tin box on the bookshelf." He took our plates to wash up and left me to follow his instructions.

I grabbed the tin and started to open it, then slowed down and pried the lid carefully in case it was booby trapped. No traps, though, just photos and papers all stuffed inside together. On top was a used tablet with some pages left.

"There's a pad from a Howard Johnson's," I called.

"That'll work, unless you need fancy stationery—you'll have to buy that. Who you writing to? Your father?"

"Felix is my stepfather, and no way. I'm writing to Nina, who used to live next door to us." Then I regretted saying that much, in case Uncle Earl guessed I had joined Nina when I left. "Do you mind if I look at the pictures in here? You might have some cool stamps on the postcards, too."

He came out of the kitchen, drying his hands on a towel. "I don't even remember what all is in there. Let's take a look."

The postcards came from all over the world, and were signed with names followed by groups of letters like ENS, LT, LTCDR, and CDWO2. Those were from sailors Uncle Earl had served with during the war and contained some salty language. Uncle Earl tried to hide the worst cursing from me, but I reminded him I grew up in a poker club. I was used to cursing, and I wanted a closer look at all the postmarks and colorful stamps.

Next we moved onto the photographs, and it was the first time I had seen any pictures of my grandparents. They looked stiff and unsmiling, and I wasn't sure if that was because it was an old photo. When I asked Uncle Earl, he scoffed; apparently his parents had been rigid in life, too. My grandmother's severe expression had certainly carried over to her daughter, my mother.

The other photos were of people not related to us, mostly Uncle Earl's friends, with their arms slung around each other. At the bottom of the tin, I spied a bunch of yellowed newspaper tied together and when I pulled those out, a photo fell into my lap. A dark-haired woman held a baby in a lacey dress in her lap, and the man behind her held them in place with his hand on the woman's shoulder. The back was penciled with cursive I recognized as my mother's: *Mama, Papa, and Rosie, '37.*

"Who is this?" I asked and passed the photo to Uncle Earl.

He touched the baby with a gentle fingertip. "That's your older sister, Rosie. She died of influenza not too long after this was taken. They hadn't got the vaccine right yet."

I grabbed the photo back and stared again. I tried to speak a few times before I was able to say, "I had an older sister?"

Uncle Earl looked pained. "I'm sorry. I thought you knew about her. I wouldn't have dropped it on you that way if I'd realized. Your parents really never told you?"

I shook my head, mute again. Was Mama's first child a secret from everyone else, or just me? Did Rosie dying turn Mama so hard, or was it in the family line already from my grandparents? Maybe losing Rosie explained my mother's— our mother's—determination to make me stronger.

"Liza used to send me clippings from her wins." Uncle Earl flipped through the newspaper cuttings. "You can have these."

I nodded, barely listening. My attention was caught by the man in the photo and the way he looked so much like a younger version of Felix. Had Mama stepped out with his brother first, and that's how they knew each other and got together later? Felix hadn't shown up until I was eight, but since I didn't know Rosie existed, I hadn't known to ask who her father was. Mama always laughed off my questions about my father's identity, but what if I was related to Felix, too? That was an answer I didn't want to hear. I put the photo back in the tin and tried to put my questions out of my mind.

"Thanks for the writing paper," I said to Uncle Earl. I took it into my room and sat at my desk, but every time I tried to write something cheerful to Nina, my sister's face floated in front of the blank page. I flipped through the newspaper clippings Uncle Earl had handed me and saw they were for poker tournaments and exhibition games. Mama's young and eager smile gradually flattened to an unreadable expression as time marched on. I shuddered, because I had seen my own face doing that in the mirror lately. It had worked for my mother though—her winnings and accolades grew along with her ability to control her poker face.

There was no point trying to start on my letter now, with so many questions and worries swirling in my head. Maybe if I worked on something else for a bit, I could come back to it later. I went in search of my uncle in the living room.

"Uncle Earl, I have a special treat for Penny, and I thought if we give it to her together, she might get comfortable enough with me that she wouldn't have to go in her pen. Can we try before you get ready for work?"

"Yeah, let's do it now, since I still have to shower. What's the special treat?"

In answer, I got the paper-wrapped chicken livers out of the icebox. After I tipped them into a hot skillet with bacon grease, the steam got all three dogs quivered their nostrils toward the pan. When the livers firmed up, I transferred them to a plate. Uncle Earl took over, knowing his cook's fingers wouldn't feel the heat as much while he made quick work of the chopping.

I thought Nap was going to perish with impatience while they waited for the pieces to cool. He tried a full-throated demanding bay, and when that didn't work, he threw himself to the floor and groaned like he was dying. His sister tried to nudge him out of his tantrum, but he ignored Josie's insistent paw and my laughter. Penny laid down quietly, accepting that the liver either was, or was not, coming her way eventually.

Finally, Uncle Earl gave a piece to Nap and then Josie. Penny nudged his hand for her piece and took it gently. But when she went looking for another, Uncle Earl had lured Nap and Josie further away, and they crowded him with excitement. If Penny wanted more treats, she would have to brave my fingers.

I held my breath as Penny sniffed from a safe distance, her harlequin brow furrowed as she looked at me and tried to read my intentions. With tail tucked, the dog stretched on her toes and snaked her neck, the whites of her eyes showing as she delicately took the scrap of liver. After that, Penny almost crawled into my lap to reach the liver bits.

Even my giggles didn't divert the hound from her mission. When I showed the empty bowl to prove all the treats had been eaten, Penny gave a sigh and settled her head on my knee. Uncle Earl exchanged a delighted nod with me and left us to get acquainted while he bathed.

Penny let me stroke her soft ears and scritch around her neck for a while before getting up to drink some water. I stayed on the floor in case Penny was coming back, but the hound went and nosed open the door to my room instead. I tiptoed after her and was just in time to see another pillow disappear under my bed.

I retrieved the last small pillow and offered it to the watchful darkness beneath the bed. A snuffling sounded, and then the pillow slipped from my fingers. One peek showed me that the pillows nuzzled along Penny's belly like pups at a banquet. The dog's legs curled protectively around them, as if she was afraid I would take them away.

I made reassuring sounds and left Penny to take comfort from her pillow babies. Uncle Earl had finished showering and getting dressed, but he was leaving for work a little early to run an errand on the way so he didn't hang around. He grabbed his wallet and hat and called for Penny like usual, but she didn't come.

"Is she outside?" he asked me.

"No, she's under my bed. Or at least she was, last I saw her."

Both of us went to check my room, but when Uncle Earl called Penny again, her only response was a wagging tail.

I exchanged a glance with my uncle, who said, "Do we dare hope she'll stay with you now?"

That seemed to be the case, and Uncle Earl made it down the driveway without the lonesome howl following him. And I was comforted to know Penny was with me while I sat at my desk to write to my friend.

Dear Nina,

I've left home, finally, but I promised Mama to make one stop before I head to you and Oregon. Well, Mama didn't exactly know where I was planning to end up, but she knew I wouldn't stick around with her husband. But anyhow, I'm staying with my Uncle Earl. He seems nice enough, and even built me a bedroom. Nearly the whole town pitched in to build it!

Uncle Earl is teaching me to cook some things, and that ought to come in handy at the lumber camp. I can help you and your Aunt Kaja with more than the fetching and carrying. Hopefully, a job will still be waiting for me when I get there. I have a dog now, Penny, and I need to stay here a bit longer while she gets some weight on her and then we both will come.

I made a friend, Georgie, and she's a hoot. Her family has the funniest names: Fae Wood, Georgia Wood, Red Wood. My dog has patchy fur and Fae, who is Georgie's mama, told me to bathe Penny in tea, if you can believe it! I guess it's good for her skin.

That's the Woods's return address on the envelope, since I didn't want to leave a trail directly to Uncle Earl's. I know you wouldn't give me away if Felix thinks to ask you about me, but sometimes the post office can be nosy. Anyway, I'll make sure Georgie knows to watch for your letters coming to their house.

I looked up from the page and out the window for a minute, thinking what to write next, and then the quiet room filled with the scratching of a pencil again.

Chapter Thirteen

I won Penny over with those chicken livers, but the hound still looked to Uncle Earl for affection. She didn't try to run after him when he left for work, but when he was home, Penny stayed by his side and barely gave a glance at me. I even stayed home with her, so Penny spent more time with me than Uncle Earl, only to have the dog slink under the bed when he was gone. It took some really tasty treats to lure that contrary hound out for her tea baths.

I was hurt and frustrated after days of Penny snubbing me—which may have brought the nightmare on. Or maybe it was a noise outside which woke me with a start, sure that Felix had found me. In any case, I huddled under my bedcovers, my heart pounding and too terrified to even reach for the lamp switch.

My mind raced, trying to remember whether I had locked my bedroom doors. The one on the outside had a proper lock with a key, but the one into the house only had a slide bolt. Plus, the window was open, so was I really safe? The thought spurred me into crawling from under my blankets long enough to drop to the floor, where I rolled under the bed.

I laid there, trembling, as I struggled to hear over my own ragged gasps. The house was quiet; in fact, Nap and Josie hadn't barked. Eventually, I recognized the danger wasn't real and waited for my body to realize it, too. Then I became aware of a furry body pressed against my side, and the brewed-tea smell of Penny in my nostrils. I turned my head and found Penny's face was only inches from my own. The dog stopped panting long enough to stare intently back at me. At least her breath didn't smell too bad.

"Hey," I whispered. "Sorry to drop in on you like this." I snorted a giggle at my joke.

Penny's tail thumped and then she licked the tears from my face, hugging me to her chest like one of her pillow babies—or even a real puppy. I laughed aloud and squirmed so I could see her face again. She usually shied away from eye contact, but this time she gazed back with curiosity. We laid there so long, her fur against my skin, that our breaths synchronized. I almost didn't want to move and risk breaking the spell, but this floor was not very comfortable.

"Thanks for helping, but I think I'm going to go back 'upstairs' to my bed," I told Penny. "You're welcome to come up there, too."

Though I called her softly from the nest of warm covers, Penny stayed under the bed. With a sigh, I settled down to try to sleep. Then some rustling noises drifted up to me and a dog with a pillow in her mouth landed almost on my face. I giggled and scooted over to make room, and then scooted over some more when Penny insisted on bringing every pillow baby onto the bed, lined up between the dog and me. Where we would all be safe together.

Penny was still in my bed when I woke up the next morning. I expected her to get up as soon as she felt me stirring, but instead she leaned over and licked my face. Was she being affectionate, or did I still have salty cheeks from crying? Only time would tell if I was her person now.

I had slept a little late since I'd had that midnight interruption, so Uncle Earl was already cleaning up after his own breakfast when Penny and I came out. "Good morning," I said, waiting for him to notice the hound at my heels.

He turned and grinned, nodding smugly. "It's about time. I've got meals ready for both of you."

He pulled a plate with fried eggs and potatoes out of the oven and set it before me, and a tin of leftovers for Penny from the fridge. He sat at the table while we dug in.

"Doc Marsh came into the diner yesterday. He asked after Penny and was glad to hear she's doing well, but he has to check on her in person on behalf of the county. He's going to stop by today."

I nodded as I chewed. Then I asked, "Will she let him examine her?"

"I think so. She remembers him from when she was recovering from the surgery."

"Do you know what time? And will you be here?"

Uncle Earl nodded, but before he could elaborate, a knock sounded on the screen door. The dogs had been too busy begging for a taste of my breakfast to notice they had a visitor, but now the pack rushed to the door.

"Oh no, vicious hounds." Georgie's voice went high with mock fear, and the dogs lapped it up.

My mouth still full, I ran over to unhook the screen door and let my friend inside. Nap and Josie immediately jumped on Georgie and they rough housed while I went back to my breakfast, since Georgie had already eaten.

"Don't eat so fast, Bet. You're enjoying a meal made by a world-famous chef," Uncle Earl said.

"Famous because you gave somebody food poisoning in every port?" I asked innocently.

Georgie laughed and Uncle Earl narrowed his eyes. "So, Mrs. Ridgeway had it right and Georgie is a bad influence on you. You're spreading slander about my cooking just to make her laugh."

"Yep," I said with a shameless grin. "But I thought you might laugh too."

Uncle Earl did laugh, and shook his head. "All right, you two troublemakers can play. I have some pie crust chilling and we'll all test my cherry pie for poison when Doc Marsh gets here."

I gave Uncle Earl a one-armed hug to make up for teasing him, before I jumped into the pile of dogs with Georgie. We all wrestled until we ran out of breath, and then Georgie picked up the sack she'd brought with her.

"You mentioned your room at your parents' was decorated, so I brought some magazines. You could cut out some pictures to put on your wall, if you want. Mom sent some gardening ones from her stash, and one of the hunters in town saves me his magazines so I can use the photos for my carvings. We'll need some scissors and thumbtacks."

Uncle Earl pointed to the junk drawer. "You weren't thinking of 'accidentally' losing some of those thumbtacks on my chair, were you, Georgie?"

"What do you think I am, an amateur?" she scoffed. "Besides, that would violate our Prank Treaty terms."

I held up two pairs of scissors and a box of thumbtacks. "Got 'em! Let's go to my room."

I remembered to call, "Thanks, Uncle Earl, for the breakfast and the thumbtacks," before I shut the door to the kitchen. Then I had to open it again when Penny scratched to be let in.

Georgie and I sat on the bigger rag rug and spread the magazines on the floor. We got into a rhythm with me dog earing pictures I liked, and Georgie cutting them out. Then I sorted them into piles of flowers, animals, and movie stars. By luck, one of the older magazines had a full spread on my favorite movie, Harvey.

We were just tacking up the last of the flower pictures when a car pulled up outside, and the dogs started barking. I scrambled up to go back into the house, and Georgie started attaching wildlife photos to the walls.

At the door, Nap and Josie greeted the tall, blond man like a long-lost friend. Penny stood back a little, but wagged her tail in an encouraging way. Doc Marsh shifted his bag to one hand so he could offer the other for Penny to sniff. Once she was satisfied she knew him, Penny turned and trotted back to my side. The veterinarian's eyes widened, and he chuckled.

"Have you been replaced in Girl's—I mean, Penny's—affections, Earl?" Doc Marsh asked. "I never thought I'd see the day."

Uncle Earl laughed and Nap and Josie pranced around at the sound; Penny stayed at my side, but her tail thumped against my calf. Doc Marsh lowered onto the footstool by Uncle Earl's chair and beckoned to me and Penny.

"Can you bring her closer so I can get this stethoscope on her chest?" he asked softly.

I approached him with Penny pressed so close against my leg that her fur tickled my shins. Doc Marsh listened closely to Penny's breathing, then peeled back the dog's lips to see the color of her gums. Last, he kneaded her stomach, including the area with the scar, before grinning at me.

"I don't have to ask if you've been taking good care of her. She's doing fantastic. The tea works then?"

I enthusiastically confirmed the tea treatment, as well as the weight Penny had already put on. "The hardest part has been keeping her home, and me stuck here with her. When can she run around?"

"I'd say another week of good food, maybe, before any all-day adventures. Meanwhile, you can start building her up with short trips. Make sure if she stops to rest, though, you respect it."

Just then, Nap leaped up in Doc Marsh's lap, like he had forgotten he was no longer a tiny puppy. The vet wheezed as the long-legged beast knocked him backward. As I helped untangle them, Penny gave a bark like she was scolding the younger dog.

"You tell him, Penny," I called.

After we moved to the table, where Georgie joined us for the cherry pie Uncle Earl was serving up, I asked, "What about walks to Georgie's house? Is that close enough?"

Doc Marsh thought about it as he chewed a bite. "Yeah, I reckon that would be okay. Can you walk there, though? I know Georgie usually only has one speed—full speed!"

"Hardy har har," Georgie grumbled as we all laughed, but she didn't bother denying it. "Mom would be glad to see how Penny's doing, whenever you bring her. Cami will be all over her, too."

We chatted through seconds on pie, and I decided I liked Doc Marsh. I'd been on guard a little since it seemed like he was checking up on Penny for the county, and maybe he'd find my care lacking. And then he might try to take her away, but he seemed easy-going and cheerful enough. I'd put him on the "maybe" list of people to trust.

"Doc, I was wondering," I said during a gap in the conversation. "What kind of dog do you think Penny is? Her breed, I mean."

He looked at Penny with a critical eye. "Josie and Nap are definitely Plott Hound mixes. But Penny—with those red-and-white patches, she's a beagle through and through. See those black hairs mixed in on her back? I'd say she's more of a pied, like a hare-pied or a badger-pied, than a tricolor. Her puppies were particularly handsome, but perhaps not purebred beagle." I didn't understand any of the "pied" talk, but I filed it away to look up later at the library.

"She's talkative like a beagle," Uncle Earl chimed in. "Sometimes she'll go out on the porch at night and bay."

The vet shook his head ruefully. "Well, there you go. You've got yourself a little red-and-white beagle."

But I didn't have Penny, not really. "What do I need to do to make Penny my dog? For sure my dog, I mean, like how her puppies got homes."

"She's not cleared for a home yet, but you can always fill out the paperwork so it's ready to go when she is. I can put in a good word for you, too."

Overcome with a rush of emotion, I leaped up and nearly hugged Doc Marsh before skipping over to hug Georgie instead. My friend squawked and tried to push me off before awkwardly patting me on the shoulder. Red-faced, Georgie abandoned her last bite of pie and fled to my room.

"What was that all about?" I asked, bewildered by the reaction. Didn't kids our age hug our friends, or were we too old for it?

Uncle Earl looked like he was trying to stifle a laugh, but only shook his head in answer.

"I expect most of Georgie's friends are boys, and she'd sock them if they tried to hug her," Doc Marsh said mildly.

I took in this information and followed Georgie. I wasn't sure if I should apologize to Georgie if I'd crossed a line by hugging her, but I got the feeling Georgie didn't want to talk about it since she was avoiding eye contact. Probably best to let Georgie take the lead for showing affection; I knew what it was like to grit your teeth through unwanted hugs.

"Should we finish hanging up the pictures before we go to your house?" I asked.

"Yeah, it's mostly done."

I tilted my head to one side and inspected our handiwork on the walls. Between the gardening magazines and the hunting magazines, we'd had enough photos to create a woodland wonderland. Or maybe a miniature fairy woodland, since each photo was smaller than a magazine page? In any case, it brightened up the room considerably. Georgie had saved the movie stills for me to do, so I carefully arranged them around my desk vanity mirror. I mixed in some of Mama's clippings too, since she was a celebrity in her own right.

Finished, we rushed back into the house to gather a few things to take to Georgie's. Uncle Earl sat at the table by himself, so Doc Marsh must have left.

"I saved a slab of pie for Fae to share with Cami," Uncle Earl said. "Can I trust you two to deliver it and not eat it on the way?"

"Of course," I said sweetly, after sharing a telling look with Georgie. "Do we have a leash for Penny? I don't want her to run off on her first trip away from the house."

"Hmm." Uncle Earl got up to rummage in a basket on top of the refrigerator. "I have collars for Nap and Josie, with brass tags on them, in case they get lost hunting. Maybe I still have one of their puppy collars to fit Penny."

He made a triumphant noise as he retrieved a leather collar, well chewed on the end of the strap, but still usable. He called Penny, and she trotted over easily until she saw what was in his hand. Then her ears flattened, her head dropped, and her tail tucked. Nap barreled her out of the way and nearly snatched the collar from Uncle Earl, but he held it out of reach.

Georgie and I hadn't said a word while we watched, but now I let out a delighted laugh. Penny actually gave a little jump, and everyone else turned to stare at me.

"I thought if she sees that a collar is fun, maybe she'll change her mind. Let's make it a game." My voice was the perkiest it had ever been, and I danced over to claim the collar from Uncle Earl.

I egged on Nap and Josie's excitement, touching the collar to their noses before prancing out of reach again. Soon they were begging for it like it was a crown made of jerky. I draped it over Josie's neck and heaped the dog with praise. While Uncle Earl occupied himself with holding Nap back, Georgie joined me in making Josie into a Very Big Deal.

"Who's the most beautiful Empress Josephine now? You are!" Georgie cooed.

Josie glowed under the attention until Penny couldn't stand to be left out and stepped prettily behind us in our impromptu parade. It was simple for me to slide the collar off Josie and put it on Penny, leaving the buckle undone in case she panicked. Dabs of peanut butter for all the dogs distracted them enough for me to buckle the collar and attach the leash with no fuss.

Now the fake laughter turned genuine as the dogs made absurd faces, trying to lick the peanut butter from their muzzles. When they finally got it all, instead of looking worried, Penny looked for more peanut butter in my hand that held the leash.

"Well, I think that may have done the trick. Good thinking, Bet." Uncle Earl patted me on the head and I rolled my eyes.

"Are you ready to go, Georgie?"

"Mmfess."

Uncle Earl and I turned to see the last of the cherry pie disappearing into Georgie's lips. At Uncle Earl's indignant cry, Georgie spewed crumbs as she said, "What? I only promised not to eat it on the way."

Chapter Fourteen

Before we could leave, Uncle Earl prepared a paper for Georgie to sign: an IOU for "one large piece of cherry pie, eaten in dishonorable circumstances." Georgie showed no remorse as she flourished her signature. Nap and Josie tried to follow us, but Uncle Earl was too quick with the screen door latch.

Doc Marsh was right that Georgie had a hard time keeping pace with us. Georgie's long-legged gait put her far enough in front that it made conversation difficult. I only caught snatches of a story Georgie was trying to tell about poison oak and a boy in the neighborhood. He got poison oak where?

Finally, I said, "Why don't you run ahead and tell your mama we're coming? If she doesn't want Penny to come inside, we can sit on the porch."

"It'll be fine," Georgie hollered as her flying feet stirred up the dust.

In truth, I didn't mind that I had the dog to myself for a little while. Penny seemed so much more alert, out of the yard and house in the wider world. It was like I was meeting her for the first time, at least the real Penny underneath the shyness. The dog's quivering nose kept leading her in all directions, but when she hit the end of the leash, she would shoot a glance at me for reassurance. Every time, I met her gaze with a smile and words of praise and our connection strengthened.

We got into such a rhythm I was tempted to go past the Woods's house for a longer walk, but then I remembered this was Penny's first time out. We were supposed to be taking it easy. Besides, Cami had spotted us from the porch and shouted my name until Fae came to scoop her up.

"I don't mind dogs in the house at all," Fae called. "We just have to see how she does around Cami. I'm more worried about this little devil hurting the dog, honestly." Cami yowled and spit like a cat in her mother's tight grasp, as if to prove Fae's point.

I came through the gate slowly, with Penny pressing against my calf as the dog sensed my watchfulness. The beagle stuck like a burr as we approached the front porch, and fortunately Cami had quieted, rapt at the wonder of meeting a new dog up close. The tip of Penny's tail quivered as I introduced Fae and Cami.

Fae set Cami down, but kept hold of the back of her overalls so the little girl planted on her bottom. Penny's ears perked forward, and the tail wagged faster. Did she recognize Cami was only a puppy herself? Though I still held the leash, Penny belly-crawled up the porch steps and across the boards towards her new friends.

Fae and I stood ready to separate them if necessary, and Cami held out a sticky hand for Penny to sniff. The hound obligingly licked her fingers and scooted forward enough to lay her head on Cami's lap. The child's joyous shriek made me wince, so it must have been ear-splitting for Penny, but she toughed it out. I sat on a step and listened while Fae explained to Cami about being gentle with Penny, and how that meant no screaming, no hitting, no pinching, no pulling her fur or ears, and no biting.

I wasn't sure if Cami understood all that, but she copied her mother's soft petting of Penny's head and ears. Penny relaxed into it, not even seeming to mind strangers were so close. Fae and I exchanged a smile and let the two small creatures have their moment together before bringing them inside.

We all trooped into the kitchen, which smelled like fresh-baked cornbread. Georgie had already wedged a piece from the tin and was eating it from her hand, crumbs dropping to the floor. Fae sighed and handed her daughter a napkin as Penny discreetly licked up the fallen food. When Cami came over to copy the dog, Georgie saw the wisdom of a napkin and didn't let any more crumbs fall.

"What are your plans today?" Fae asked as she started drying the dishes beside the sink.

Georgie and I looked at each other and shrugged. We hadn't really talked about what to do next; the freedom to be lazy was the best part of summer. I was just glad I got to spend more time outdoors—and in better company, too—instead of cooped up in a smoky poker club.

"I can think of a few chores if you're bored." Fae winked.

"No, that's okay," Georgie said hastily. "I was going to work on one of my pieces for the Fair. Out on the front porch, with Bet."

Taking my friend's lead, I spoke up, "Yeah, and Georgie and I are going to come up with some ideas for me to enter something in the Fair."

Fae tsked. "I guess I'll do the ironing myself, then. The entry forms are due soon, so you'd better decide on a category. Do you think you could shell a few peas while you two talk, Bet?"

Standing behind her mom, Georgie's eyes went wide, and she shook her head in warning. But it was just a few peas, so I didn't think it would take too much time from my summer. "Sure."

My eyes widened when Fae pulled an enormous bowl of peapods from the fridge. "My peas have thrived this year. The string beans, too. I plan on doing a heap of canning in a few days."

Before I could say anything, Georgie blurted, "We definitely have plans on canning day. I'll go get my carving knives and my project." She ran upstairs.

"I appreciate the help," Fae said wryly as she found another bowl for me to put the shelled peas in. "Georgie said she only likes to help me can when there's explosions. There was only one time I didn't watch the gauge on the pressure cooker close enough—one time!"

"Yeah, but we were scraping carrot off the walls for a week," Georgie interjected as she came back in the room.

We all laughed, and I lugged the giant bowl out to the porch, while Georgie carried the roll of leather holding her tools, plus a basket piled with unfinished projects. Penny followed us and laid next to my chair, to catch any falling peas. I was glad her appetite was strong enough to mooch now.

Through the screen door, Fae called, "Do you girls want some lemonade? Or cornbread?"

"Not right now," Georgie said. "I'll come in and get some in a while, thanks. Can you turn on the radio so we can hear it?"

So the strains of "Your Cheatin' Heart" gave me a rhythm to fall into while shelling peas. The rasp of Georgie's tools against the wood matched the *tink* of peas in the metal bowl. Along with our humming, the two sounds made a curious backup band.

"You shelled peas before?" Georgie asked. "You're pretty quick."

"Yeah, I used to help my neighbor, Mrs. Nowak. They had a garden behind their house, and a big family, so she canned as much as she could. Mama Nowak was the best cook." At Georgie's scoff, I hastily added, "Apart from your mom and Uncle Earl, obviously."

We went back to our tasks and I said softly, "Mama Nowak joked that all her kids were American hoodlums, and one more child underfoot didn't make a difference. If it wasn't for her sharing some of her home canning, I would have been as desperate for food as you seem to be."

Georgie rolled her eyes at my joke, but asked, "Did they offer to take you in after your mom died?"

I shrugged. "They might have, but they'd already moved away by then. Mr. Nowak got a job down by Modesto and off they all went." Well, all except for Nina, who went to her aunt in Oregon, and who was expecting me to join her any day now. But I was still keeping that to myself—even from Georgie. That reminded me I still needed to ask about the mail.

"Say, Georgie, do you mind if I get mail here? Just some letters from a friend."

Georgie gave me a funny look, but nodded. "Do I need to head off the mailman, or can my mom know about it? I'm guessing it's something secret from Earl."

I shrugged like it didn't matter. "It might be better if your mom doesn't know, so she doesn't slip up and mention it to Uncle Earl."

"All right. And hey, we'd better talk about your fair entry for real, or Mom will find more chores for us. Do you have any idea what you want to do?"

"When are the entry forms due again?" I asked.

"In two weeks, but then you deliver the actual entry in the week before the fair starts on July 4th. So you only have a little while to decide, but then you have another three weeks to make your handicraft. Growing prize flowers or vegetables is out, since you would have had to start the seeds months ago, like Mom does. Do you just want to participate, or are you aiming to win?"

I snorted. "Win, of course."

"Then you should look at the sure bets. Ha, sure Bet!" Undeterred by my groan (like I'd never heard puns on my name before), Georgie continued, "Now, you don't have to grow the veggies yourself to enter the food preservation category, but you'd be up against my mom there and she always wins. Winning in baking would mean beating out Mom and Earl, which only Mrs. Garcia has ever done. I still have dreams about those coyota pastries she made!"

I sighed. "Okay, so I know the ones not to enter. What's left?"

"I don't remember. To be honest, I don't pay much attention to anything but the woodworking. Mom!" Georgie hollered the last word.

Fae came to the screen door. "Georgie, I'm right here. You don't need to yell so loud every mom in the neighborhood thinks their child is calling."

Georgie grinned, unrepentant. "Next time, I'll call for Fae instead. Do we still have the guidebook for the fair?"

"Yes, I think so. I'll get it." Fae disappeared back into the house.

I asked if I could try one of Georgie's finished whistles and tootled an out-of-tune version of "Chew Chew Chew Your Bubblegum" while dancing a jig.

Georgie commented, "Well, you won't win the talent show with that, but people might toss you some pennies on the corner."

I stuck my tongue out at Georgie and danced faster. I was out of breath by the time Fae came onto the porch, carrying a tray with two glasses of lemonade.

"I found the guidebook, plus my camera still has some exposures left on the film. Maybe you could enter some photographs—unless you've come up with something better?"

"I was thinking of the talent show," I said, ignoring Georgie's scoff, "but maybe I'd better have a backup plan. You don't mind if I use up your film? I'll pay to develop it."

"No, it's fine. I don't even remember what all is on here. I don't have much time for things like photography since Cami came along. It's better for the camera to get some use than to sit on a closet shelf. Just play around with it and see what you come up with."

Fae gave me a demonstration of how to use the view-finder to see her subject, and how to advance the film. "This little window shows a four, so there are eight exposures left. That should be enough to start with and see how you like it."

"Okay, thank you," I said. "I'm about halfway through the bowl of peas, so I'll finish those first."

Georgie coughed into her hand while saying, "Apple polisher!" I ignored her insult and when Fae went back in the house, Penny slipped inside with her. While I continued shelling peas, Georgie read categories from the guidebook.

"Canning we've already talked about, and cakes too. There's lots of livestock—maybe you could put Fidget in a pig costume and enter her? She's getting big enough to fetch a good meat price at auction."

I glanced at Cami, who was with Penny in the sun patch inside the screen door. Cami squealed as she lay on her belly, inching like a worm, while the dog copied her. It looked like Penny was smiling and the light hit them just so. Putting a finger to my lips to warn Georgie, I stood up and pointed the camera at the pair.

Bracing the camera against my belly, I squinted at the tiny image in the viewfinder to line up the subjects. The shutter made a soft click, making them glance over, and I carefully turned the dial on the side counterclockwise until the number five showed up in the little window. I only had the one chance to capture the scene because the duo rushed over to the screen door, wanting out. Cami's little hands clutched the wooden scrollwork like prison bars.

I called over my shoulder to Georgie, "The prisoners want out. Should I let them into the yard for exercise?"

"You can if you stick with them. The yard is fenced, but Fidget has figured out how to open the gates, so we have chains on them now."

"Okay, there might be things to take pictures of in the garden, so that works."

The button on the screen latch was hard to open, which was probably why Cami hadn't gotten out yet. I finally got the trick of it and Penny and Cami pushed past me. Cami disappeared into the jungle of the front garden almost immediately, calling for her new furry friend.

Penny hesitated, looking at me, until I said, "Go ahead. I'm coming too."

As soon as my foot stepped off the bottom stair, Penny shot away to find Cami. I kept them in hearing range—easy to do, since Cami kept up a constant babble—and wandered with the camera in hand. Taking pictures of pretty flowers seemed too obvious, so I got creative.

There was a weird vine with flowers which looked like Uncle Earl's tobacco pipe, and I tried to line up the blazing sun so it sat right in the bowl. I snapped a bee the size of my thumb as it buzzed around a hollyhock flower, but I was afraid it might just be a dark blot against the tissue-paper petals. I even laid down in a dusty hollow under a lilac bush, pointing the lens at the interlocking branches and filtered sky above.

It was there that Cami and Penny found me, and I curled around the camera to protect it from the tickling, licking assault. My attackers were relentless. They were joy personified, and instead of scolding them, I decided to join in.

"Georgie, Georgie, save me!" I called in mock terror. "The prisoners are revolting!"

Georgie's frowning face poked between the leaves. "Ugh, you're right, you're all revolting. I should hose you all down."

Cami shrieked and bolted deeper into the garden with Penny hot on her heels. Georgie helped me from under the lilac and we gave chase. After we caught Cami, her big sister lifted her over her head like a strongman, posing for me with teeth bared in a grimace. Then Georgie swung Cami in a circle while Penny tried to catch her flying heels.

Is this what it would have been like if Rosie had lived and been a big sister to me? Would she have given me a funny nickname? Maybe we could have stood up to Mama and Felix better if there were two of us, instead of just me. Uncle Earl made it sound like their hard childhood had made him and my mother closer when they were younger. But then Uncle Earl had gone off to the Navy and left Mama with their parents, until she found her own way out with her card skills. Just like I'd taken my way out when Mama died. Was it just an unbreakable cycle? Before my thoughts could go too much darker, the screen door squeaked open.

"You're going to make that child sick," Fae called from the porch. "That's enough of that, and I whipped up some honey butter to go with the cornbread."

There was a scramble as we all ran to the house, and I picked up Cami when she fell behind. The cool lemonade washed the dust from our teeth and the honey butter was heaven on the cornbread. After clearing the plates, Georgie and I settled back to our tasks with satisfied bellies.

Chapter Fifteen

It only took about half an hour for me to take the last three exposures, and then Fae helped me advance the film and remove the cartridge. After I finished shelling the peas, I wanted to take Penny home to rest after her eventful afternoon with Cami, so Georgie promised to drop off the film at the camera store the next day.

Nap and Josie ran to meet me and Penny at the end of the driveway when we got back to Uncle Earl's; he had already gone to work and left me a plate of cheese and lunchmeat for a sandwich in the fridge. I fed all the dogs and made a towering sandwich to eat. Grabbing a book from Uncle Earl's shelves, one of many with a cowboy on the cover, I sat at the table to eat. I thought maybe it was a book I could read to Penny, but decided all the gunfights might not be to the dog's taste.

After we all ate, we sat on the porch for a while. Nap and Josie soon ran off after something in the bushes, but Penny stayed leaning against my leg. I scratched her and asked, "Is your skin feeling any better? It looked like you had a good time with Cami today."

I wasn't really expecting any kind of answer, of course, but she seemed to like the sound of my voice, so I kept talking. "I bet you miss Cami already, but don't forget you're my girl now. And I'm yours. We'll be going to Oregon as soon as you're able, just the two of us."

It occurred to me that Penny really might miss Cami, and Uncle Earl, and everyone and everything she knew here in Amberfields. Would I be enough for her? Maybe the fresh smells in the lumber camp would help her forget her early life, the bad along with the good. After all, this town and my friends had made the poker club seem like a long-ago nightmare for me. The lumber camp was bound to feel like home in no time, once I had Nina around again.

In the morning, Uncle Earl seemed to be sleeping in, so I tried to be quiet while I fed the dogs their breakfast and made a bowl of cereal. But the quiet didn't last, because when I turned on the kitchen tap the water sprayed out, soaking my shirt and the counter. Excited by my screech, the dogs crowded me as I fumbled to turn the tap off.

Blinking water from my eyes, I crouched down to look at the faucet and saw a piece of chewing gum crammed in it. Just like putting your thumb over the end of the hose to make it spray wildly. A noise from Uncle Earl's room got the dogs' attention, and he opened the door and stepped out fully dressed. He must have been waiting in his bedroom for me to discover his booby-trapped faucet.

"At least you know you're safe for a while, since you got pranked today." He grinned at my sopping clothes and hair.

"Yeah, that was a good one," I admitted grudgingly. "Are you going to cook me a real breakfast to make up for it?"

"It looks like you already had cereal, but I have some pastries for this morning hidden in the back of the fridge."

When I bit into the delicious perfection of a sticky pecan roll, I decided to go easy on Uncle Earl with my next prank. It turned out I didn't have to put it off too long, because both of us had forgotten the chewing gum was still in the faucet. As Uncle Earl finished his pastry, he went to wash the powdered sugar off his fingers and got sprayed, too.

We both laughed and Uncle Earl said, "Okay, I've been pranked too, so you can't get me back today."

"I'm not sure if that really counts, but it gives me time to think up something fitting." I gave an evil laugh and ducked as Uncle Earl threw the dishrag at me.

"Actually, it's good that we're both already wet," Uncle Earl said. "I have something in mind for today."

"Like what?"

"Well, you had asked what you can do to help around here, and at the time I said as long as you clean up your own messes, we'll do fine together. But I thought of a chore—I mean, an opportunity for you to help me out."

"That doesn't sound suspicious at all," I said dryly. "Are we making moonshine?"

He laughed. "Nothing that ambitious. I thought you could take over the garden."

"What garden? I haven't seen one here."

"It's across the road. That's my property too, part of the old farm fields. I haven't done much with it in the last few years, but maybe we can get it going again. Fae said she can give us some plants, since she always starts too many seeds."

"Let's go see," I said. "The dogs can come, right?"

"Sure, they can help us dig."

After we all walked down the long drive and across the road, we entered a gate into an overgrown patch. Wooden pallets and wire made a cobbled-together fence to keep the deer and rabbits out, although the holes dug underneath showed it wasn't completely successful. The entire garden area was about half the size of a football field, and dry as dust under the overgrowth. Along one side, a bright tumble of yellow flowers grew leggy, reaching out to take over more parts of the garden.

The dogs immediately started rooting and Uncle Earl called for them to be careful of snakes, as if they could understand him. Since Nap and Josie slowed down, maybe they could. Penny seemed more interested in the shade cast by some big, umbrella-like leaves.

"How far does your property go?" I asked.

"You see those cottonwoods down there? That's the Bear River, and my parcel goes down to its banks. It floods, though, so I don't do anything with that end. The river curves around and runs practically in Fae's backyard before it follows the edge of town again."

"You could have a huge garden, then!"

"Hmm, let's start with this. I didn't think it would be this bad," Uncle Earl said, hands on hips. "But I can see the Jerusalem artichokes survived—those are the yellow flowers— and some things might have reseeded on their own. Yep, some tomatoes are taking over that corner back there. This might be more than a couple hours' work like I had hoped."

"Maybe Georgie can come over when it's cooler tonight and help me, since she knows plants. She's trying to get out of helping Fae with her canning, though, so maybe she should help her mom."

Uncle Earl scoffed. "Georgie's not afraid of hard work, but I don't blame her for skipping out on canning. It's miserable, unless you have a separate summer kitchen so your house doesn't get steamed up. Fae might grumble about it, but truth is she loves canning. Says she appreciates seeing a line of jars she made, and she's generous with sharing. That pie I made was some of her preserved cherries. I used to send over produce from my garden, and she'd send back a few jars."

Uncle Earl found a long stick and used it to part the grass for a closer look at his former garden. "Hey, look at that, strawberries! And those big leaves are probably squash or pumpkin. Maybe these plants won't put us so far behind in the season after all."

His stick disturbed the nest of some kind of small, furry rodent, and before Nap and Josie had even turned their heads, Penny was diving after the critters. *Snap, snap, snap,* and they disappeared into her gullet. She licked her lips and perked her ears to listen for any escapees.

"Whoa," I breathed. "I guess we know how she kept herself and her puppies fed when she was running wild."

It was too hot already to do much, so Uncle Earl agreed to stop by Fae's on his way to work and see if Georgie wanted to come by later. That left me and the dogs at home to cool off as best we could on the porch. The latest tea bath for Penny helped, and then a nap.

Georgie found us on the porch, dozing, and a book dangling from my hand. I woke as Georgie took it from me and I smiled blearily at her.

"I've been busting my tail all day trying to finish my carvings, and look at you, lazybones!" Georgie said with a grin.

I frowned, feeling bad she had been working all day and here I was asking her to do more. "Are you really too tired for the garden? I can at least make you something to eat."

Georgie laughed. "No, we can work on the garden. I was only teasing. Mom sent some cookies, but I wouldn't say no to eating."

"Do you ever say no to eating?" I teased as we went into the house. "I'll make us some sandwiches."

Georgie watched as I stuck some pieces of bread in the toaster, and while those turned golden, I thinly sliced tomatoes from the garden. Next, I chopped sweet onion, but instead of putting it directly on the toasted bread and ham, I tossed the onion in oil and vinegar.

"Oooo, fancy," Georgie teased.

In return, I put on a snooty expression as I sprinkled on some dried herbs. The plain ham and cheese sandwich took on a sweet and sharp bite from the onions and herbs.

Georgie chewed thoughtfully. "Okay, this is my new favorite. Do you eat this a lot?"

"Not this kind all the time. I started making sandwiches as soon as I could pull a chair up to the counter, since no one else was feeding me. I had to get creative with whatever we had on hand, or what I could get from the store for cheap. Usually Spam or bologna, but Uncle Earl has better food."

"Yeah, chicken livers are cheap, which is why Mom buys them so often, yuck. What's your favorite food you've ever had, whether or not you made it?"

I swallowed a bite before answering. "Has to be the pierogi our neighbor, Mrs. Nowak, made. They're like these dumpling things with meat or potato filling and then you fry them in butter and onions. The absolute best, and even better if you throw some kielbasa sausage in there with it."

Georgie moaned, "Mmm, now you're making me hungry."

I laughed so hard I nearly choked. "Georgie, you're complaining of being hungry while you're actually eating! Nap is the only other one I know who would do that."

Georgie blushed and smiled weakly. "Penny might do it too—if you've gone hungry, it never really leaves you. I'm always thinking ahead to the next meal, to make sure there is one."

I felt bad for my joke and nodded gravely; of course I could relate. "I get that. I've been so hungry before that my stomach just heaved dry. Mrs. Nowak was a lifesaver whenever there was no food in the house."

Even though we were sharing confessions, I couldn't bring myself to admit I had gotten so desperate that I'd stolen from Felix's wallet while he slept. I didn't know where he got the silver money clip engraved with initials that weren't his, but it always held a fat wad of cash. I convinced myself he wouldn't notice a few dollars missing here and there. The first time Felix caught me stealing his money was also the first time he beat me in front of my mother.

He dragged Mama into the bedroom by the hair when she tried to stop him. More blows sounded as I pulled and kicked at the locked door, until the sobs in the room turned to soft words that coaxed and charmed. And then the only sounds were soft gasps and moans. I slept outside the door and Mama almost stepped on me while sneaking out after he fell asleep.

She wouldn't look at me as she said, "He's seen sense that a child needs to eat, and there'll be a shopping allowance from now on. You'll have to make do with whatever money he sees fit to give, and not take any from him again. I'll make sure he doesn't forget." But of course, my mother lost track of her promises during her next binge, leaving me and my belly hollow once more.

Georgie and I finished their last few bites in silence, then I asked, "What's your favorite food? If it won't make you too hungry to talk about it."

Georgie's smile lit up. "Sacher torte! Chocolate cake with apricot or raspberry jam and even more chocolate. We had it at a fancy department store cafe once, and now Mom makes it for my birthday every year."

I groaned. "That does sound good. We'd better head to the garden before we eat all the food in Uncle Earl's fridge."

Georgie and I dropped our dishes in the sink and got two pairs of gloves from atop the hutch, where we kept them out of Nap's reach. We loaded some tools into the wheelbarrow and the dogs trotted ahead to the garden. I expected Georgie to turn around again, once she saw the job ahead of us, but she dug right in with a hoe. She even shared some useful tips.

"This plant is mallow, and most people call it a weed, but it has lots of uses. Mom makes remedies with it, but even she can't use all of this. We'll save some for her, and the rest we can chop up to start a compost pile. Just getting it out of the way should give us a better look at what's not mallow. Oh, there's purslane—Mom pickles that and it's fantastic."

Georgie was right; there were lots of other plants trying to survive under the blanket of mallow. Other greens (called weeds by those who didn't know how to use them), plus some survivors or descendants from Uncle Earl's garden. The compost pile we started in one corner was as high as the fence by the time we finished. Plus, we had a wheelbarrow heaped with foraged plants and Jerusalem artichoke tubers. The garden still looked wild instead of neat rows, but the individual plants could breathe again.

It was getting dark by then, so I would have to bring some water to the plants the next day. I was sore but proud to have accomplished something. I would get this garden whipped into shape as a present for Uncle Earl before I leave.

Penny and I walked Georgie home with the full wheelbarrow, so I could bring it back empty. Georgie's mom was delighted with the bounty and sent me off with a slab of zucchini bread.

Georgie called after me, "Hey, I almost forgot. The film should be ready tomorrow. Come by after ten and we can fetch it."

"Okay, but promise you won't go early and look at the pictures without me!"

Georgie's raspberry was the only promise I got. I slipped Penny bites of bread as we walked together, and the warm light from the lamp in Uncle Earl's window welcomed us home. I frowned, realizing I was already thinking of this place as home in spite of my plans in Oregon.

My mother and I had moved around a lot when I was growing up, so there wasn't one place which was "home" for me. We'd stayed put after Felix moved in, but it was not home with him there. More like an asylum, I thought with a snort. Uncle Earl's definitely felt like home, especially the little room all my own, where I curled up with Penny and slept that night like one of the rocks we'd dug up from the garden.

Chapter Sixteen

I was surprised to see Uncle Earl up when I came out of my room; he usually slept a little later than eight after a night shift. I gave him the side eye as I poured myself a glass of milk, in case he had a prank waiting for me.

As if he could read my mind, he laughed and said, "No tricks this morning, don't worry! I thought we could see what still needs doing in the garden together."

"We pretty much finished it last night. But how do you get water to the plants? Do you lug buckets from the house?"

"I have a way. I'll show you. But first, since we have extra time, have you ever had a spaghetti omelet?"

"Isn't there a rule about not being allowed to prank after you've said you weren't pranking the other person?"

"No, this is the real deal. It was a good way to use up leftovers in the galley. You scramble up some eggs and pour them in with whatever you have in the fridge. Today, that's leftover spaghetti and meat sauce. You said you wanted me to teach you all my specialties."

I agreed to try it, and it was better than it sounded. The dogs must have tried it before, because their begging went into overdrive. I may have slipped them each an eggy noodle, but then so did Uncle Earl. Once everyone had their breakfast, Uncle Earl and I headed outside to the old stable.

As I helped move things to get to the water tank, I asked, "Is there anything this old place doesn't have? Seems like whatever we need magically appears."

"That's because those of us who lived through the hard times in the thirties never throw anything away. I made this from some old milk cans and tiller parts the farmers left behind."

He pointed like a showman to his creation. It looked like he'd welded the milk cans to a metal frame mounted on wheels. Even with ten gallons of water in each can, it moved screechily but surely as he pulled it behind. He stopped at the garden gate in astonishment.

"Wow, this looks fantastic. You even thinned the Jerusalem artichokes, and I bet we'll get some pumpkins off those vines."

I helped him water the plants we were keeping, and then Penny and I took off to meet Georgie. She sat on the curb in front of her house, whittling a stick.

"What are you making this time?" I asked.

"Just a tootle for Cami—it's what she calls these elderberry whistles. She drives Mom crazy with them, so they 'disappear' after a while. Until I give her a new one."

Georgie pocketed the unfinished whistle and her folded knife, and dusted off the seat of her shorts. "Let's go to the camera store. I bet you're dying to see your pictures."

I suddenly smacked my forehead. "Ugh, I forgot about Penny. Is it far?"

"It's right by Doc Marsh's office, so not too far. It would be a good way to add a little distance to her walk."

Relieved, Penny and I fell into step with Georgie and headed into town. Everybody seemed to know Georgie and greeted her, but I was surprised by how many people knew my name, too. That must be small-town life. I appreciated the folks who had a kind word for Penny the most, as I saw Penny try her best to be friendly back.

We passed Doc Marsh's clinic just as he came out the door, and he exclaimed, "Isn't she a shiny new Penny? You're really doing a good job with her, Bet."

I blushed under his praise and laid my hand on Penny's head possessively. "Yeah, she's coming right along. I don't have to bathe her in tea so often now her fur is growing back."

After a little chat, Doc Marsh went on his way and we continued to the camera shop. As I was walking in, I spied a display of Philco AM radios with a clock dial—the green one would be perfect for my bedside table. I bought it and paid for my prints, while Georgie waited with Penny outside, and then we hustled back to Georgie's. Penny and Cami found each other immediately and ran off to play, but Fae joined us at the kitchen table as we opened the paper envelope. I thumbed through the photos to find the six I took and handed the rest to Fae, since those were the ones already on the roll of film.

I only half-listened as Fae and Georgie exclaimed over their prints, since I was trying to look at my own with a critical eye. The one taken under the lilac and looking up at the sky wasn't nearly as artistic as I'd hoped; it was just busy looking with all the crossed branches. And as I'd feared, the bumblebee I'd snapped was an out-of-focus, dark blur. I hoped I'd be good at this right out of the gate, but no such luck.

The photo I'd tried to take of Cami and Penny playing inside the front door was blurry from the screen, but the snapshot of Cami dressing up Penny in an old nightgown and lacey cap made me smile. I would have to think about whether it was good enough to enter. The last photo in the group made me pause; the more I looked at it, the more I liked it.

I had caught Georgie intent on adding details to the fox carving cupped in her hand. The way the afternoon sun came from behind Georgie's shoulder, it lit up her face and the fox's. They looked more like two luminous creatures gazing at each other in wonder than a carver and her creation. I didn't realize Georgie was calling my name until she also knocked on the table.

"I was asking if you have a winner in there?"

I answered, "Most are garbage. There's one I like an awful lot, but maybe it's just me."

Fae gestured. "Pass them over here, and Georgie and I will take a look."

I handed them to Fae without saying which photo was my favorite. Georgie and her mom made hmming noises as they studied the handful of prints before lining them up. The photo of Georgie was at the top, with Penny and Cami playing dress-up ranked below.

"I would love enlargements of both of these if you're going to get some printed for the fair," Fae said. "Georgie looks like a perfect angel in this one."

Georgie blushed and rolled her eyes at her mom. Then she fetched the entry guidebook so we could review what size enlargements I needed to order. At least eight by ten, plus they would also need to be mounted on cardstock with a white mat around the image. Mr. Diaz at the camera store should be able to help.

"I could enter both perfect angels," I said with a wink at Fae. "It's only twenty-five cents for each photography entry."

"I don't think the others are garbage, by the way. You're just starting out. They show a good eye for detail, but you need to get the hang of depth of field. That will come with experience. Are you going to enter anything else?" Fae asked.

I stared again at the two pictures we'd set aside as favorites. "I think Georgie's could win if she says it's okay to enter it," I mused. "But I'm thinking I want to challenge myself more, too. I don't need to deliver the actual artwork until a few days before the Fair, right?"

Georgie nodded and read aloud, "Photography entries must be dropped off July 2nd by six in the evening, and picked up on July 7th by noon."

I looked to Fae. "For what I have in mind, I would need to borrow Cami and Georgie along with your camera. Would that be okay? And I'll need to find some old dresses or nightgowns."

Fae raised her eyebrows. "Sounds intriguing. Do we get to know what you're planning?"

My laugh was full of mischief, like when I was planning a prank. "Not yet. I need to think on the details some more."

I carefully filled out the form for submitting photographs, one entitled "Creation" and the other "Storytime." That should be vague enough that even if my original vision didn't work, I would have some wiggle room to change it and still fulfill the title.

"They haven't picked up the mail today, so you can put the envelope in the box at the curb," Fae said. "I have a stamp here if you need one."

After we put the registration in the mailbox and raised the flag, Georgie turned back to the house, but I spoke up. "Uncle Earl said the Bear River runs behind your house. Is that true?"

"Yeah, it's just down a path. You can walk along the banks all the way to the park in town. Do you want to see?"

I grinned and nodded. "I should get Penny so she doesn't think I've left her."

But when we went in the house to find the dog, and to tell Fae where we were going, Cami shrieked she wanted to come too. Georgie tried to pry her little sister off her leg and looked at her mom.

Fae raised a brow and said, "I wouldn't mind a few moments to myself, if you two promise to watch her. Maybe she'll take a nap later if she gets some of her energy out."

Georgie heaved a sigh, but took Cami's hand. "I'm not carrying you, Fidget. And you have to do what we say. I mean it."

I attached Penny's leash, and we walked to a gate in the back corner of the yard. A loop of chain over the gate and post kept curious Cami fingers from opening it, but Georgie deftly opened it and led her sister through. Penny and I followed, latching the gate behind us.

The path was blazing hot in the midday sun, until we reached the welcome coolness of the oaks along the river. Insects buzzed in the tall greenery and a bird gave a sleepy peep as we disturbed its siesta. Cami couldn't resist brushing her hand through the nodding seed heads on the grass, despite Georgie's warning of "that's where ticks wait for succulent little girls to walk by."

The chuckle of running water turned louder as we stepped to the water's edge. Tiny frogs fled into the river with a squeaking sound, catching the interest of Cami and Penny. The pair tried to follow the jumping frogs into the shallows, but Georgie held tight to Cami's hand.

"We're not going in the water right now. We're showing the river to Bet," Georgie said over the howl of protest. Penny didn't help things by stepping daintily into the shallows and lying flat to cool her belly. She could almost be teasing Cami with her smug dog grin.

"Do you go swimming here? Is the water safe?" I asked, eyeing the white froth churning in a faster-moving stretch of water close to the other bank.

"There are lots of places that look safe to wade, but the drop-offs dump you into the deep parts before you have time to catch your breath. Some of us kids spent a summer moving rocks to make a swimming hole downstream."

We walked along the river trail, passing the swimming hole Georgie had mentioned, until we came out by the park in town. A long field of mown grass, dotted with shade trees and picnic tables, led to a bandstand and baseball field in the distance. Cami broke away and scampered up a small hill with Penny at her side. But the dog tired quickly and left Cami picking daisies.

Panting, Penny came to lie beside me, stretched out in the shade of a sycamore. "Smart girl," I said. "I think Cami will outlast all of us. I vote we hang out here."

A warm breeze stirred the leaves above us as we snuggled into the embrace of the cool grass. Shrieks and calls carried from Cami and Georgie as the sisters chased each other, with Georgie swinging Fidget into the air when she caught her.

As I laid apart from my friends, but still close enough to join in if I wanted to, it was the most peaceful I had felt in a long time—my whole life, maybe. Even the good times with my mother weren't peaceful, exactly, since Mama didn't sit still for more than a blink. Since the Nowaks had left, I had gone back to life as an only child, and I missed playing with the younger kids. Cami was an entire pack of hoodlums on her own, so maybe I wouldn't miss the others as much.

In between dozing, I tried to build a picture in my head of the photograph I wanted to take. Inspired by Cami playing dress-up with the dog, I envisioned a Mother Goose (Fae or Georgie?) reading to a rapt audience of dogs and Cami. All of them in old-fashioned dresses and bonnets, or nightgowns and caps, kind of like a Saturday Evening Post cover. It made me smile just to think of it.

A chuff from Penny was the only warning I got before a small form cannon balled into my belly. I gasped and tried to fend off tickling hands, but Cami was surprisingly good at finding any gap for wiggly fingers.

"Come play!" Cami insisted. "I broke Georgie."

I struggled to sit up and spied Georgie collapsed on the grass, trying to catch her own breath while red-faced and sweating.

"Yeah, you did a good job wearing her out, Fidget. I know a game we could play; it's called Let's Go Home and Find Something Cool to Drink and Have a Snack. Sound good?"

"Sounds perfect!" Georgie wheezed.

Giggling, Cami said, "You sillies! I want to play."

Desperate for help, I looked to Penny. "I bet Penny's hungry. You don't want your friend to go hungry, do you?"

Penny obliged me by rotating her head at every spoken "hungry" and then getting up for a wagging stretch. "See? Want to go see what your mom has for us to eat?"

With a sigh, Cami agreed before going to torment Georgie into standing. Cami ran back to hold my hand as we walked. Laughter announced our arrival back at the house, and thankfully Fae had iced lemonade and thumbprint cookies waiting for me and Georgie. And some bologna for Penny. Cami got sent to nap in her room, where she fussed for about ten minutes and fell asleep. The rest of us were able to play a board game without interruption, until Georgie won and I headed home again.

The few streetlights had bats circling them, snapping up the moths attracted to the buzzing bulbs. Penny, refreshed by her own nap, snuffled in the ditch and reminded me of when I couldn't stay out of the ditch the first time I walked to town with Uncle Earl. Maybe Penny really was a girl after my own heart.

Chapter Seventeen

The next morning I woke up Uncle Earl with the sounds of moving furniture. I had tried not to make too much noise, but the chair legs screeched as I pulled them across the floorboards. When Uncle Earl poked his tousled head out to see what I was doing, I had already cleared the furniture from the space in front of the fireplace. I'd dragged the larger rag rug from my room to fill the bare floorboards and added the stool Uncle Earl used to reach the higher book-shelves.

"What are you doing?" Uncle Earl grumbled.

"This is going to be my photo studio later today. Do you mind if I neaten up your books? Just so they don't look like a tornado landed them there."

"Yes, I mind. I know where everything is. You can pretend your backdrop is a messy library. Is your photo studio going to infringe on my sleep time?"

"No, the Woods aren't getting here until after noon. Is that okay?"

"Yeah. Do you have anything quieter to do right now?"

I tapped my chin in thought. "I was going to see if Mrs. Grant had some old dresses I could buy. I can grab some money and go do that."

Uncle Earl yawned. "Dresses for you? I thought you don't like to wear them."

"No, for the dogs and Cami, and maybe for Georgie."

"Well, it'll be a challenge to get dresses on the dogs, but wait till you see the fit Georgie pitches. Good luck with getting her into a dress. But do you remember the big wardrobe in the stable? There were some old clothes in there. Probably smell of mothballs, but you might be able to use some of them."

I grinned. "Okay, I'll try not to make so much noise in there that you can hear it all the way from the stable. Go back to sleep."

He waved as he shut his door and I headed out to the stable. A pile of stacked chairs blocked the wardrobe, so I had to move those, plus some small side tables.

"The junk in here breeds like mice," I muttered to Penny. The dog's ears perked, and she looked around. "Do you know that word, mice? I don't mind them too much, as long as they don't startle me. But you probably think they're a delicacy."

I tugged on a stubborn drawer in the wardrobe, the wood squealing enough to make me wince. The potent smell of mothballs made me cough before I said, "This must be the right place, since Uncle Earl warned us about the mothballs."

Brittle newspaper from the 1920s encased several parcels, and I carefully separated the bundles. In the first one, I found pin-striped woolen pants, in an older style and cut.

They were a little too long for me when I held them up, so I set them aside. The matching fedora went on Penny's head, and the dog froze in place until I removed it. Next to come out of the paper wrappings was a man's striped shirt, the collar darkened with oils. I wrinkled my nose at the scent of rancid pomade and wrapped the shirt back up.

The next few shirts were smaller, like from a boy my age and size, and they didn't have the stained collars, so I put them with the pants. Discouraged, I hadn't come across a single dress by the time I emptied the drawer. Just a bunch of boys' Sunday-best, likely outgrown before they got too worn, and put away for the next wearer.

It wasn't until I moved enough junk to get one of the upper doors open that I struck gold. Faded flour sack dresses, the lace collars on them limp and grayed with dust, hung between yellowed nightgowns. The aged colors wouldn't matter so much for photos, since those would be black and white, and the range of sizes should fit my subjects.

Carrying the crate of clothes made me sneeze at the lingering odor of mothballs. Instead of bringing them in the house, I detoured to the clothesline and hung the garments to air out. Now that I could see them better, I cocked my head and made matches with my models.

The yellow, flowered dress would fit Georgie, and a big sunhat would complete the Mother Goose look—if Georgie would wear them. One dress in my size had buttons all the way up the front, so that one might work the best for Nap, since he rarely stood still. I could attach a few buttons to hold it on, while someone else bribed him with food. Josie loved attention so she should be easier to fit, and Cami would be the same. Since Cami dressed up Penny every time she came over, the hound was a veteran.

Leaving the stinky costume pieces to freshen in the breeze, I cautiously poked my head in the screen door. The house was silent, so Uncle Earl must still be sleeping. I decided to check on the garden and then go to the Woods's to see if they had anything to use as nightcaps, since the wardrobe had come up empty on those. I filled the water tanks and hoped the squeaky wheels wouldn't bother Uncle Earl as I pulled it down the driveway. Penny followed without me needing to say a word, as if she had always been at my heels. Nap and Josie stayed behind, probably to try to convince Uncle Earl they hadn't eaten breakfast yet.

Now that it was free of the mallow and other choking weeds, the garden grew robustly, making up for lost time. The tomatoes were loaded with ripening globes, and the pumpkin vines sported miniature gourds among the blossoms. The entire green patch was a calm oasis, with the faint hiss of the sprayer in my hand joining the bird and insect songs. I wondered if assigning me to the garden was part of Uncle Earl's plan to get me to put down roots in Amberfield. When I finished watering, I stashed the empty tank inside the garden gate so I could fetch it on the way home.

Cami answered the door when I knocked, and she and Penny scampered off immediately, leaving me to find everyone else on my own. Fae was in the kitchen, stirring pots of bubbling purple goo.

"I knew you were a witch," I teased. "Want me to add some eye of newt to the pot?"

Fae laughed and threw a sticky pit at me. "It's plum jam. Are you here to help? Keep stirring while I run to the bathroom."

I took over. When Fae came back, I said, "I wasn't planning on staying long—I'm still getting stuff ready for the photoshoot later. You didn't forget, did you?"

"No, that's why I started the plum jam so early. I'll be finished in plenty of time, and Georgie will be back from errands by then, too. Did you find the costumes you needed?"

"I've got dresses and nighties so we can see which work best, but I came up empty on nightcaps. Do you have anything that might work?"

Fae frowned as she took over the stirring again. "They've never been my thing, so no caps here. But a neighbor gave me a stack of doilies; maybe we could do something with those? I won't have time to sew anything, though."

I shrugged. "They only need to look like caps for a few minutes, so that should be fine. What do you want my help with before I go?"

Without missing a beat, Fae handed me a bucket of plum pits. "Could you take these to the compost? And maybe bring in the crates of jars from the back porch?"

I finished some chores for Fae, including helping her pour the plum jam into jars. Like Georgie had warned, it was steamy and sweaty work for a summer's day.

"How'd you get so good with plants? Did you grow up on a farm?" I asked.

Fae huffed a laugh. "We did have a truck garden, but I hated that way of life when I was younger. We lived on the edge of a swamp and everyone in town called my mama a

witch. We made more money from her potions and oint-
ments than the produce though, so somebody was buying
them. I ran away to the city as soon as I thought I was old
enough to hold a job."

"How old was that?" I asked, not looking at her. I felt bad
I'd called her a witch.

I felt her glance at me before she said, "Thirteen. I had
no clue how hard it was going to be on my own, though."
Her gaze went far away, and she stopped stirring. "Those
first few years were tough, and I fell in with some bad people."

Not me—I was trying to run away from the bad people,
even if they were my parents.

I cleared my throat and Fae jumped at the sound before
continuing, "I guess I'd absorbed more of the plant lore than
I realized, because when I needed some income when I
moved to Amberfields, it all came back to me. I'm sure some
people call me a witch behind my back, but it doesn't seem
to bother Georgie the same way."

Fae wiped her hands on her apron and said, "Look at me,
using up your summer day! You should go take a dip in the
river. One of us ought to have a little fun this morning!"

Georgie hadn't come back yet, so I went to reclaim my
dog from Cami's clutches. The little girl wailed at being separated from "her" dog until Fae came to calm her so I could
leave. Penny and I ran to the back gate, and I made sure it
shut securely behind us. Once we left the shade of Fae's garden, the heat sucked all the moisture from us. There was
only one thing for it: the river and its shock of cold eddies.
Penny led the way down the well-worn trail to the green

strip along the water. We walked downstream, looking for the rock pool Georgie had pointed out.

The tangled grass was so tall it brushed my shoulders and I lost sight of Penny. I stepped carefully around the black-berry bushes with their still-green fruits, but still had to stop to loosen a catch of thorns from my clothes. When I got to the pool's edge, Penny was already up to her belly in the sun-dappled water, whining like she did when her bath-water was too cold.

But as soon as I hollered and jumped in, Penny paddled in circles as I splashed. The water was only as deep as my waist, so I flipped onto my back and spun like a water bug in the softer current. But the river flowed down from the mountain snow and the temperature could be over a hundred in the air, but only in the sixties below the surface. The cold gripping my lungs eventually became too much, and I hauled out on the bank.

I cozied into a hollow around the roots of a pepper tree, deep in the shade of its hanging branches, and Penny stretched next to me. But for the occasional twitch as we tried to dislodge the troublesome flies, we were soon lost to a summer nap. In my dream, my mother was floating right beside me in the sun-warmed river, our hands touch-ing every time the current brought us together.

I woke with a start when Penny scrambled to her feet. The hound's ears curved forward, intent on something in the water.

"What is it, girl? Did you spy an otter?"

Penny glanced back at me, acknowledging that I'd spo-ken, but then focused right back on the water. Now she stood, every line of her body stiff with—worry? Fear? A shiver ran through me, and it wasn't from the cool shade or the lingering chill of the river.

I sat up and shaded my eyes, trying to see what caught the dog's attention. I was still scanning for an otter, or maybe a goose, so at first my eyes passed right over it. Just a limb flailing out of the water, a wide-open pink mouth, and then a swirl of pale fabric. A tiny gasp carried over the sound of the water.

My stomach dropped as I scrambled to my feet. "Cami?"

Penny couldn't wait any longer and splashed into the river, steaming towards the little figure being carried downstream. I screamed Cami's name again as I waded into the water. But the water was moving faster than I could, so I slogged back to the bank to run along the path.

Gasping now, I tripped over rocks and popped back up to run again. The small dot of a child, with the head of a dog trailing along behind it, seemed further away than was possible. They disappeared around a bend and I crawled up a steep bank to try a shortcut into the park. The people sitting at the tables in the park stared at me, bleeding from scrapes on my hands and muddy knees.

"The baby!" I hollered, still running. "Cami Wood is in the river!"

Some young men reacted first, leaping up from the benches and running to catch up. I cut back over to the bank and came out on a small spit of sand, searching the waters for signs of Cami and Penny.

"No, no, no," I cried as the river flowed unbroken. The men breathed hard as they came up next to me, all of them shading their eyes, desperate for a sighting. More people came running as word spread, voices murmuring in worry and some women sobbing—and then, a cry of "They're here!"

Out at the end of the spit, where the current curled in a spiral, Penny's head struggled to stay above the surface. And in her mouth a wad of cloth, with Cami still tangled in it, her body limp and buffeted by the current.

The current kept Penny from getting any closer to the shore; after all, the child weighed nearly the same as the dog did. Two of the men waded in and one grabbed Cami and the other Penny, and they dragged them up onto the spit.

I fell to my knees beside them, Penny's sides heaving and her eyes rolling as she tried to catch her breath. But Cami—Cami wasn't breathing at all. A man turned her on her side and walloped her a few times on the back and we all held their breaths as we waited.

And then, a gout of water from her blue lips, and a wet coughing. Cami opened her eyes to see strangers hovering over her and she cried. Weakly at first, and then loud enough to bust an eardrum. It was the sweetest sound I had ever heard—as good as Penny's wet snuffle in my ear a moment later.

After the brief lift of Penny's head to lick my ear, she didn't try to move again. The voices and bustle around me swirled into static while I comforted my dog. I was vaguely aware of someone driving their car out onto the grass so they could load up Cami, but they seem to have forgotten me and Penny.

Chapter Eighteen

"We should still get Cami to the doctor," one woman said, taking charge. "And her mother needs to know."

I was torn. Penny needed me, but should I go with Cami? Or should I be the one to let Fae know about—just trying to find the right word for Cami nearly drowning made me shudder. I couldn't shake the feeling it was my fault, and if I blamed herself, then surely the Woods would blame me too.

A hand on my shoulder made me jump, and I looked up to see an older woman smiling kindly at me.

"Do you think you can carry your dog to my truck? She oughta see the vet."

It took a moment for me to get my legs under me, but I finally stood with Penny in my arms. Even wet, Penny felt frail and light, as if she was made of papier mâché. The lady led us to her battered blue truck, and only when we were seated in the cab did I look around again. I couldn't see Cami, so they must've already taken her away.

As if the realization gave me permission, I burst into fresh tears. The lady patted me on the shoulder, only pausing to shift out of reverse.

"Cry if you need to, but I have a feeling the little girl and your dog will both be okay. I'm Mrs. Jones, by the way. I was there the day we built you a room. I had no idea then I would get to chauffeur a couple of heroes."

The words, meant kindly, only made me cry harder. Penny was a hero for sure, but what if I hadn't closed the gate and Cami had followed us? I was sure I had closed it, but it was so hot I'd just wanted to get to the river, so maybe not. Felix's voice in my head seized the opportunity to remind me that mistakes have consequences. This is what came of thinking only of myself. Panicking, I gasped for breath.

But it didn't take us long to get to the veterinary clinic, and somehow the news must've already reached Doc Marsh because he came out to meet us at the truck.

"Let's get this girl checked out. Bet, were you in the water too? You might need to see the doctor yourself."

I shook my head before I replied, "I only have lots of scrapes from running to get help. I think they'd be okay, and I'm more worried about Penny and Cami."

Doc Marsh nodded and led them into the clinic. Mrs. Jones followed, saying, "I can take care of Bet's scrapes while Penny gets her exam."

The vet laid Penny on a high table, and Mrs. Jones had me hop up onto the counter. She helped herself to iodine and cotton and set to work; I barely felt the sting as I craned my head to see over Mrs. Jones's shoulder.

"Is she okay? What will you need to do to Penny?"

Doc smiled reassuringly. "She's probably getting the same workup as Cami. We need to make sure she doesn't have fluid or inflammation in her lungs, and we'll monitor her for a few days to make sure it stays that way. Give me a moment of quiet to really listen now."

I held my breath, afraid that even that would be too loud through the stethoscope. But Doc Marsh's frown of concentration cleared as he gave me a thumbs up.

"I think she'll be fine," he said. "She's just tired out. We'll give her some antibiotics to make sure she didn't catch anything from all the water she took in."

I started crying again, and Mrs. Jones patted my shoulder. I grabbed her hand and squeezed it instead.

"So she won't get sick again? With an infection like she had before?" I asked in between sobs.

Doc Marsh chuckled and then caught himself. "I'm sorry. I shouldn't have laughed when you're so worried, but she definitely won't get sick like that again. Did Earl tell you what happened?"

I shook my head. "Only that it had to do with the scar on her belly."

"Well, when Penny was brought in, she was very sick with pyometra and she had surgery to remove her infected uterus."

"What?" I didn't think I would have been able to make sense of all those words even if I hadn't been so shook up.

Mrs. Jones tsked. "He means Penny doesn't have her womb anymore, so she can't get sick that way again. Of course, she'll never have puppies again either, but she might be glad to have a rest."

He nodded. "That's exactly right. And rest is what she needs right now, so I'll keep her at least overnight."

"Can I stay—" I was interrupted by somebody calling my name.

Uncle Earl pushed through the door and spotted me. He grabbed me in a bear hug, with my face smushed into his apron. The smell of hamburger grease and bacon was more soothing than I would have guessed as I clung to him. It reminded me of the hugs Mrs. Nowak gave, and felt familiar and comforting.

"I overheard someone saying a girl was pulled out of the river and I was afraid it was you," Uncle Earl cried. "I was already running out of the diner when I smacked into a friend, and he told me you were here."

Mrs. Jones murmured something about leaving as she passed me and Uncle Earl, so I called "thank you!" as the lady exited.

"I'm going to set Penny up in a cage in the back, and you can come say goodnight later," Doc Marsh said, leaving me and my uncle to talk together.

My subdued words sounded loud in the now-quiet exam room. "I'm sorry I worried you. I was safe, but Cami or Penny could have died. It's my fault, Uncle Earl!" I was so tired that instead of sobs, only a sigh escaped now.

"I'm sure you did your best. Are you sure you didn't swallow any water? We can take you by the doctor," Uncle Earl said.

"No, I only waded. And floated a little."

"Let's get you home to bed, then." He helped me up.

Inside my head, I berated myself for making a mistake that put Penny and Cami in danger, but I was also upset about opening up my heart to this pain. I'd learned time and again that it was safer to keep people at a distance, to save myself from hurt when they left. Or when I left, in this case. I listlessly followed my uncle only vaguely aware of voices around me.

"Say, Earl, can I give you two a ride home?"

"Much appreciated, Hal. I don't relish the walk home in this heat."

I fell asleep in Hal's backseat, and Uncle Earl prodded me awake when we got home. I stumbled to my room and laid in bed. Coming awake enough to realize it felt empty without Penny, I hugged one of the pillow babies to my chest.

When I woke again, bright sunlight made me wince. I laid there a moment, rubbing my eyes, before I remembered what had happened. Swinging my legs out of bed, I still felt disoriented and overtired. Maybe that was why it took me a while to realize the birds sounded more like they were singing for morning than for evening, like I expected.

I came out to the kitchen and spied Uncle Earl reading in his chair. I fended off Nap's and Josie's enthusiastic greeting as I asked, "What time is it? Can we go see Penny?"

Uncle Earl set aside his glasses and smiled at me. "You slept all night. How are you feeling?"

"All night? But I was supposed to see Penny! Why did you let me sleep?" Josie flinched away from the anguish in my voice.

"Because you needed it, and so did she. We'll go see her after you've had breakfast, and if we're lucky, she'll be ready to come home. Sound good?"

I scowled at him, since I should have been able to decide for myself whether to keep sleeping. But I sat at the table anyway when Uncle Earl brought a stack of pancakes from the oven, where he'd been keeping them warm. The fluffy bites, dripping with melted butter and maple syrup, earned Uncle Earl a little forgiveness.

"You should have asked me," I grumbled. "Penny might think I've abandoned her."

Uncle Earl shook his head, putting on a thoughtful expression. "So, I should have woken you up to ask if you were still sleepy? Wasn't the fact you were sleeping answer enough?"

When he put it like that, it sounded silly, but I didn't want to admit it, so I said, "Hmph."

"Don't forget, Doc Marsh already nursed Penny through a terrible infection. She trusts him, and you should, too."

He made too much sense not to listen to. The resentment left my shoulders, and I hurried through the rest of my meal, so we could go to the vet clinic.

"Do you want Nap and Josie to come with us?" Uncle Earl asked. "They've been looking for her overnight."

I bit my lip in indecision. "Have you had any updates on Penny? If she's still weak, these wild beasts might be too much for her."

"I haven't heard anything. If we wanted to stop and visit Cami, though, we probably shouldn't bring the dogs along."

Shame made my stomach drop all over again. Those pancakes weren't settling so well now. "How is Cami? I was afraid to ask."

"I haven't heard any updates on her, either. I've been thinking about getting a phone installed, and it seems like it's time for us to join the modern age. Maybe Doc Marsh has heard something, or someone we meet along the way can tell us what's happening with Cami?"

Nodding in agreement, I stooped to put on my shoes—they wouldn't let me in the doctor's if I was barefoot. While Uncle Earl was in the bathroom, I snuck into the pantry and grabbed some money from my sock stash, in case we needed to pay for Penny's care. Then Uncle Earl grabbed his hat and we were on our way, with Nap and Josie following us to the end of the driveway. The hounds' heads and tails drooped when they got the news they were not coming along.

I didn't talk much as we walked, my head whirling with questions: how did Cami get to the river? If I had left the gate open, would Fae and Georgie ever forgive me? Could I forgive myself for such a careless mistake? What if I was a jinx and anyone I cared about would pay the price, like Mama did? It was all too much and made me want to run for Oregon right now.

Just then, we passed the Woods's house; it felt vacant and lifeless, and I suddenly grabbed for Uncle Earl's hand. He winced at how hard I gripped, but then he nodded and pulled me onward. A few doors down, a neighbor called out to us from her laundry line.

"Have you heard from Fae?" the woman asked, shaking out a shirt. "I talked to her last night."

Uncle Earl tipped his hat and joined the neighbor at her picket fence. "No, you probably know more than we do. How is the little girl?"

"They took her to the hospital in Yuba City as a precaution, but Fae told me Cami's sitting up in bed and talking the ears off the nurses. Georgie bought her so much candy, it's a good thing the child is in the hospital, if she gets sick from too many sweets."

Uncle Earl turned to me. "You hear that? It sounds like she's back to normal."

I looked up from drawing lines in the dirt with the toe of my shoe and tried to look happy at the news. I was glad, of course, but I couldn't help thinking about what would happen after Cami came home. The Woods might never want to see me again. And I couldn't blame them one bit.

"Is this the girl?" the woman asked Uncle Earl. "The one with the dog?"

I blanched at the question, thinking the whole town knew Cami's accident was my fault by now. Without waiting for Uncle Earl, I started walking quickly, head down and fingernails biting into my palms. At that moment, I wanted nothing more than to get my dog and disappear along with her to Oregon.

"Whoa there," Uncle Earl huffed as he caught up with me. "Mrs. Thompson wanted to tell you how grateful she was for helping Cami."

"I just want to check on Penny." And if she was doing okay, it might be time for me to get serious about leaving town.

Uncle Earl gave a funny look at my flat tone. But by now we were across the street from the vet clinic, so he didn't say anything further. He held the door open for me and I practically ran inside. A woman sitting at the front desk looked startled at my sudden entrance.

"I'm here to see my dog," I blurted.

The woman nodded and said the doctor was with another pet and would be with us shortly. I reluctantly sat down to wait, chewing on my fingernails while Uncle Earl exchanged small talk with the lady. Doc Marsh soon stuck his head out the door and gestured for me to follow him.

As my running footsteps sounded on the tile, the vet put a finger to his lips. "We have other patients resting today, too, so let's be quiet."

I nodded, holding my breath as we walked into the back room. Surely he would have said something starting with "I'm sorry," if Penny wasn't doing well? My eyes searched the cages until I saw a familiar coppery head.

Penny saw me and leaped to her feet, tail wagging madly. A bracelet of gauze encircled one leg, but otherwise she looked fine. Though she was not usually as talkative as Nap or Josie, Penny gave a holler that showed her Beagle heritage. I tried to shush her but was giggling too much at the tongue sticking through the cage bars, desperate to reach me.

Uncle Earl came to stand beside me, and the little hound's entire body wagged now. "I guess she's feeling better," he said with a chuckle.

"Yep, you can take her home," Doc Marsh said. "But I'll need to check on her the next few days to make sure there aren't any further problems from aspirating water. Otherwise, she can go back to her routine. We gave her some antibiotics through an IV."

I joyfully unlatched Penny's cage and gathered the dog into my arms. Penny didn't feel nearly so frail now, but I was happy to hold her so the dog had an easier time licking my face.

"What do we owe you, Doc?" Uncle Earl asked as he reached for his wallet.

Before I could say I had money, the vet answered, "No charge. She still belongs to the county, so it's part of the work I do for them."

The men shook on it, and Uncle Earl and I took turns carrying Penny on the way home. After greeting the rest of the pack, Penny took inventory of her pillow babies and went straight to sleep. It looked like she hadn't slept in days, and maybe she hadn't slept well during the first night away from us. I sat at my desk, reading a book, so I would be the first thing Penny saw when she woke up.

Chapter Nineteen

A bit later, I woke with my head on my desk as Uncle Earl carefully set down a plate with a sandwich and pickle spears on my desk, and another one with chopped sausage.

"I'm going to walk into town and take care of a few errands," Uncle Earl whispered. "Do you need anything?"

Answers, maybe? Even while I'd slept, the same worries about Cami and her family seemed to be stuck in my head, with dreams of terrible outcomes running through my mind like a flipbook. I shook off the dire images and answered, "I forgot to ask, are we supposed to bring Penny back to Doc Marsh to check on her, or is he coming here?"

"Good question. I'll stop in and find out. Do me a favor and stay away from the river while I'm gone, will you?" He said it half-jokingly, but I could tell he was seriously worried.

"We will. I might go down to the garden, though."

Uncle Earl gave me a brief hug around the shoulders and left. When he was safely out of sight, I pulled out the money I'd grabbed before and replaced it in my secret stash. I turned to find Nap and Josie watching me expectantly from the pantry doorway, like they hoped I was getting a snack.

"Sorry, moochers, but I already have my sandwich and chips waiting."

Nap and Josie came in my room to lie on the rag rug and watch me eat, and Penny tucked into the sausage Uncle Earl had cooked for her. Nap and Josie got the crusts off the bread. Afterwards, the dogs started wrestling in the living room while I washed dishes, so Penny must be feeling better. Would I ever be able to shake off scary experiences like that and be joyful in the moment?

Needing to feel busy, I decided it was time for another training session with the dogs. In every spare moment, I'd been working on training all three of them since I'd gotten the idea for my photo. Getting Nap and Josie to sit and stay was the biggest challenge, but it helped that they thought any kind of food was worth working for. Penny, however, was much pickier about treats and would only move for chunks of cheese. She was great at holding still—so good at it that she often fell asleep in whatever position I put her in. That was especially true that day, so I didn't work Penny too hard.

While Penny napped, I took a shower, leaving my hair wet afterwards so the walk to the garden would be cooler. Penny followed me and the rolling water tanks, putting fear into any lizards and squirrels along the way, but Nap and Josie decided to stay at the house. I did the watering and then checked if anything was ready to harvest.

Most of the tiny pumpkins were larger now, and I picked an entire basket of tomatoes. The peaches should be ripe in a few weeks, and the grapes were swelling now they got water regularly. More Jerusalem artichokes were ready, but if I ate any more of those gas-causing tubers, I'd float away like a helium balloon. I turned my back on the overgrown yellow flowers and surveyed the garden.

For a moment, I let myself imagine my mother was also enjoying the garden, just out of sight, singing her own version of "Dream A Little Dream of Me." I pretended we had left that Devil before things got worse, and instead we were both happy and healthy living with Uncle Earl. Mama and Fae would be best friends, like their daughters were. But if my mother was in the garden, it was only her ghost, and it was harder to find comfort in that. With a sigh, I closed the garden gate behind me and headed up the driveway with Penny.

Penny's ears perked, and she took off for the house, so Uncle Earl must have gotten home while I was busy in the garden. "I know he's still your favorite!" I teased Penny.

Uncle Earl heard my voice, and he came out on the porch, calling, "This was either the best prank or the worst one—I can't decide."

I squinted up at him, where he stood under the shadow of the porch roof. "What are you talking about? I didn't prank you. Did Georgie leave a booby trap for you to find?"

"I'm talking about this." Uncle Earl dug in his pockets and pulled out torn and crumpled papers.

They overflowed his hands and as they fell, I glimpsed the faces of presidents.

"Is that money?"

"It's fake though, right? I just got home and found these scraps of bills on the porch, mostly where Nap was laying.

You really don't know where they came from, either? They're all wet, but it could be slobber."

And then I remembered my sock full of cash in the pantry, and Nap's fixation for socks. Without another word, I pushed past Uncle Earl and into the house. As I got closer to the pantry, a smell of vinegar and herbs assaulted my nose. My fears came true when I saw the shattered jar of peppers which had guarded my money.

Nap must have spotted the sock when he'd followed me in there earlier, and waited to grab it. He came up behind me now, nudging with his nose like he was asking for more stuffed socks to play with. I knew it wouldn't do any good to get mad at him; I couldn't blame anyone but myself for leaving it within his reach.

Uncle Earl came over and peered around me. "What's that smell? Did one of the dogs get a craving for Fae's peppers?"

"No, I hid my money behind them," I confessed. "In a sock."

"Ohhhh." Uncle Earl understood immediately. "Maybe we could try putting the pieces together and the bank would honor them? How much did you have?"

I didn't know how to tell him Nap had destroyed over two hundred dollars, since that amount might bring up questions about who it actually belonged to. The law wouldn't care about how long I'd worked at the poker club and never been paid, even though my skills had earned Felix thousands of dollars. Anyways, it was not like Uncle Earl would have that much money lying around, and he'd already helped me so much I'd feel funny taking it.

I avoided answering his question by saying in a strained voice, "Why don't I go check Nap's nest?"

Sensing I needed some time to myself, Uncle Earl nodded and pulled out a pan to heat some leftover soup for dinner. But as I unlatched the screen door, he called softly, "Bet? You're not going to disappear on me, are you?"

I choked on a sob before I answered, "I think you're going to be stuck with me for a while."

I pushed my way out the door and onto the porch. Stumbling on the stairs, I sat down hard as the loss fully hit me. Nap had destroyed my plans for Oregon along with that money: it was supposed to cover a train ticket, food, and a ride the rest of the way to the lumber camp. Without my savings, I would be just another lost girl hitchhiking. That was worse odds than if I'd stayed working at the poker club. I'd have to earn some money before I could leave.

Trying to shake off the hopelessness, I made myself walk to Nap's hollow under the blackberries. In his dugout, I found a few more pieces of cash, but it still was nowhere near all of them. The rest might be in his belly, but I figured the bank would draw the line at replacing bills that had passed through a dog. A half-hysterical laugh burst out of me at the thought, and suddenly I was rocking in the dust. This was not the way things were supposed to go.

After a while, I stopped by the water pump to wash off as much dirt as I could, then swung around the house to my room and changed out of my dirty clothes. Squaring my shoulders against defeat, I went in the kitchen to eat with Uncle Earl before he left for work. We made small talk about the weather and the garden—anything to avoid talking about money. I caught Uncle Earl sneaking worried glances at me, like he still wasn't convinced I wouldn't run.

I forced a smile, saying, "You never told me if I need to bring Penny to the clinic tomorrow?"

"Yeah, he said you could come around early, since it's not an official appointment. You could go by the Woods's on your way there or your way back. Cami's coming home to-morrow."

The lost money had almost shoved my worries about Cami aside, but now they came back. All of my troubles felt tangled together like Nap's blackberry patch, and I didn't see a way out. Hearing my shaky sigh, Uncle Earl patted my hand sympathetically. I tried to look grateful, but I was too exhausted and dragged myself to bed after I ate.

Later, Uncle Earl stuck his head into my room, where I lay curled around Penny. I wasn't quite asleep, so I heard him whisper, "I know it was my dog who did this, so I'll try to make it up to you."

The next morning, I lingered in bed after I woke up. I braced for the loss of the money to hit me all over again, but instead I felt oddly relieved. I still grieved my broken plans, but the money itself—it had always felt dirty. None of Felix's businesses were clean: the poker club, the "boarding houses" only housing women and their male visitors, the cash loans that landed people deeper into debt. Sure, Felix always said he never forced anyone through the doors, but he knew all the tricks to make them stay and hand over their money.

I was ashamed I'd ever been even a small part of it. Even though I'd be starting nearly from scratch to replace my savings, I could see this was a fresh chance to earn the money in a different way. A way that didn't make someone else's life worse—or could even make it better, although I didn't know what that would look like yet. Since I couldn't leave without some cash in my pocket, I would have more time to find out.

In the middle of a yawn, I sat up suddenly, remembering I was supposed to be up early to take Penny in to see Doc Marsh. Uncle Earl had left a note reminding me not to be late, and asking me to feed the dogs so they'd let him sleep. I fed them as quietly as I could—which was not all that quietly, since Nap and Josie wanted to wrestle. I left them grappling on the porch and hoped they would leave Uncle Earl alone while Penny and I were gone.

I started out carrying Penny, but it seemed the dog had put on weight since I had hefted her to the truck a few days ago. Either that, or I wasn't caught up in the moment like I was then. Penny got to walk the rest of the way on leash, although she didn't jump in and out of the ditch so much. Whether she was still tired or affected by my gloomy mood, I didn't know.

Penny paused at the gate to the Woods's yellow house and my stomach dropped. I didn't know if they'd gotten home yet, but I wasn't ready to face them, anyway. I tugged on the leash, trying to get out of there before someone saw us, and Penny reluctantly continued walking.

The door to the vet clinic was locked, but Doc Marsh heard the rattle and came to let us in. He made quick work of Penny's exam and gave her a friendly pat.

"Let her rest up a bit more, and then you can go back to your normal routine. Isn't Cami getting back today? Maybe that little spitfire would rest if Penny napped with her."

My relieved smile fell away. "Yeah, maybe."

Doc Marsh raised an eyebrow. "I thought you were friends with them? Earl was telling me you had some special photo project planned?"

I nodded. It seemed like so long ago when I'd been excited about the photo shoot. "It was supposed to be the day of...the day Cami went in the water. But now I don't know if it will happen. It's okay if it doesn't."

"Are you trying to convince me or yourself?" Doc Marsh gave a wink, but I didn't even smile in return. I knew it would be utterly crushing if I'd lost the friendship of Georgie and her family, too.

"When do I need to bring Penny back again?" I asked instead.

"You're welcome to visit any time I'm free, but she won't need to come back for a recheck. Unless she starts coughing or has trouble breathing, that is."

I nodded absently, and Doc Marsh asked, "Is there something else worrying you about Penny? I thought you'd be happier she's doing so well."

I replied, "Sorry, I have a lot on my mind. I am happy. Thanks for everything." I shook his hand before leaving.

Penny tried to stop at the Woods's again on the way home. This time, I could see the front door was open behind the screen. I fidgeted in place, undecided on whether I should go knock. Before I could make up my mind, a car drove slowly past, with the people inside pointing to me and

Penny and all of them talking at once. I wasn't sure what they were saying, but I didn't like being singled out like that.

My face heated, and I whispered frantically at Penny to walk on. Thankfully, the dog obeyed, and we made our way home. Nap and Josie met us at the foot of the driveway, and I took all three of them to check on the garden before heading to the house.

When the screen door slapped shut behind me, Uncle Earl called from the bathroom, "Is that you, Bet?"

If I'd been feeling more myself, I would have answered, "What if it's a burglar come to steal the leftover Swedish meatballs in the fridge?" But being worried so much was taking its toll, so I just said, "Yes, it's me."

Uncle Earl came out, dressed for the day and with his dark curls still damp. "I was expecting you'd stay at Fae's a while."

"No," I said, explaining no further. "I checked on the garden, but I didn't water, so I'd better go do it." I scurried back out the door with all the dogs, leaving Uncle Earl scratching his head at my strange behavior.

The garden was a good place to hide out, and after I did the watering, I did just that. I laid on the damp earth under the umbrella of pumpkin leaves and the dogs were happy to snooze beside me. Something about the dappled shade let me set aside my sadness and doubts long enough to fall into a doze myself. Other than dive-bombing flies or clumsy bumblebees, the morning passed away in a comfortable drowse until the sound of tires on the street roused us.

Nap and Josie raced to the garden gate, barking to get out. "Shh, you'll give away our hiding place," I scolded. I let them out, and they ran behind the car, now turning into

Uncle Earl's driveway. I recognized Mr. Grant's car, stuffed with passengers plus a lot of stuff tied to the roof. And the pale face in the back window, spying me at the gate, had to be Cami.

I hurriedly stepped back into the shadows; I couldn't quite see to the house from here, but I could hear a commotion as everyone piled from the car. Then it quieted before the car left again, with only Mr. Grant at the wheel. Penny and I slunk back to our spot under the cooling leaves, but somehow it seemed less relaxing, and more shameful, to hide from my friends.

Nap and Josie came rushing at the gate, and I started to crawl out to let them back in, but Georgie's voice froze me in place.

"Hi, Bet. We're all waiting for you up at the house."

Chapter Twenty

I slowly came to the gate; no sense in trying to hide now. "Waiting for what? Are you all going to yell at me at once?"

Georgie cocked her head. "What? Why would we do that? We're here for your photo, now that Cami's feeling better."

I blurted, "Yeah, but how did Cami get to the river? Did I leave the gate unlatched?"

Georgie shook her head. "We checked after we got home. Fidget dragged one of the empty crates off the back porch and used it to climb over the fence. The gate was latched tight, like you left it."

I swallowed hard. "Really? Your mom isn't mad?"

Georgie's loud laugh made me jump. "Are you kidding? You're her hero, you and Penny both. You'll be lucky if she doesn't cover you in lipstick when she sees you. Come on, so you can get it over with."

I joined Georgie, and we walked back together, but only made it a few steps before I hugged Georgie tightly. "I'm glad you're still my friend," I whispered. Maybe it was worth staying a little longer to feel like this. After the Nowaks had moved, I didn't want to feel that kind of loss again.

Georgie surprised me by hugging me back, before she awkwardly cleared her throat. "Me too. Wanna race?"

In answer, I pushed Georgie away hard enough to make her stumble, and then ran for the house. After a squawk of outrage, Georgie's pounding feet followed. The circling dogs slowed her enough that Georgie and I reached the porch at the same time, laughing and breathing hard. Fae threw open the screen door and attacked me with kisses, just as Georgie had predicted.

I caught only a few words like "grateful" and "little monster," though I didn't think those last two words were about me. Then Cami realized I was home, and she shrieked as she raced to hug my legs, only abandoning me to fall on Penny. It was chaos for a few moments, and I grinned from ear to ear in relief and happiness. They were still my friends. Almost family, really.

"Bet was worried we were here to yell at her," Georgie said.

"Only because you hadn't been to see us sooner so we could thank you," Fae said before she went back to kissing me. "Why would you think that?"

I explained with a sheepish laugh, but Fae knew what to say. "Oh, I hate to think you were worried all this time. We would have called to let you know it was this daredevil taking risks, and nothing you did—except to save her."

"We're getting a telephone line installed soon," Uncle Earl chimed in. "And maybe I'll start looking around for a cheap car, too. We'll be caught up with the twentieth century. Now, do you need my help setting up before I leave for work?"

"No, I think we can manage," I said. "But what about lunch? Did I miss it?"

Fae immediately opened a box and pulled out a huge quiche, fruit salad, and a round of sourdough. While she and Uncle Earl plated everything, Georgie gave me a tour of the other things they'd brought.

"We have the doilies you asked for, and the small chairs from the play table at home. What are we doing with all this again?"

Before I could answer, the grownups called us to the table, and we had lunch together. Soon we were as stuffed as the dogs, who had been treated with a meatloaf Fae made for them. When Uncle Earl said goodbye, a lackluster farewell met him, since I was too full to walk him to the door. Fae ended up leaving at the same time, since she had things to do at home.

After a while, I roused myself to say, "We should start going through this stuff so I can see what I'm going to use. The light coming through the window should be better in about an hour."

Cami, Georgie, and I dove into the boxes and sacks, laying out nightgowns and other clothes. But when I got to the part of my explanation where Georgie would be dressed as Mother Goose, Georgie flatly refused.

"If I won't wear a dress for Mom, no way will I wear one for a picture. Mom would probably hang it in the living room for everybody to see, not to mention all the people who would see it at the fair. You'll have to think of something else."

"We'll start getting the dogs into their nightgowns and you can have time to think about it," I answered.

Georgie grumbled she would not change her mind, but she started wrestling Nap into one of Fae's old nightgowns, printed with large cabbage roses. I earned his cooperation with bits of chopped boiled egg.

"You know those dogs are going to have the worst egg gas tonight, right?" Georgie asked, as she smoothed the fabric in place.

Cami giggled as she brought over a doily to drape over Nap's ears like a nightcap. "Now who's stinky?" Cami teased.

I shrugged. "Only Penny sleeps in my room, and I'll just leave the window cracked. Okay, that's Nap done. Let's do Josie now."

In half the time as it took to dress Nap, we had Josie in a blue nighty spangled with stars and moons. I was trying to attach the doily nightcap when I glanced over at Cami. Wearing a trailing dress, the little girl was standing on a footstool, looming over Penny and Nap lying before her. She looked like a lecturing schoolmarm, finding fault with her students.

"Did you change your mind about being Mother Goose?" I asked Georgie. When Georgie only rolled her eyes, I added, "Because I have a different idea, but you'll need to help me, so we're done in time. Do you know how to draw fancy letters?"

While I changed Nap and Josie into dresses, and then got Penny into one of Cami's old dresses, Georgie sat at the table with a large piece of paper torn from an old sketchbook.

She carefully drew flourished lettering with a pencil, filling them in so they were dark and bold against the white.

It came to peer over her shoulder. "It's perfect! I grabbed this book to fit it over. It will look real in a photo, I'm sure."

Georgie helped to line up the dogs, posing as students instead. Cami relished her role as a picky teacher, holding a switch in one hand and a book now entitled *Etiquette for the Unmannerly*. I was nearly overcome with fits of laughter because the scene looked so much like I had envisioned—hopefully the judges at the fair would think it was funny too.

"Everyone stay still," I warned as I hit the shutter button. Before my subjects could move, I took a few more.

"Did you get what you wanted?" Georgie asked, holding onto Nap and Josie so they wouldn't lose their spots.

I bit my lip. "Not quite—something is missing. I'm not sure if it's quite believable as a teacher and students."

Georgie and I stared at the tableau, brows furrowed. Then Georgie grinned, saying, "Hey, I thought of something. Turn around and I'll set it up."

I had already gotten some good photographs, so I did as Georgie said. I heard whispers behind me, plus the rustle of cloth, and then Cami cried, "P U!" I almost turned around to see what was going on, but then the smell of mothballs hit me. Was Georgie dressing up as Mother Goose after all?

Finally, Georgie called, "You can look now."

I turned to see Cami and the dogs posed like they had been before, but now there was a new addition. Georgie wore some of the old clothes from the stable: the striped Sunday-best shirt and trousers, and even a necktie. She perched on one of the tiny chairs with knees akimbo, holding a doll-sized saucer and teacup with her pinky in the air.

"Do you get it?" Georgie asked. "Now she's dragged her unmannerly, older brother into playing school."

I doubled over with laughter, which got the dogs so worked up they broke character and came to lick my face. With the help of more egg bits, we got the dogs back in their places again.

"I love it!" I said. "We'd better hurry and get the pictures, though, before the dogs get sick of eggs."

I captured a few shots, and then directed Georgie to frown like a resentful older brother, while still raising her pinky finger. "I think that's the one! Let me finish the roll of film since we're all here. Pose however you want."

Georgie and Cami made goofy faces with the dogs, so I got closer with the camera to fill the frame. Then Georgie took a few of me and Cami, and I ran to put on my one dress so Georgie could take a "real" portrait of me and Penny and Cami. After spending the last few days in a twist of worry, having fun with my friends was a welcome relief.

"Okay, that's the end of the film roll," I said with satisfaction as I advanced it and removed it from the camera. "Do you think the camera store is still open?"

"Even if it's not, there's a drop box you can put it in. Grab an envelope and write your name on it in case we have to leave it in there."

Nap and Josie collapsed into a doze, full from all their bribes. Georgie and I boxed up all the borrowed stuff and left it on the front porch for Mr. Grant to pick up later, then showed Cami the garden on the way back to the Woods's house. Cami didn't even pitch a fit we were dropping her and Penny off with Fae, and going into town without her, she was that tired. Penny happily jumped up next to Cami and went to sleep herself.

We just made it to the camera store before it closed, and I could come pick up the prints in a few days. "Ugh, waiting is going to be so hard!" I cried as we left. "Should we stop at the diner and get ice cream sundaes? Unless you're too full from lunch earlier, that is."

Georgie gave me a pitiful look and slung an arm over my shoulders. "You'll have to help me get there. I'm faint with hunger."

I laughed and wrapped an arm around Georgie's waist and we lurched like we were running a private three-legged race on the way to the diner. The bell above the door rang as we pushed inside, both trying to squeeze through at once.

One of the waitresses spied us and called out, "Here comes trouble! Earl, I think one of these belongs to you."

Uncle Earl stuck his head out of the kitchen and grinned. "Let me guess, one fried egg sandwich and one meatloaf special, right?"

I shook my head. "We're here for sundaes—"

Georgie interrupted, "Hold on. I never turn down free food."

Uncle Earl stepped behind the counter, wiping his hands on his apron. "Who said anything about free? And didn't you have thirds at lunchtime?"

Georgie gave a long-suffering sigh. "Just the sundaes, then, with extra cherries on the side."

The waitress motioned for us to sit down, and Uncle Earl went back to his greasy domain. Georgie and I had only been apart for a few days, but we had a lot to talk about. Georgie insisted I tell the story of Cami's rescue again, and Georgie told me about their hospital stay.

"It wasn't all bad for Cami. She had nurses to wait on her and we spoiled her with candy and toys. The doctors took great care of her—especially a young guy who took a shine to Mom. I almost expected him to cry along with the nurses when they sent us home."

The sundaes arrived then, and we didn't talk anymore while we dove in. Uncle Earl came and sat with us on his break, but then I needed to get home and feed all the dogs. I walked Georgie home, where I was once again covered in Fae kisses, and came away with a sack of treats. Penny trotted next to me with her nose pressed against the bottom of the cloth sack, in case it tore open and the food tried to get away.

The next few days were a blur of running back and forth to the Woods's, except for the morning when I had to stay home to wait for the telephone crew. Once the phone was installed, Georgie and I could call to say we were coming over—or we talked and tied up the line.

"Didn't you two see each other half an hour ago?" Uncle Earl teased. "How do you even have anything left to talk about?"

Finally, the call came from Mr. Diaz at the camera store that my prints were ready. I immediately dialed up Georgie to see if she wanted to come along and pick them up.

"How did Mr. Diaz even get our number?" I asked Georgie. "You're the only one who calls, so I almost answered the phone with a peacock sound." I demonstrated by screeching into the phone.

"You know I hate that peacock call! It would serve you right if you'd embarrassed yourself," Georgie replied. "Haven't you figured out this is still a small town? Earl's phone number had probably been added to the church directory before the installation finished."

I nodded, then remembered Georgie couldn't see me. "Probably. So, do you want me to stop by on the way?"

"I'll meet you outside the front gate, so Little Miss Fidget doesn't try to come along."

I thought about bringing Nap and Josie too since I'd been working with them on leash. Three dogs were a lot for one girl to handle, though, and I snorted as I pictured them running down Main Street with me trailing like a kite behind them.

As promised, I found Georgie sitting on the curb, waiting. I let go of Penny's lead so the dog could greet Georgie properly with an attack of kisses and dusty paws. Then we walked into town all together.

When we got to the camera store, I poked my head inside. "Mr. Diaz, do you mind if Penny comes inside with us? It's too hot to leave her tied up outside, but I can leave her at the vet clinic if you don't want her."

Mr. Diaz waved us in. "You've got some tremendous photos, young lady," he said in his soft Spanish accent. "Are you entering the County Fair?"

I hurried over to take the envelope from him. "Yes, I'll have two entries. I just need to decide which two I like the best."

Georgie led me to a table set up for the customers and we spread out the prints. We laughed so hard over the funny-face pictures, even if they weren't destined for the photo competition. The handful of posed photos presented a dilemma, however.

"I like all of these," I moaned. "How am I going to choose?"

"Try picking the ones you don't want until you're left with the best one," Georgie suggested.

There were only six of the photoshoot prints, and Cami had her eyes closed in one of them, so there was one gone. A closer look showed another one with Nap's ears blurry—it must have been when he was starting to shake his head. Of the four left, my two favorites were very close, with only slight differences in Georgie's posture.

"This one," I declared. "Do you think we stand a good chance of winning with it?"

Georgie grinned. "I would have picked that one too. I tried to imagine smelling something terrible, so I'd look fed up and disgusted."

"It worked. Next stop, Hollywood."

We laughed and Georgie offered to order the right size print for me, since her mom wanted prints too. I agreed and flipped open a catalog sitting on the table. It might be a good idea for me to get a camera of my own, if I was going to keep going with this photography thing. The Brownie Hawkeye was a good value for the money—it only cost seven dollars, and then there was a jump to really good cameras starting in the ninety-dollar range. I would be spending over half of the twelve dollars I had left from Nap's chewing spree, but if I won the photo competition, I could pay myself back for the Brownie.

Chapter Twenty-One

I walked to the counter where Georgie and Mr. Diaz were talking. During a break in their conversation, I asked, "Mr. Diaz, do you know how to mount the photos for the Fair? I was thinking eleven by fourteen for the prints. Eight by ten inches feels too small."

Mr. Diaz nodded. "Yes, I can do all the mounting for you. It's not a requirement for you to do it yourself."

"I brought the negative with me for the one of Georgie." I fished in my pocket for the envelope, and then held the film strip up to the light and pointed out which one I wanted. "Georgie, did you already tell him which one I wanted from the other batch?"

"Yeah, plus I ordered a bunch for Mom to have. Is that okay? They're your pictures."

"It was a team effort, and it's Fae's camera, so print whatever you want. I'd like to order one of these cameras too, please, Mr. Diaz."

After we left, Georgie said, "Where to next, the diner?"

"We can't bring Penny inside. Unless you want to get some food to go, and bring it back to your mom and Cami?"

We decided to do that and gave our order to Uncle Earl through the kitchen's screen door. While we waited, Penny checked to see if the racoon family was hanging around the dumpster. She whined her disappointment until I shushed her. I tried to pay Uncle Earl for the bags of food, but he said if it was for Fae, then no charge.

"I'll have to remember to bring Mom with me every time, then," Georgie said with a grin.

"Get on with you." Uncle Earl shooed us away. "Don't forget I have a poker game after work tonight, Bet. I probably won't see you at home until late morning."

Fae looked tired when we got there, so she seemed grateful when we occupied Cami with a cheeseburger and fries. Fae unwrapped her Reuben and turned to Georgie.

"Did you—" she started to ask, before Georgie interrupted.

"Yeah, we got all the prints ordered. Even the embarrassing ones."

Fae didn't seem upset at Georgie's rudeness and responded with a smile. "Good. Bet, did you want to spend the night tonight?" Cami gasped, almost choking on a French fry in her excitement.

I looked up from my patty melt, my eyes wide. "Could I? I'd need to go home and feed the dogs and grab some stuff. Is Penny invited?"

"I don't think any of us would get any peace from Cami if you left Penny at home."

"Or Georgie could sleep over at my house," I said. "Uncle Earl won't be there to be bothered by us being loud."

"That might be all right, since you have a phone there now. You know, so Georgie could call if she gets scared of the dark and needs me to come get her." Fae winked at her daughter's indignant scoff.

"No, stay here!" Cami protested. "All the dogs too!"

Fae sighed. "Why not do both? Have your fun at Earl's tonight, and then Bet and Penny can stay here tomorrow night. I like that idea—it gives your uncle a break, too."

Georgie nodded. "Good plan. I'll go get my things."

Cami's howl of protest gave wings to Georgie's feet as she rushed upstairs, and Penny took advantage of the chaos to knock a plate off the table. Unfortunately for her, it was Georgie's plate, and she only got a few crumbs.

While I waited for Georgie, I called over to the diner and made sure it was okay with Uncle Earl for Georgie to sleep over tonight. And for me to go to the Woods's the next night. After he agreed, I ran upstairs to let Georgie know.

Once the sleepover started, I set aside worrying about money and getting to Oregon, and let myself just have fun. We had so much fun I didn't get any sleep until after Georgie went home the next day. Then we did it all over again that night at the Woods's, this time with Cami joining in our she-nanigans.

Fae woke up the next morning to find a pile of kids and Penny asleep on the living room floor. The smell of pancakes and sausage soon roused us, and one by one, we found our way into the kitchen for breakfast.

"You all have time to bathe and change clothes," Fae said, "and then we're going to the park."

Georgie perked up. "Oh, yeah. It's Saturday."

I piped up, "What's at the park?"

"It's a secret," Cami whisper-shouted.

Georgie and Fae exchanged looks, and then Georgie said, "It's a town celebration. There will be food, games, and even the newspaper photographer."

"Maybe I can get some advice from them about photography," I said.

Penny came over to Georgie at the table and looked hopefully at her, since Cami had finished eating and wasn't dropping anymore crumbs. Georgie made sure Fae wasn't looking and slipped Penny a bite of sausage. I shook my head and laughed—Georgie must really like Penny if she was willing to share her food. If I had tried to take a bite off my friend's plate, I would have gotten a fork stabbed into my hand. Georgie saw me watching them and winked.

"Who wants to shower first?" Fae asked.

"I will, I'm quick," Georgie answered before she stuffed the last of her pancakes in her mouth. She dashed up the stairs, leaving me in the kitchen with Fae and Cami. Fae stifled a yawn, and I jumped up to gather the dishes.

"You don't have to do that," Fae said. "I'm just taking a break."

"It's all right. We probably kept you from getting enough sleep last night. I like to be useful."

She eyed me shrewdly. "Do you actually like to be useful, or you've been told you have to be useful?"

That question hit too close to home. Felix didn't like to see me sitting and reading, or even doing my homework. He would always find something else for me to do, and I'd learned if I kept busy, I faded into the background. It was much safer in the background.

"No, I like to be useful," I insisted brightly. I don't think I fooled Fae though because she got up to help with the dishes.

Georgie came back into the kitchen and shooed me towards the shower. After I was clean and dressed, I walked into the kitchen to find Fae on the phone.

Fae turned away as she said, "Okay, see you there." She hung up the phone and told me, "That was your uncle. He's going to meet us at the park."

It struck me as strange, but I shrugged. "He doesn't want to stop by your house and walk with us?"

"I guess not. It's hard enough to get Cami out the door, so I'd rather we get there in our own time," Fae said with an eye roll.

It was another half an hour before everyone but Cami was ready to go, and then another fifteen minutes before Cami quit her dawdling and put her shoes on. Georgie carried a hamper with picnic blankets, plus some toys to keep Cami occupied. Penny led the way, trotting at the end of her leash, and as we got closer to the park, it grew more crowded. Everyone seemed grouped on the lawn near the bandstand, but thankfully, the trees offered shelter from the sun.

Georgie and I ran ahead to find a shady patch for the blankets, and I grinned like a Cheshire cat when nearly everyone we passed greeted Penny, too. Once we claimed our spot, Georgie and I tore off to see if any of our friends were there yet. Well, most of them were Georgie's friends, but I was welcome. If I allowed myself to think of staying, they could become my friends, too.

Georgie dragged me into the kids' baseball game for a while, then I reclaimed Penny from the dugout and went to find something to drink. The iced punch was popular, so it took me a while to get a cupful. After I drained it, I took Penny in search of a water fountain so the dog could have a drink. It wasn't as hot as it had been lately, but then it was only around ten thirty and would still get hotter.

I was planning on watching the ball game, but I spied Uncle Earl arriving—with Nap and Josie, too. The dogs wound their leashes around each other and us as they excitedly greeted each other. Uncle Earl and I could hardly see to untangle them, we were laughing so hard. Eventually, we got them separated.

"I didn't know you were bringing the other dogs," I said. "Can they go off their leashes and all run around together?"

"Are you kidding? With all the food around here? Nap and Josie are not above stealing candy—or a hot dog—from a baby. I know you've been working with them on leash training, so I thought I'd give them an outing. They need more training, by the way."

I led Uncle Earl to where Fae and Cami lounged in the shade. Fae and Uncle Earl chatted for a while, when Fae casually mentioned, "It's almost eleven."

Uncle Earl got to his feet and pulled Nap and Josie with him. "Come on, Bet, have you seen the bandstand up close yet? I helped build it."

Alarms went off in my head as I thought of all the odd behavior this morning. However, I didn't think Fae would help in the setup for a prank, so I followed Uncle Earl as he wound through the patchwork of blankets and quilts spread on the lawn. Just as we approached the bandstand, a man leaped onto the stage and faced the crowd with a micro-phone in his hand.

"Hello, everyone!" He called, waiting for the whistles and cheers to die down before he continued. "Most of you know why we're here today."

"I'm here for the burgers and beer!" someone yelled, get-ting a laugh.

The man on stage shook his head. "There's always one in the crowd. Okay, Chris is here for the eats, but the rest of us are here to celebrate someone special. Bet Carter, can you come up here, please?"

Everyone clapped and cheered, but I looked at Uncle Earl, not sure if I'd heard right. He smiled and nodded, gesturing for me to climb the steps onto the stage. I tried to hand him Penny's leash, but he shook his head.

"Take her with you," he said.

Penny and I climbed the stairs, and I braced myself for a prank. I had to admire Uncle Earl for getting the entire town to go along with it, though. I came to stand beside the man with the microphone and the cheers and whistles got louder. My smile went a little stiff, as I got nervous about what was going to come next.

He held up a hand until everyone quieted. "Like Chris said, we love any excuse for a party and beer, but we also wanted to celebrate these heroes. Bet here is Earl Wain-wright's niece, and she's only been in town a short while. She made friends with the Woods, and they have cause to be thankful because this girl and her dog pulled young Ca-mellia Wood out of the river."

I bit my lip, wanting to say that wasn't exactly what hap-pened. Penny did most of the work, and it was someone else who pulled the dog and Cami out of the water. But this didn't feel like the time to quibble over how it went, considering all the beaming faces looking my way in the audience. Plus, a photographer kneeled in front of the stage, with his camera lens pointed at us.

The microphone man noticed the photographer at the same time and sucked in his gut before saying, "Fae Wood says she's already thanked Bet and Penny with home cooked food—and will continue to do so until they burst, I suspect—but the people of Amberfields wanted to recognize these two in a special way. You see, Penny is one of the dogs seized in a cruelty case a while back, and Earl was caring for her on behalf of the county.

"Even while Penny was at the vet clinic recovering from her dunking, she belonged to the county. However, a few of the puppies from the same case have found new homes, so Earl argued it could happen for Penny, too. In fact, some of her puppies are here to cheer on their mama!"

A line of five people leading beagle puppies, almost as big as Penny but not grown into their ears and paws yet, paraded in front of the bandstand. I stepped forward and pointed them out to Penny, who wagged her tail but otherwise seemed unimpressed.

The man shook his head and said, "Well, I, for one, was expecting more excitement from Penny. Anyways, we petitioned for the county to surrender Penny to Bet's care and I'm glad to tell you all the county supervisors saw sense—"

Here, he was drowned out by loud laughter and catcalls before he could finish his sentence. "I'm glad to tell you the county saw sense and have made it official. Penny now belongs to Bet!"

He handed a fancy certificate to me, and I saw it had Penny's and my name on it. He also handed me a new collar with a dog license and an engraved tag with Penny's name and address. I couldn't help crying a little as I kneeled to hug *my* dog.

The man joked, "Wait until Joe takes a photo to cry."

Penny and I posed with the certificate, and the man with them. If he'd ever said his name, I had missed it, so I just pumped his hand and uttered a sincere, "Thank you, sir!"

Chapter Twenty-Two

My arm was sore, so many people wanted to shake my hand. What I really wanted to do was to get a closer look at Penny's puppies, named Scout, Daisy, Snoopy, Teddy, and Sinatra. Sinatra was apparently quite the singer. They swarmed all over Penny, but again, she seemed mostly resigned to their rambunctiousness.

After playing and eating, and playing some more, we were all tired and ready to go home—even Cami. Georgie and I staggered across the grass with armloads of blankets and gifts of food. The surprises weren't quite over, however. We hadn't walked but a few feet down the sidewalk before Uncle Earl called to us.

"Hey, where you going? Wouldn't you rather ride in style?"

Georgie and I turned to look, and Fae was already loading a sleepy Cami into the backseat of a car. Uncle Earl stood with one foot on the running board, gesturing to the Packard's faded green paint as if the car was on a pedestal in a showroom.

"Whose is that?" I asked. Nap and Josie leaped into the front seat, and one of them laid on the horn before Fae shooed them into the back with Cami.

"Ours," Uncle Earl replied. "Fae and I went in on it together and we're going to share it. We both needed something to taxi around all these kids and dogs, and one of my buddies gave me a deal."

The last of the picnic supplies got stowed into the trunk and Fae climbed into the front seat. That left the back seat for three dogs and three girls, and fortunately, we all thought it was great fun. Uncle Earl slid into the driver's seat and pulled slowly out of the parking spot. He honked all the way through town, showing off.

"She may not look like much, but she runs smooth." He patted the steering wheel fondly, like it was another stray dog he'd picked up. "We'll have to think of a name for her."

It wasn't a long drive to Fae's house, but Georgie, Cami, and I spent it shouting suggestions for names: Merrylegs, Stinky, Old Paint, Taco, Dumpling, Duchess, and Ivy. Ivy was actually Fae's idea, but Cami repeated it like it was hers, since no one else had liked Stinky. And in spite of Georgie coming up with a few more food-themed names, there was only one which stuck.

"See you later, Old Paint!" Georgie called as Uncle Earl and I pulled away. I waved through the back window and Nap and Josie stuck their heads out to bark all the way home.

"Aren't you glad you don't have to work today?" I asked as I released the hounds into the yard.

Uncle Earl huffed a laugh. "Yes! We had to scramble to plan your party on such short notice, but Rufus was able to cover my shift. This whole thing was Doc Marsh's idea, by the way. He thought you needed cheering up, and we all agreed Penny was nobody's dog but yours. Mr. Diaz printed up that gorgeous certificate."

I blushed, but this time it was more of a warm feeling than embarrassment. The rest of the afternoon and evening was quiet, partly since the dogs were so exhausted they fell right to sleep, only waking long enough to eat their suppers. We appreciated the break from Nap and Josie's mischief and spent the evening reading in our own spaces. Uncle Earl promised to build a frame to display Penny's certificate, but for now, it was propped on my desk. I could almost imagine it shone like something precious, even after I reached over and switched off my pineapple lamp.

If we had hoped the next morning would bring some peace and quiet, though, we were wrong. The phone rang early and Uncle Earl stumbled from his bedroom to the kitchen to answer it, cursing all the while. It was the first of many calls from friends congratulating him, and me, on the front-page article of the local newspaper, The Amberfields Flag.

I came out of my room, grouchy at being awakened earlier than I wanted, but the news of the newspaper's feature cheered me up.

Uncle Earl rubbed his eyes and said, "Well, I guess I'd better drive into town and fetch a stack of papers. Fae will want one, and maybe some people will want the heroes to sign them."

"Really? Even Penny?"

He laughed. "Are you kidding? A newspaper signed by a dog would be worth a fortune one day. Everybody will want one."

I brightened. "If you're going to town, maybe you want to pick up some donuts?"

Uncle Earl opened the fridge door. "Did you forget we have the pies Mrs. Miller sent home yesterday? Plus, leftover beanie weenies and corn pones. And all the burgers Mack burned when he wasn't paying attention to the grill, saved for the dogs."

"Hmm, those sound like meal choices. Donuts are more of a treat. Besides, doesn't a hero like me deserve a raspberry jelly donut?" I made my best puppy dog eyes. And then I laughed at myself, since I'd so quickly been spoiled by easy access to food.

"Oh Lord, that article is going to turn you into a monster, isn't it?" Uncle Earl said. "Well, you can stay here and answer the phone so all your fans can gush over you and Penny."

Uncle Earl changed out of his pajamas and whistled for Nap and Josie to join him in Old Paint, and off they went, with loud barks announcing their progress down the driveway. I served myself a piece of blueberry pie—well, it was more like half a pie—and put some sausage and corn pones in a pan to heat. I crumbled up a couple of cold, charred hamburger patties for Penny, too.

I had barely lifted my fork to my mouth when the phone rang. The lady on the line said she was Mrs. Felda, and was this the girl with the dog from the paper? Before I could answer, Mrs. Felda launched into an avalanche of chatter.

I tried to answer questions or speak up, but I didn't get much of a chance. "Yes—no, she's a—when? Of course—maybe—what do you...?"

Mrs. Felda chirped a goodbye and I was left holding the phone as it buzzed a dial tone. I looked at Penny and shrugged. "I have no idea who that was."

The next few days were just like that. I could be walking Penny down the street, and someone would wave a news-paper at me to sign. Fae gave me a jar of beet juice and I trained Penny to offer her paw so I could use it as a stamp. That never failed to get a laugh. I was going to know every-one in town's name at this rate. If I wasn't careful, this place, and these people, might start to feel like home. The thought didn't seem so awful anymore, but I wasn't ready to aban-don my plans for Oregon yet.

Instead, I decided to use my newfound fame among the town to play an ambitious prank on Uncle Earl. Around the corner from the diner, Georgie and I set up a card table with a homemade sign saying: "Help us prank Earl Wainwright!" Nearly everyone in town stopped by to see what it was about and agreed to take part.

All day long, Uncle Earl's friends came into the diner and asked, "Say, Earl, did you hear about the restaurant on the moon? Great food, but no atmosphere." The first time he heard it made Uncle Earl laugh, the second time made him chuckle, but after the tenth time or so, he demanded to know who had put them up to it. From our spot, we could even hear him throw a few of his buddies out for telling him the joke, even when he warned them not to. We laughed so hard every time we heard him roar in indignation.

Eventually, Uncle Earl came around the corner and found us, hands on his hips as he said, "I should have known you two had a part in this. Was this your idea, Georgie?"

Georgie shook her head as she pointed to me with pride. "Nope, this one was all hers. I didn't think it would go on this long, but it's the best prank yet. You sounded like a mad bear!"

Uncle Earl grudgingly admitted it was a good prank. "Although, pranking me while I'm at work is going on the list of forbidden tricks. I'm not sure my boss would appreciate it."

"Nah, he was in on it," I said with an impish grin. "Mr. Perkins thought people might stick around to watch, and buy more food, and he was right."

"Hmmph," was all Uncle Earl had to say about that. He gritted his teeth every time someone told him the joke over the next few days; it was impressive how long everyone kept it going.

Meanwhile, being a local celebrity was fun and all, but a little overwhelming for Penny and me. We took to hiding in the garden again, or hanging out in Georgie's room. After about a week, folks found other things to distract them, and we could walk around town again in peace. On the morning that I was going to the store to pick up some nice stationery and envelopes, only a few people stopped me to talk.

An old man on a bench outside the office store watched us walk up. "I know that dog!" He lurched to his feet and pointed at Penny.

Penny had come to love the attention lavished on her, but at the man's voice, she tucked her tail and tried to cower behind my legs.

I frowned, but politely said, "You probably saw her in the paper. This is Penny." No chance I was going to offer this guy an autograph.

I went to step around him, but he blocked my way, getting even closer. "No, that's one of my dogs. She's Lousy Dog."

At the name, Penny started shaking, and I felt wetness on my heel. Had Penny peed, she was so scared? She hadn't done it since Uncle Earl first brought her home. I bristled in defense of my dog.

"She's not a lousy dog. She's my dog, and my best friend." I backed up, putting more space between us and the man, but he shook a finger in my face.

"You don't know what you're talking about, girl. My dogs were stolen from me, and I want this one back."

Could this be Penny's former owner? What had Uncle Earl called him—Mr. Bundle? No, Mr. Bindle.

"Mr. Bindle, the county took your dogs because you didn't treat them right." I tried to sound firm, but my voice shook as he loomed at me. I was frightened, too, but I could be brave for Penny's sake. "Penny is my dog, and it's all legal. Talk to the sheriff if you think you can take care of dogs now."

I didn't want to turn my back on him, so I crouched and picked up Penny's shivering form. I cradled the dog close and tried again to get around Mr. Bindle, to make it to the safety of the office store. As I put my hand on the door, the old man seized my shoulder and whirled me around.

"You're not taking my dog from me, not again," he barked. "Gimme that mutt!"

I screamed as he grabbed at my dog, and we tussled over Penny. Mr. Bindle gouged his filthy nails into my hands and arms, and I cried out, "You're hurting me! Stop it!"

At the sound of my pain, Penny transformed into a snarling, snapping defender. She latched onto her former master's hand, not letting go once she had hold. Now Mr. Bindle was howling in pain, too, and passersby rushed over. A man came out of the office supply and attempted to calm things down.

"That's enough, now! You two take a couple of steps back."

Penny let go of Mr. Bindle's hand so she could lick the tears from my face, and the old man continued to holler.

"That dog attacked me for no reason! It ought to be shot! Now that it's tasted human blood, none of you are safe!"

A few spectators murmured in horror, but I stubbornly spoke up, "That's not what happened at all! He was trying to take her, and look, he scratched me all up. My dog was only trying to protect me." I waved my bloodied arm to show the wounds, still holding Penny tight with the other hand.

The man from the store nodded, crossing his arms as he said, "I saw it, and it was definitely not for no reason. He was bothering the girl and dog."

People started arguing about who was in the wrong, and I sobbed harder when Penny and I were mentioned as often as the awful old man. I'd thought we'd made friends in this town, but some folks were so quick to believe Mr. Bindle. I wanted to run home with Penny and lock us in my room, but I also wanted to make sure Mr. Bindle was punished. I couldn't find a familiar face at all in this crowd.

A sheriff's car pulled up to the curb, and a man in uniform got out. "I heard there was some kind of commotion going on. What's happened?"

Everyone talked at once, and my explanation was lost in the crowd of voices. Mr. Bindle shoved his dripping hand into the sheriff's face. "Look at what that vicious dog did! You need to shoot it!"

The sheriff looked at the old man's bloody wound and pulled a clean hankie out of his pocket. "This looks bad, Mr. Bindle. You ought to get the doctor to look at it. You may need stitches."

"It is bad! But what about the girl and the dog? They can't be allowed to roam the town and attack people!" Mr. Bindle insisted.

The sheriff glanced at me and Penny, huddled together in misery, and his face softened. "I tell you what, I will take these two back to the station with me. You go get that hand seen to and then come to the station so we can get this sorted out. Can someone see Mr. Bindle makes it to the doctor all right?" He directed this last part at the crowd.

A man volunteered and led the still-hollering Mr. Bindle towards the doctor's office. Everyone else milled around, grumbling and taking sides, until the sheriff approached me.

"Hello, Miss, I'm Sheriff Nicholls. If you will come with me to the station, I'd appreciate it."

I nodded, but then asked, "What about Penny? My dog."

Sheriff Nicholls eyed the dog. "If you think you can control her, she can ride in the back with you."

"She listens to me," I said wearily. "She only went after him because—"

"We'll have plenty of time to talk about it at the station. We can call your uncle from there."

Before I could argue, he had opened the back door of the car and was waiting for me to climb in. I weighed my chances of running, but the sheriff would only find me at home later, since he knew who my uncle was. Hopefully, he would believe me when I explained Penny was defending me.

Penny curled as small as she could in my lap as we drove to the station, and I rhythmically smoothed her fur, to comfort us both. Now that I wasn't in immediate danger, the scrapes on my arms stung and throbbed more. I would probably get tetanus from the old man's dirty hands. When I climbed from the car, I stumbled as my knees went weak.

"Delayed shock. You'll be okay," the sheriff said.

Sheriff Nicholls followed us into the station, which thankfully had air conditioning even though it struggled to cool the shabby central room. We passed mostly empty desks in the bullpen, but a few deputies shuffled paperwork or talked on the phone. I spotted a couple of holding cells in the corner, the metal bars open to the room like in a Western movie. This place must be old—the Sacramento police stations had done away with those years ago, at least in the places I'd been to retrieve Mama after a bender.

The sheriff's tiny office was hotter until he turned on a desk fan. He pointed at me to take a seat in one of the two chairs across from his desk, but before he could say anything, his phone rang.

"Hello? Oh, Earl, yeah, she's here with me." He held the phone away from his ear for a moment and I could hear faint shouting. "Instead of yelling at me over the line, why don't you come down here so we can get this sorted out?"

He hung up without waiting for an answer. "Your uncle doesn't want me 'interrogating' you without him here, so make yourself comfortable."

His eyes fell on my arms. "We should get those cleaned up so they don't get infected. Wait here and I'll get the first aid kit."

I stayed in the office, but my nerves wouldn't let me sit. Penny and I paced the small space, passing in and out of the cooler stream of air from the fan. It did nothing to help my anxiety—I didn't have friendly thoughts about most officers, since Felix was always complaining about them sticking their noses into his businesses. As his businesses weren't strictly legal, it seemed like he should have gotten used to that. Plus, back when Mama was out drinking so much, she had a standing reservation in the drunk tank. I was the one to retrieve her, as often as not. Some police were sympathetic, and some thought I was just a smaller version of the same trouble.

A lady in uniform came in to clean my arms, saying the sheriff thought we might be more comfortable around her. Although the iodine stung like a yellow jacket bite, the woman was gentle enough that I was able to relax a little while we waited for Uncle Earl. I still couldn't help thinking I should have run, though, and taken Penny with me. I hoped this didn't end as badly as my clenched gut said it would.

Chapter Twenty-Three

The lady brought me a cold soda, plus a bowl of water for Penny. We both guzzled them down, thirsty after walking in the heat and then getting into a scuffle. A few red spots bloomed in Penny's water, swirling into pink before disappearing. I wiped her muzzle with my shirttail, getting the last of the blood off from her "victim." Her villain was more like it.

We waited alone in the office long enough for me to get bored, and then sleepy from the still-warm air. I stretched out across the chairs and Penny crawled beneath; I left one hand dangling to stroke her fur. We must have dozed off, but loud voices woke us up.

I peeked out the door and saw a handful of people at the front counter, all talking at once. Uncle Earl was there, plus other people I recognized. Sheriff Nicholls tried to restore order, but then a few more of Uncle Earl's friends came in and started jabbering too.

"All right, everyone calm down," Sheriff Nicholl's voice carried over the rest. "Earl, you come back to my office, and the rest of you wait your turn for my deputies to take your statement. You'll all get a chance, although I don't recall your faces among the witnesses of the incident."

The sheriff opened a door for Uncle Earl to come through to the bullpen, and two deputies stepped to the counter to take names and statements.

Uncle Earl spied me in the doorway and hurried over. "Are you all right, Bet? Both of you?"

I displayed my badges of courage, a row of Band-Aids covering the deepest gouges. "Mostly. We met Mr. Bindle, and he tried to take Penny. He shouldn't ever be allowed to have a dog again."

Uncle Earl glanced at Sheriff Nicholls as we took seats in his office. "Hopefully after this, the county will see that, too. They're dragging their feet about a judgment."

The sheriff shook his head. "It's not so simple, Earl, since Penny doesn't belong to the county any longer. We have to take Mr. Bindle's accusations seriously—the bite wounds looked nasty."

I leaped to my feet. "She wouldn't have bitten him if he hadn't hurt me! You can't shoot my dog because he says so."

Earl nodded vigorously. "She's right, Bill, this isn't the Wild West where people can just shoot dogs."

The sheriff dropped his head in his hands. "I'm aware of that, Earl. Let me be clear in saying Mr. Bindle does not have the power to shoot your dog, nor to condemn it to be shot. I am waiting for him to come in and give his version of events, and to see if there are any useful details in the stack of papers my deputies recorded. Meanwhile, Doc Marsh needs to get back to me with Penny's rabies vaccination info, so we know whether to worry about it being in the mix."

Earl sat back in his chair, pulling me down beside him. "You're right. I'm sorry for—I've known you for years, and I should have known you wouldn't do anything hastily. I could bake and frost a cake in the time you take to lay down your bet at our poker games."

Uncle Earl's apology and joke helped to cut some of the tension between them. It was good timing for a knock to sound on the door jamb, and to see Fae standing there with a plate of cookies. Cami hung onto her leg, and Georgie stood behind her.

"I thought maybe everybody could use a cookie break," Fae said.

Sheriff Nicholls threw his hands in surrender. "Why not? It's not like I'm working or anything. Let's go to the kitchen. My office is tight enough with three people in it." His smile showed he wasn't really put out by Fae's arrival. He grumbled about small towns and the speed of gossip as he led us to the back of the building.

Penny ran to the end of her leash towards Cami, but I pulled her back. I didn't want a scratch or bruise to add weight to Mr. Bindle's accusations. Once we got to the kitchen, though, Cami sat on the floor and I let Penny climb into her lap. The rest of us made small talk as we nibbled cookies, conscious we were avoiding talking about anything important. Then Mr. Bindle arrived, so the sheriff went to escort him to his office—where he shut the door.

Uncle Earl glanced at the Woods and leaned in to say softly to me, "A deputy is supposed to take your statement now that I'm here. If they ask outright whether I'm your legal guardian, I don't want you to lie. We'll say your mama's deathbed wish was for you to spend some time with me, but if anyone specifically asks if your father knows you're here, you'll have to fess up."

I wasn't happy, but I nodded. I could still change my story in the moment, but if they actually contacted Felix, my lie would unravel quickly. My best bet might be to play along, and then run with Penny the first chance I got. As if he could read my mind—or maybe he could read my face—Uncle Earl pulled me in for another tight hug. It gave me the strength to take a deep breath and follow the deputy when he came for me.

Penny sat in my lap while I gave my account, which, even though it felt like a huge thing, didn't actually take very long. Then it was back to the kitchen to wait for the sheriff again. I was too numb to be scared at this point. Georgie tried to liven up the somber group by telling a funny story, but Cami was the only one who paid attention. When Sheriff Nicholls returned, we all held our breaths.

"All right, you can go home, Bet." When I made for the door, he held a hand up. "I'll need to keep Penny, though. Her rabies vaccine is up to date, but the bite was serious enough that I'm required to open an investigation. Part of it will be observing her for behavior."

"What do you mean, keep her? How do I know you won't shoot her?" I pulled Penny's leash in tight.

"Yeah, can't she stay in the house?" Georgie added.

Sheriff Nicholls wiped a hand down his face. "I need to be able to watch Penny, to judge for myself if she's a danger. I was thinking of putting her in one of the old holding cells, where the staff and I can all see for ourselves how she does.

That would also make it much harder for me to discharge a firearm in the middle of the station, if that helps."

I wasn't sure if he was joking, but I refused to be diverted. "No. I have to stay with her. That's the only way she can be here. Somebody could tease her or scare her and then she'd—"

I broke off, not wanting to suggest Penny could bite again under any circumstances. "I'm not leaving her here alone. End of story."

The sheriff shook his head. "I don't have staff to babysit you, in addition to a dog. There's only one person in the station overnight, and we don't do room service. Not going to happen, young lady."

I stared at him as a wild impulse came over me. I wordlessly handed Penny's leash to Uncle Earl, and before anyone knew what I was planning, I kicked Sheriff Nicholls in the shins as hard as I could. I was wearing shoes, so he doubled over in pain and surprise.

"There. Now I've attacked an officer, so you have to lock me up, too." I stood with arms on hips, daring him to contradict me so I could kick him again.

Georgie didn't bother to hide a snort of laughter, and when the sheriff started to argue, she helpfully held the plate of cookies out to me so I could pelt him with cookies too.

"Stop!" Uncle Earl roared, making Penny and I cringe. Everyone else froze, not used to hearing Earl yell like that.

Seeing he had our attention, Uncle Earl frowned and added, "Stop wasting those cookies!"

With his stern expression and my misbehavior, it was such an unexpected thing to say that Fae guffawed before covering her mouth. Cami tittered uncertainly until we were all laughing, and I even had tears streaming down my face. Just like when I'd climbed the tree at Uncle Earl's, tears and laughter went hand in hand.

After our mirth trailed off, Uncle Earl spoke again. "Now that we got that out of the way, why don't we see if we can figure out some way to make this work? I'll start: I know between me and Fae, we can easily keep Bet and Penny fed here, so they're not eating on the taxpayer's dime. Right, Fae?"

"Of course," she said.

Sheriff Nicholls looked skeptical. "And who's going to babysit her? Especially overnight?"

I opened my mouth to argue, but Uncle Earl winked at me. He'd used humor to make his point before, so I decided to try it. "I haven't woken Uncle Earl up once for a feeding or diaper change since I've been here. I'm old enough to be a babysitter. What kind of trouble can I get up to in my sleep?"

Sheriff Nicholls snorted. "I don't know you well enough to give examples of the trouble you could get up to. Besides kicking me like a mule."

Georgie raised her hand like she was answering a question at school. "But you know me! I'll stay here with Bet at night. We were going to have more sleepovers before school starts, anyway. I never dreamed they'd be in a jail cell, but there you go."

The sheriff scoffed, but he chewed his lip like he was considering Georgie's offer.

"I want a sleepover too," Cami whined, breaking the thoughtful silence.

Fae jogged Cami on her hip. "I hope you're much older before you stay in a cell." She took her younger daughter out of the kitchen as she wailed.

"You asked me how you could know I wouldn't shoot your dog, so I'm asking how do I know you won't run off and leave me with the consequences?" Sheriff Nicholls asked me.

I took a moment to answer, so he would know I was taking the question seriously. I couldn't really use examples of promises I'd kept—to Mama and to Nina—since that would give away my plans. But I could say it in less specific ways. "Because I keep promises. If I make you a promise to stay here for as long as you say, I'll do it. As long as you swear Penny is safe."

"Promises aren't conditional, so it's not a good start."

Uncle Earl spoke up. "It didn't sound to me like she was adding conditions, as much as she was asking for your promise in return. A little give and take from both sides."

"But I can't make that promise," Sheriff Nicholls replied. "It's not entirely up to me what happens to Penny. I have to report my observations to the same committee who ordered the dogs seized from Mr. Bindle. They will ultimately decide Penny's fate. I'll tell them the truth, so can you live with that?"

I didn't know what to think—trust didn't come easy to me, or to Penny. But Penny was trusting me to speak up for her. I looked at Uncle Earl, but he shrugged.

"It's not my decision," he said. "This is between you and the sheriff. If it helps, I trust him."

I scratched at the Band-Aids on my arms as I considered. What were my other choices? Make a run for the door with

Penny, and just keep on running? Or to pretend I was okay with Penny staying there and staging a jailbreak?

Either one of those might put too much attention on my situation. And if Felix dragged me home, no way he would let Penny come with me. Or if he did, he would use the dog's health and happiness as a way to keep me in line—which was why I'd never dared to have a pet before Penny. Both those scenarios made trusting the sheriff a lot more appealing. I'd just have to run the odds on each one.

"How long would we need to stay?" I finally asked.

"For a rabies quarantine, it would be ten to fourteen days. For this, I would think five days would give me an idea of how she behaves when you're not being threatened."

Hmm, five days, so four nights. "Uncle Earl and Fae, can you keep us fed for that long? If not, I'll call it a hunger strike."

Georgie scoffed. "I'll stay the nights with you, but I'm not signing up for any hunger strike. I don't like you that much, Bet."

The sheriff ignored Georgie, keeping a steely gaze on me. "Do I have your promise not to run away, Bet?"

I sighed, still not pleased at having to say it. "Yes, I promise I will stay here for the four nights and five days you asked."

"And Penny too?"

That sheriff was just too sharp. "And Penny promises too. We can both shake on it."

True to my word, I shook the sheriff's hand, and Penny offered her paw when prompted.

"Good enough for me," Sheriff Nicholls said. "Now let's go see about setting you up a cell. They haven't been used for a long time, since we built the jail."

Each of the two holding cells had a window which didn't open, plus a bunk that looked more like a wooden bench. I spotted the toilet in the corner, open to everyone's view in the bullpen, and I turned wide eyes to the sheriff.

He laughed. "We won't expect you to use that. You can use the squad bathroom down the hall—it even has a shower—and you'll have to take Penny out in the equipment yard to do her business. That would have been the perfect way to escape, if you hadn't both promised me."

I smiled but didn't confirm whether I had been thinking the same thing. Uncle Earl said he had an old Army cot he could bring by for Georgie, plus some bedding for both of us. With that settled, the sheriff closed Penny and me into a cell so he could see if the lock still worked. Penny walked forward to sniff the door before stepping between the bars and out of the cell, wagging her tail as everyone laughed again.

Chapter Twenty-Four

Penny and I had been at the station through lunch, so Georgie ran to the diner to get food for herself and us two "criminals." Uncle Earl and Fae left to gather things we would need to stay there that night, and the sheriff had other business to attend to. So Penny and I stewed in the holding cell.

A few of the employees smiled as they walked by, but otherwise the room was just a background of buzzing sound. The noise and my relief almost soothed me to sleep in the folding chair I slumped in, but the arrival of food and drinks perked me right up. The lady cop, who had the unintimidating name of Peggy, let us eat in the kitchen.

"I can bring some games, cards, books, stuff like that," Georgie said between bites. "Is there anything of yours you want me to get from Earl's?"

"Some clothes would be good. I don't want Uncle Earl digging in my underwear drawer." We both laughed until Peggy shushed us from her desk outside the kitchen door.

"And one of Penny's pillows from my bed," I added in a low voice.

Georgie nodded. "Will do. I was planning on coming in and out during the day, if that's all right, but I'll stay here all night."

"That's fine. The hardest part is being stuck inside, but I'm good at entertaining myself. I'll be glad of the company while we're sleeping."

"Who gets any sleep at a sleepover?" Georgie asked with a wink. We finished eating and Penny and I went back to our cell, and Georgie went to run her errands before returning for the night.

But in spite of my claims of being good at entertaining myself, I found it was less true when I didn't have something to occupy me. A book, a deck of cards, some drawing paper—anything would be welcome. Penny was snoring under the bunk, and I didn't want to disturb her to work on training. Things were winding down at the station as the support staff left for the day, and only a few officers lingered at their desks to finish paperwork.

I had nearly worked up the courage to ask one of the deputies for a pencil and scrap paper when a familiar face came through the front door. Doc Marsh spoke briefly to the desk worker, and they waved him through. He shook his head as he approached the cell.

"Look at you two jailbirds," he drawled. "I came to take a gander at Penny to see if she's okay from today's encounter."

At the sound of her name, Penny stepped again through the bars so she could get close enough for petting. Doc

Marsh obliged by rubbing her ears the way Penny liked. "How's it going?"

I replied wryly, "She's the one under investigation, and she can come and go as she pleases. But she's fine, I think, just a little nervous still." That made two of us.

"I brought a book to lend you. Earl says you've been working on training the dogs." He slipped a book through the bars. "Careful, some pages are 'bout to fall out. It's been well read."

On the worn red cover, some gilding remained to pick out the title Practical Dog Training by S.T. Hammond. I took it hesitantly; the books on dog training I'd found at the library advocated whipping dogs to "bring them in line." When I opened this one, the subtitle caught my eye: Training vs Breaking. Maybe this book would be more useful, since I wasn't planning on whipping Penny ever.

I thanked him and Doc Marsh turned to leave, but I called out to him. "Wait, do you need help in the kennels? I need to earn some cash, and I thought maybe you want to hire me for cleaning and feeding."

Doc Marsh narrowed his eyes. "I don't know if I'd feel comfortable hiring on an ex-con. Would I have to keep track of your hours for your parole officer?"

I barked a laugh. "I promise to leave my crimes behind me." That was a promise I'd already made to myself, so it was no hardship to make it to Doc Marsh, even if he was giving me a hard time. "Penny too, if she can come along."

"It would be early in the morning, before we open, but yes, we can try it out."

Doc Marsh waved and went on his way, while I happily settled into the folding chair to read my borrowed treasure.

The pages so absorbed me that Uncle Earl had to say my name a few times before I looked up. The pile of bedding in his arms hid his face, and I could smell the fresh linen scent from my chair.

I rushed to help him, and since the officer with the cell key wasn't around, we had to pass the blankets, sheets, and pillows through the meal tray slot. The folded Army cot fit sideways through the bars, and the same with a rickety card table and a second folding chair.

Deputy Ramirez, the youngest officer, had overnight duty, and he finally unlocked the cell door. It made it easier to hand over the bags Uncle Earl had brought—after Deputy Ramirez searched them—containing playing cards and other things to occupy my time. Uncle Earl eyed the door, once again locked.

"Is it safe to lock Bet in there with only you on duty? What if there's a fire or emergency?"

Deputy Ramirez scratched his head. "Then I'll let her out."

"Just now, you were away from your desk, and it took you a while to find the key when you came back. She's already promised the sheriff not to run, so can't you leave it un-locked?" Uncle Earl's voice was gentle but firm.

"I don't have the authority to decide."

"How about we call someone who does?"

The deputy's eyes shifted nervously. "Sheriff Nicholls is probably sitting down to dinner right now. I hate to bother him."

Uncle Earl sighed, like he was trying to find the patience to get through to the younger man. "If there was any other question, what would you do?"

"I'd have to figure it out for myself," he answered. "I'm only supposed to call a superior if it's something serious."

I felt a little sorry for the deputy. He didn't look much older than Nina, and even his uniform hung a little big on him, like he was expected to grow into it. "What if I also promise you I won't run away?"

He nodded in relief, and I solemnly spoke the words, with Penny shaking his hand like we'd done for the sheriff. Now satisfied, Deputy Ramirez turned the bolt with the cell door hanging open, so it couldn't be locked closed. He saluted us and returned to his desk with a jaunty whistle.

Since Uncle Earl could come in to help, we got the cell looking shipshape in no time. The built-in bunk and cot were crisply made up with sheets, and a blanket lay folded over the foot in case it got chilly (not much of a risk with the struggling air conditioner). The card table had two chairs waiting for Georgie and me, and a stack of cards and cribbage boards stood ready. Uncle Earl had even delivered some meals and snacks to the kitchen's refrigerator, which was handy now that I could come and go from the cell as I pleased. Penny got her dinner, too, since she'd only had part of my sandwich before. Then she curled up with her pillow, in the nest I made under the bunk, and watched her people.

Uncle Earl clapped his hands together in satisfaction. "Whelp, this is better than some motel rooms I've stayed in. Do you want me to stay until Georgie gets here?"

"No, I'm fine," I said as I gave him a hug goodbye. "Doc Marsh brought me a book, so I want to try some training with Penny."

By the time Georgie arrived, I had taught Penny a new trick. "Watch this!" I spun my hand in a circle as Penny watched carefully. Penny dropped her bottom into a sit.

"Wow," Georgie said dubiously.

"No! She's supposed to spin." At the word "spin," Penny's ears perked forward, and she stood up before circling. I sighed. "We're still working on it."

Georgie handed me a canvas bag. "Here, this has some clothes and a toothbrush, stuff like that."

"Thanks." I stowed it under my bunk and came to sit at the table. "What do you want to do until bedtime?"

"Did you eat dinner yet?"

I rolled my eyes and led Georgie to the kitchen, where we dug into the macaroni salad Uncle Earl had left.

"Needs more cheese," Georgie mumbled. "And not so many vegetables."

"It's better than the gruel they feed you when you're in real jail," I countered. But I had to admit Uncle Earl's meatloaf and burgers, and pies and milkshakes, were a step above this food. The macaroni salad was still better than trying to sneak a meal at the poker club or finding things at home to throw together for me and Mama. "He probably wanted to use up veggies from the garden. Plus, I'm not sure there's any way to heat stuff up."

Her mouth full, Georgie pointed to a hotplate in the corner, and a dented pot and skillet hanging on the wall nearby. An electric kettle and a toaster rounded out the kitchen appliances, but the sign saying "Do Not Plug in More Than One at a Time" had me worried.

"We're not too far from the diner, so maybe with more planning, the other meals will be hot," I said hopefully.

"And I'll make sure Mom knows we were stuck with macaroni salad," Georgie said with a shudder. Although she didn't stop eating it, so how bad could it be? I wouldn't start craving this every day, but it was better than greenish ham on day-old bread. Or old ham on greenish bread, both of which I'd had.

After we finished eating dinner, we dug into the blueberry pie Uncle Earl had left. First, I cut a hefty slice and took it to Deputy Ramirez. He came to thank us afterwards, and we had a hard time not laughing at his purple teeth. It was a good thing he was only answering the phones overnight, so no one could see it.

The company cheered me up, and maybe my incarceration wouldn't be so bad. Normally at a sleepover, unbrushed teeth were a badge of honor, but I didn't want purple teeth all night. "You said you packed me a toothbrush in this bag?" I asked as I retrieved it from under my bunk.

"Yeah, and there's some clothes for tomorrow. I figured we'd be sleeping in what we're wearing tonight since otherwise the whole station would see us in our pajamas in the morning."

I nodded absently as I dug through the bag, feeling for a toothbrush and paste. "What—are these pajamas? I thought you said—" I broke off as I pulled the black-and-white striped fabric out and saw it was a prison uniform. Pants, a shirt, and a cap with numbers on it.

As Georgie doubled over with laughter, I turned to her in amazement. "I'm impressed you got this prank together on such short notice. How did you manage it?"

"Cubby Parr wore it for Halloween last year, and I traded him a pocketknife for it. Are you going to wear it tomorrow? I didn't pack you anything else."

I grinned. "Would it count as your prank or mine if I'm wearing it when Uncle Earl gets here? I could sing 'In The Jailhouse Now'. Maybe Penny will join in."

Georgie shook her head. "My prank was to deliver the suit. What you do with it is your business, so I think it would count as yours."

"And now you're stuck here with me while I think of a way to get you back." My grin turned wolfish.

"Do your worst," Georgie snorted. "You're always nice with your pranks. Instead of writing something rude on my face while I was sleeping, you made me up like a doll with Mom's Avon samples."

I shrugged; I'd actually thought Georgie would hate the makeup worse than if I'd written "booger" in grease pencil on her forehead. I was content to let Georgie underestimate me, so she'd be that much more shocked when I finally pulled a glorious trick on her. Georgie would be just as surprised as the marks at the poker club, if they figured out a little girl had bested them at the card table.

I watched in delight as Georgie pulled some tubes of M&M chocolates from the battered blue suitcase she'd brought. "I saw Earl brought you cards, so do you want to play poker?" she asked. "I know your stepdad had a poker club, so I'm sure you know how. We can bet candy."

I chewed my lip, hesitating. Although I didn't want to go back to using the tricks I'd learned from Mama on real marks, surely returning a prank was okay? Georgie had practically dared me to step up my game.

Nodding, I said, "I know how to play. I'm better at poker than blackjack, that's for sure."

Georgie covetously eyed the chocolate, her favorites. "Maybe we should start out with blackjack then and work up to poker."

I agreed reluctantly, as if that hadn't been my aim the whole time since it would be much easier for me to win at Blackjack. I even risked holding out the cards to Georgie, asking, "Do you want to shuffle and deal?"

"Go ahead." Georgie shrugged. As I shuffled the cards like a pro, Georgie looked like she regretted her choice.

"We oughta make sure all the cards are here, that it's a full deck," I said. With a deft hand, I fanned them in a long row, face up, so we could count. "Fifty-two, though we won't need the jokers."

I set the jokers aside and gathered the cards up for one last shuffle. I held them out again to Georgie, asking if she wanted to cut the deck, but Georgie shook her head and frowned. Maybe she wasn't used to somebody being better than her at something?

And I was better than Georgie—after several hands, nearly all the candy was on my side of the table. I'd lost a few hands here and there, but Georgie was beginning to suspect those were on purpose. After I won again, Georgie leaped to her feet.

"No one's that good! What are you, some kind of card sharp?"

I froze, because those words never ended well at the club. But I reminded myself this was just a friendly game, with a friend, and grinned. "What'd you expect? Didn't I tell you my mother was the best card sharp in the Western states? And maybe even the entire country, but she hated to travel very far, so she never put it to the test."

Georgie sank back into her chair. "So, you've been cheating this whole time?"

"If I was seriously cheating, you'd never be able to tell. This was just for fun." I set the rest of the deck in the middle of the table, saying, "Jack of spades, four of hearts, six of clubs, ten of spades, and queen of diamonds."

"What?"

"Turn over the next five cards in the deck," I urged.

Georgie did, and found they were the cards I had listed. Dumbfounded, she blurted, "How did you know that?"

"I memorized the cards when I spread them out, and then only pretended to shuffle. I was only using my skills to prank you back. You don't actually mind, do you?" I bit my lip.

Georgie tested me on a few more cards and then stared as if she was meeting me for the first time. "I'm...flabbergasted. You're the coolest friend ever, Bet. I can't believe you had this talent the whole time I've known you—it's like finding out a superhero's secret identity. We could have so much fun with this." She rubbed her hands together in glee.

I sighed, since I'd only talked around some of my past before. But I had a feeling Georgie would continue to beg me to trick friends unless she knew the whole truth. I leaned forward to whisper, in case the deputy could overhear us.

"Sorry, but I don't use my superpowers for evil anymore. Pranking you is one thing, but I've seen all the lives my stepfather ruined with gambling debts. It's not anything I want a part in." As it was, I had already been forced into some things which didn't sit well with my conscience.

"Felix and my mother were partners. If they were working a mark, sometimes Mama was the one doing the tricking, and sometimes she was the distraction while Felix ran some con. And they were training me to take part. Which is why Felix likely isn't too happy I'm gone, especially since Mama isn't in play anymore." Well, that plus the two hundred and six dollars I had stolen from his emergency stash.

Georgie's face screwed up as she adjusted to what she thought she knew about me. "So, you're on the run from some kind of crime family?"

I laughed. "My grandfather's not Al Capone, if that's what you mean. Felix has…properties around Sacramento he makes most of his money from, but he likes to keep his hand in the poker club. Pun intended."

With a sigh, Georgie said, "Okay, so we're not going to get rich from your superpowers. But can you maybe play one game against Cubby and win my pocketknife back? I liked that one."

"Since it was to get the prison uniform, I'll allow it." I offered my hand, and we shook on it. But her gaze was still on me, and this time it looked sad.

"What?" I asked nervously. Did she think badly of me because of what I'd revealed?

She frowned before saying, "You're really smart, but how come you never let on? I bet they don't even know how smart you are in school. Except for people you really like, you mostly stay quiet and watch everyone else."

I didn't answer right away. Finally, I said, "How I grew up, it's safer to not be noticed. Besides, you can learn a lot of cool things by listening in when people forget you're even there."

"That sounds lonely. How can you ever be yourself if you're trying to pretend you're not even there?"

I didn't have an answer, so I wordlessly pushed some of the M&Ms back to Georgie's side of the table, hoping she'd drop it. She gave me the side eye like she wasn't fooled, but crammed a handful of chocolates in her mouth.

Chapter Twenty-Five

We did eventually get to sleep, and I woke early to find the deputy's head down on his desk too. I made sure to slap my bare feet extra loud on the tile as I passed him on the way to the bathroom, and he awoke with a snort. He had time to grab a cup of coffee before the sheriff arrived.

"How did it go?" Sheriff Nicholls asked.

"Good," Deputy Ramirez and I said at the same time.

The sheriff's eyes narrowed as I opened the cell door to take Penny out. He looked askance at his deputy, who quickly filled him in on Earl's concerns about our safety.

"I suppose it's all right. Did you get those statements sorted, Ramirez?" the sheriff asked as they started their workday.

The station gradually got busier and louder as other employees arrived, and Georgie sat up with a start. "I forgot where I was," she said with a yawn.

We took turns using the shower, and it turned out Georgie had hidden some fresh clothes for me in her own bag after all. I pulled on the prisoner uniform over my clothes and we waited for Uncle Earl or Fae to show up with breakfast. Fae came to bring us food, but when Cami ran ahead to the cell, she took one look at me in the uniform and started screaming. The commotion started Penny barking, too.

Fae calmed her daughter down, but the sheriff's scowl showed he didn't appreciate the disruption in his station. "It's bad enough to have the drunks yelling as they come in. What was that for?"

Fae turned red. "A while ago, I went to the movies with a friend and had to bring Cami with us. I thought she would sleep through it, but she woke up when they were e-x-e-c-u-t-i-n-g a prisoner and now she thinks they're going to put Bet in the e-l-e-c-t—"

As Georgie and I stifled our giggles, Sheriff Nicholls put his hand up. "I get it. Just keep in mind this is a place of business, or this whole experiment will stop."

With a chorus of "sorry" from me and my friends, we went to the kitchen to eat breakfast while it was still hot. Fae even brought Penny cooked chicken livers and rice, which the hound gobbled up enthusiastically. After we finished, Georgie left with Fae and Cami, and I took Penny out to the fenced equipment yard again so we could both get some air.

The rest of that day was a repeat of meal deliveries, and visitors coming to see me and Penny or to drop off a character reference. The prison uniform got more laughs, so it seemed Cami was the only one afraid I was destined for the electric chair. Georgie and I stayed up late, until we couldn't keep our eyes open any longer, but got up a little earlier the next morning so we could spend some time outside before it got too hot. The next day was pretty much the same, and I understood a little bit of how tedious it could get for real prisoners.

By lunchtime that third day, the novelty of the jail cell was wearing off for me. I'd read the dog training book from cover to cover more than once, and tried to sketch Penny, but time passed a lot slower during the day without Georgie there. Penny was tired of training and now pretended to be asleep whenever I looked her way. I would have found some trouble to get into if Mr. Diaz hadn't come in on his lunch break carrying a box of things for me.

He unpacked my mounted and matted prints and laid them on the kitchen table; I couldn't hide a squeal of delight. Fae was going to love the copies they printed for her, too. Peggy wandered in to take a look and said she was sure I would win at the Fair.

"What do you think, Mr. Diaz?" I asked.

"I was most impressed, especially since you are so new to the form. I brought you some books so you can refine your eye."

"Books, thank goodness!" My fervent answer made him smile. "I only have one on dog training with me."

"I'm lending you The Amateur Photographer's Handbook and The Complete Book of Press Photography, but the copy of the Photo Amateur's Pocket Book came free with your new camera, so it's yours to keep. It has handy pages to keep track of your camera settings as you learn."

Next to come out of the box was my handsome new Brownie Hawkeye Flash camera, along with a few packs of film. It even came with one Kodachrome roll for color pictures! Mr. Diaz walked me through loading the film, and took a picture of me in my uniform to test it.

"Look more remorseful!" he called before he hit the shutter. My laughter got Penny up out of her fake sleep, and the dog came to visit Mr. Diaz.

"Pleasure to see you again, Penny," he said solemnly as she offered her paw to shake. "So you've been working on training her?"

"Yeah, but we're getting bored. She knows sit, stay, lie down, spin, pat-a-cake, dead dog—well, she knows them when she wants to know them. That's getting to be more often."

"You must be good with dogs."

"I think it's mostly us learning how each other thinks and finding common ground. Even though we don't speak the same language, dogs are a lot smarter than most people give them credit for. I've learned a lot from Penny and Nap and Josie. It's not so much about making them listen, as it is listening to each other. And they are living examples of how to be joyful."

Mr. Diaz rubbed his chin in thought. "I've just had an idea. There's a dog show one day of the Fair, and I take the winners' photos. If you want to be my assistant, I could use your expertise with the dogs and you could get some hands-on training for photography."

My eyes went wide. "That would be great! Would I get paid anything?" Then I realized how that sounded and hastily added, "I'm grateful for the opportunity, of course, but I also need to make some money this summer."

Mr. Diaz winked at me, so he must not have been offended. "Some of the dog owners give tips, so you can certainly keep those. Then, when you're good enough, they might hire you on for these events, like they do for me. Now, do you want me to leave this box here with you, or drop it at the diner with Earl?"

"What could be safer than a police station?" I asked with a grin. "I'll put them in the cell and Uncle Earl can take them home later. He's got the day off, so he should be here soon."

Mr. Diaz had to get back to the store, and I barely had time to crack a photography book before my next guest showed. Uncle Earl brought fried egg sandwiches, plus Nap and Josie. Those two were too chaotic for the small kitchen, so we all went out to the equipment yard. After Earl pulled over a couple of empty crates for the people to sit on, the dogs started wrassling and I bit into my sandwich.

Uncle Earl caught me up on all the gossip from the diner—Penny's and my incarceration was still very much on folks' minds—and mentioned he'd been over to Fae's for dinner.

"Georgie was grumpy about something," he said, "and I eventually got it out of her that you whupped her in black-jack. Took all her chocolates."

I sighed. "She wasn't supposed to spread it around. If people think you're cheating all the time, you can never have a game for fun. And I shared the M&Ms with her."

"Oh, she didn't volunteer your secret. I guessed it after she mentioned y'all had played cards. Your mama discovered her talents at your age, and was traveling the circuit of professional card games within a few years. Are you planning on supporting yourself the same way?"

I emphatically shook my head. "Maybe I'll bring it out as a party trick, but I'm not interested in that life."

"Glad to hear it. It didn't bring Liza happiness in the end."

I'd had a lot of time to think over the last few days, so I commented, "I don't know if she was unhappy. I think to be happy or unhappy, you have to let yourself feel things. One way or another, Mama avoided that."

"That's pretty astute for you to spot the difference. Are you talking about the morphine?"

"Even before then, there was the drinking. The doctor said her liver might have held up better under the morphine if it wasn't already nearly sick to death from the alcohol. But I meant that when things got too hard where we were—with creditors at the door, or her latest romance gone wrong—we'd just move on. Leave behind all the old complications until the new ones got too big, and we'd move again."

Uncle Earl asked, "Were things too complicated with your mother to work things out before she died? What was she like with you?"

I sighed before I spoke. "She didn't make things easy. Mama could be flighty and forgetful—we used to joke she was only ever on time for a scolding for being late. And when she'd get her head turned by a new man, sometimes I wouldn't see her for days. Then it would end and she'd shower me with toys and kisses, saying we only ever needed each other. Those promises just made it worse when she disappeared again. If I could get her to talk about it, the situation had been completely revised in her head to make her out to be a hero or a victim. Never the cause. She often said she was so hard on me to protect me from making the same mistakes she had made. But what about the mistakes she was still making, over and over?"

Uncle Earl heard me out and nodded, as if that fit with his memories of his sister. "She was careless of others' feelings, and of consequences. Especially when she showed her ruthless side at the card table." He pushed on with another question, "What about Felix?"

I mused, "He was sweet at first, and bought us fancy things. All of Mama's friends told her how lucky she was to have landed him. Instead of her disappearing with him and leaving me alone, he moved in with us. He wanted me to call him Papa and for a while it was kind of nice to pretend that he was. Like we could finally have a more settled family. But after he showed what he was really like...I tried to avoid him."

"And what was he really like?" Uncle Earl prompted.

"He always had to be in control. And was too worried about how things looked to other people. If you messed up either of those things for him, you'd pay."

Seeing Uncle Earl was about to put an arm around my shoulder, I stopped talking and leaned out of reach. "I'm not telling you this so you feel sorry for me. I'm only telling you what it was like."

Uncle Earl put his arm down and cleared his throat. "I'm sorry you had a hard time, but I'm not sorry for you—I think you'll be just fine. Eventually. Do you believe that?"

I frowned, thinking, but I ended up nodding. "I guess so."

I stood and brushed crumbs from my lap, and let the dogs lick the egg yolk from my fingers, so Uncle Earl realized I was done talking for now. But he had something to say.

"I came to find you and Liza, you know, a few years ago. I saw a flyer for an exhibition game Liza was doing in Sacramento, and I showed up at the club. Your mama was already boozed up and only wanted to play her hand. She said, didn't I get the hint that she didn't want nothing to do with me when she'd returned all my letters before? She told me to get out of there or Felix would beat me again."

He rubbed absently at a scar on his temple. "It wasn't Felix himself who'd done the beating, of course, but that's another story. I asked Liza if her daughter wanted to come stay a while, but she wouldn't tell me where you were. One of the waitresses pulled me aside and told me the address. Said she was worried for you, too.

"When I got there, no one was home, and I was 'bout to leave when I heard some children playing. I recognized you straight off. You looked so much like Liza. You were watching the other kids play kick the can and looked happy. Laughing and keeping score. Then a woman in the house next door called the kids in for supper and you piled right in with them. I watched through the window for a while and you looked like part of the family. Like you belonged with them, and I couldn't bear the thought of tearing you away, so I left without introducing myself."

I was kneeling to pick stickers out of the dogs while he spoke, but I had been listening.

Without looking his way, I said, "The Nowaks. I really did feel like I was part of their family—until I wasn't. They packed up and moved away, and left me to fend for myself again. It was a good reminder not to trust anyone."

"I don't know that I agree; it might as well be a reminder to look out for the good folks who come into your life. In my experience, the best cure for rotten folks doing you wrong is for good people to love you. I hope you've found a few of those good people here in Amberfields."

Instead of answering, I threw a ball for the dogs, and Uncle Earl said he hoped I'd take his words to heart. We played fetch until we were all worn out, and Uncle Earl left with a reluctant Nap and Josie pulling on their leashes.

Penny went straight to sleep on my bunk, and I tried to read, but Uncle Earl's words kept coming back to mind. I wished he'd at least made himself known when he'd come to find us before; then I might have had a choice in going with him. As for now, he was right that I'd found some good people in Amberfields and it was getting harder to feel an urgent need to leave. Unless things didn't go well for Penny's investigation. Oregon felt further away every day I stayed here.

A commotion at the front desk got my attention, and I looked up to see Mrs. Ridgeway throwing a tantrum. A deputy was trying to speak, but the old fussbudget was having none of it.

"I demand you take my statement, young man," she said. "That girl and her vicious dog wounded a good friend of mine."

The deputy raised his voice, either to keep her from talking over him again or because her hearing wasn't the best. "I've explained we have all the statements from everyone who was actually a witness. You cannot give a statement unless you were there and saw it."

She banged her cane on the tile, and the sound rang like a shot through the station. "I know for a fact half the town has been in here giving statements."

The deputy stuck his finger in his ear for a moment; his head was probably ringing. "No, they gave character statements. Those are different."

"And are those character statements meant to be in support of a person, or a condemnation?"

"They can be both. Either, I mean." The deputy looked relieved when the sheriff came up behind him.

"I can help you, Mrs. Ridgeway," Sheriff Nicholls said. "Who are you wanting to make a statement about?"

Mrs. Ridgeway made no attempt to lower her voice as the sheriff led her to his office. "That wicked girl runs around with Georgia Wood, and I knew something terrible would come of it. I never dreamed she would cast aspersions on a member of such a fine, old family as Mr. Bindle…"

Her voice grew muffled as the sheriff shut his office door, and I breathed a sigh of relief. If I thought the sheriff would take the old woman seriously, I would be a lot more nervous. But so far, the sheriff had been honest with me and as fair as he could be. I would have to trust he'd see Mrs. Ridgeway for the hateful, bitter person she was and take her "statement" accordingly. Plus, all those character statements from everyone else were bound to help—they certainly made me feel more hopeful.

A few minutes later, Peggy appeared at the cell door with a cup of cocoa. "I thought you could use this," she said with an understanding smile, and went back to her desk.

Chapter Twenty-Six

I was glad Peggy had left me to my thoughts, but I was discovering another drawback for prisoners: I never had any time without eyes on me. Sure, the station was busy, and the staff wasn't staring at me for every moment, but I missed the quiet time alone in my room. That lull helped me sort out my feelings, and to recharge for the next chaotic day (usually featuring Georgie's or Nap's special brand of mischief). My own bed, in a room with a solid door that closed, was going to be heaven when I got back to Uncle Earl's house.

I needed something to occupy me until Georgie got there in a few hours. When I carried my empty mug to the kitchen, I paused at Peggy's desk. "Do you think it would be okay to take some photographs of the station, inside and out? I want to try the techniques I read about in books, and the photos might be of historical interest later."

"You make a good argument," Peggy said. "You can ask the sheriff, but wait until Mrs. Ridgeway is gone. And give me a few minutes' warning before you aim the camera, so I can touch up my lipstick."

"Will do," I said with a chuckle.

The sheriff didn't have any problem with me taking pictures, as long as I wasn't in the way. I took a few indoors when the subjects weren't looking my way—I didn't want them to look posed—and then went out to the yard. I'd never noticed the swirly plaster details where the walls met the roof on the old building, or the crumbling horse-drawn fire engine hidden in the dimness at the back of a lean-to. Everything looked more interesting through the viewfinder of my camera.

Penny and I didn't stay out too long since it was the hottest part of the afternoon, and Penny didn't feel much like posing. In fact, she was acting a little strange—she kept looking off to the distance, with her nose working overtime. I looked for any wild critters who might have caught Penny's attention, like deer, but saw nothing.

If anything, it felt more like someone was watching us. Maybe Mrs. Ridgeway was skulking in the field behind the station. It felt more like something Mr. Bindle would do, though. I wouldn't put it past him to rile Penny up, so the investigation would go against her. I retreated to the station, since it was probably the safest place for us right now.

Georgie arrived later, with more games to play, but I was feeling weighed down by all the heavy things which had happened that day and begged off. Instead, I cracked open a copy of A Tree Grows in Brooklyn Fae had sent along for me, while Georgie broke out some carvings she was trying to finish before the County Fair. Not only did Georgie have her entries still to complete, she needed to create more goods to sell in her booth.

"Would you rather work at home?" I asked. "I don't want you to lose out on money because you're keeping me company."

"Honestly, I can concentrate better here without Fidget demanding attention. And I don't have to worry she's going to sneak off with a carving tool. If you'd rather be on your own tonight, I can head home, but I'd just as soon stay here."

I thought of the watcher outside—if they were even real—and said, "I'd like it if you stayed."

Georgie said, "Hmmkay," already back to work on a piece of driftwood she was turning into a family of playful river otters. I could hardly wait to see how this one turned out, and I wished I could buy it for myself. Even though I had jobs lined up with Mr. Diaz and Doc Marsh, that money was going straight into my Oregon stash. Somewhere safer from marauding Plott hounds this time.

I didn't want to interrupt my friend again, so I waited until we took a break for dinner (meatloaf sandwiches) to tell Georgie about helping Mr. Diaz with the dog show at the fair. "Plus, he said some people make a business of this, traveling around to the dog shows. The kennel clubs need the photos to document winners, but the owners and handlers love seeing their dogs in perfect form. I know I'm new to photography, but I could see myself doing this for a living. That would be a dream job, to spend time with a camera and people who are just as crazy about dogs. Want to come on the road with me?"

"Nah, you should come with me to San Francisco. I'm going to have my own furniture and art gallery someday. You can take pictures for the catalogs, and we can have as many dogs as we want in our gigantic mansion overlooking the Bay. You can have the walls for your art, and I'll furnish the rooms with mine."

"Georgie Wood, you have hidden depths," I marveled. "You've obviously put some thought into this—it sounds fancy. But why San Francisco?"

"Mom has an old friend there, and we went to visit last year. He lives in North Beach and teaches at the California School of Fine Arts. He took us to galleries and shows all over the city, and there were so many people and places to inspire me I can't imagine going anywhere else. Plus, it felt like...I belonged. It doesn't hurt that Mom has a connection there, too, in case I want to go to school there or for when I open my own space. Do you want to come?"

I laughed. "I'd love to, but I might need a few years to give you a real answer. School was never in the cards for me—pun intended, since Felix would rather see me earning than studying. Uncle Earl is insisting I get my high school diploma, though, so maybe the California School of Fine Arts you mentioned has a photography program for after."

"Okay, but I'm holding you to that. I expect an answer in a year or two. In the meantime, maybe we could have Mom or Earl take us into the city and I'll show you what it's like."

Georgie's expectations sobered me suddenly; I'd only been playing along, but Georgie was serious. It was great to be wanted, but I didn't know for sure where I would be in two months, let alone two years. I dreaded telling Georgie I was leaving, especially after finding out she'd included me in her dream mansion life. But I knew how it felt to be left behind, and knew I owed Georgie a proper goodbye—later, when it was time. Plus, I had promised Uncle Earl I would talk to him before leaving town. How did a quick stop at my uncle's turn into weeks? I kept finding more reasons to put off my trip.

Speaking of reasons to stay, Uncle Earl had outdone himself with a triple berry pie for dessert. The blueberries, blackberries, and strawberries oozed juicy goodness when I cut into it. Georgie's full attention was on gobbling it down, so at least I got a much-needed break from conversation. What was it about today that made everyone want to have heart-to-heart talks with me? It was all so complicated.

But as we got ready for bed later, Georgie threw one more complication my way.

"I almost forgot," she said. "One of those letters came for you."

She handed me an envelope with Nina's handwriting, but the return address was in Sacramento. At my frown, Georgie picked up on the shift in mood.

"Want me to take Penny out to the yard one last time, and you can read your letter?" she asked.

"Yeah, thanks," I said as I slowly tore it open.

I barely noticed Georgie and Penny had left as I pulled out a few folded pages. My stomach sank as a photograph fell into my lap: a smiling Nina, dressed in a smart houndstooth suit, with her natural curls styled into a soft, short cut. She looked like a grown woman instead of sixteen, and the chic outfit was certainly not something she'd wear in a lumber camp.

Sure enough, Nina's letter was full of gushing chatter about starting secretarial courses in Sacramento, after her aunt followed the lumber camp workers to Idaho and Nina opted not to go with them. The students shared apartments and Nina's roommates sounded so modern and worldly, especially since Nina had lied about her age to get in and her new friends were older. It almost felt like an afterthought when Nina closed the letter with an offer to put in a good word for me, when I was old enough to attend in a few years. She said maybe it was a blessing that Felix had gotten her family evicted, because they'd all gone on to better things.

That last bit of information shocked me to learn, but more importantly, Nina, my last Nowak friend, was leaving me, too. And taking my dreams of starting a new life with her—what was the point of continuing to run, if I didn't have a place to run to? Feeling tears prick my eyes, I flew to the bathroom so Georgie wouldn't see me crying like a baby. I locked myself in a stall and sobbed like I hadn't done since Mama died, to the point where I started heaving. Berry pie and meatloaf sandwich were not nearly as enjoyable when they came back up—I might not ever be able to eat them again.

As I leaned against the stall wall, limp and emptied, I couldn't escape some hard truths. If I was being honest with myself, the lumber camp had always been Nina's escape, and I was only tagging along. Even away from my parents' control, I hadn't come up with anything better. Georgie was nearly the same age as me, and she had all these big dreams and plans. How sad was it that working in a lumber camp was the most I had let myself dream?

That needed to change, and it would have to be me who did the changing. But maybe from now on, I could let myself accept some help along the way? What perfect timing for me to hear a scrabbling at the bathroom door. It creaked open and Penny ran to me, wiggling into my lap. I hugged her tightly, nuzzling the dog's forehead.

"Sorry, she wanted in really bad," Georgie said. "Are you okay? It sounded like you were sick."

"I think it's over now," I said dully. "Give me a few minutes to wash my face and I'll be out."

Georgie didn't answer right away, and I heard a shoe squeak on the tile before she said, "Okay. I'll see you out there. Unless you want me to stay?"

"No, thanks." I rubbed Penny's ears and waited to hear Georgie leave before I pushed myself up. I felt as old as Mrs. Ridgeway as I shuffled to the sink. The water cooled my eyes and cheeks and mostly took away the awful taste in my mouth. Eventually, I felt enough like myself to shoo Penny off my feet and to leave the sanctuary of the bathroom.

Peggy wasn't at her desk, and the cell was empty, too. Had Georgie taken me literally and gone home? I picked up the letter and photo where I'd dropped it on the floor and tucked it into my book before laying on the bunk. Penny jumped up with me and there was just enough room for us both, if I curled around the dog's tight coil.

I heard voices approaching, but stayed where I was. Georgie called my name softly, and I finally turned to look. She stood with Peggy and the sheriff, and they all smiled tentatively at me.

"Bet, your uncle's going to come pick you and Penny up," the sheriff said. "Get your things together, please."

Peggy and Georgie stepped into the cell and started gathering items and folding bedding.

"I don't understand," I said. "We're supposed to be here for a few more days, aren't we?"

"You've done your time. All the evidence shows the bite was provoked, and I'll be saying as much in my report. No reason to stay here now, especially if you're sick. That would be cruel and unusual punishment."

Hardly believing it, I looked to Georgie, but she wouldn't meet my eyes. Had Georgie said something to the sheriff? Is that why he was sending me home early? Georgie wasn't usually a tattletale, so she must have been truly worried about me. I wanted to confess I wasn't sick—not sick like the flu—but I had done enough talking today. Being able to go home to my room and shut my door sounded like paradise.

Uncle Earl arrived and had a quiet conversation with the sheriff while Georgie and I loaded up the car. Nap and Josie were in the backseat and demanded to inspect each item, so it took longer than it should have, but we eventually got all the blankets and bedding crammed into the car. We stopped at Georgie's house to drop off her and her belongings, and Uncle Earl and I were headed home at last.

"Okay, now it's just us. Are you really all right?" Uncle Earl asked. "Georgie said she thought you'd gotten some kind of bad news?"

I rubbed my sore eyes. "I want to sleep for a while. Maybe a week."

But my joke did not put Uncle Earl off. "I'm serious. I was at work when the sheriff called, and they expect me back, but I can get someone to cover if you need me."

"No, really, I will only be sleeping. No sense in you missing work when I'm going to be holed up in my room." When he still waited, I added, "Can't we talk another time?"

He nodded reluctantly, and we quickly unloaded the car so Uncle Earl could turn around and drive back to the diner. "I'm glad we have this car. It makes situations like this easier," he said.

I, for one, didn't want to have situations like this ever again. No jail time, no bad news, no worries about my dog being taken from me. Finally in my own bedroom, I crawled into bed with Penny close behind, and we fell asleep immediately. I woke up a few times to stumble to the bathroom and to eat the food Uncle Earl had left for me, but I ended up sleeping a solid fourteen hours.

When I woke up, my bedside clock showed it was just after noon. I laid in bed for a while, relishing the quiet and the four solid walls. Penny was not so patient, though, and scratched at the door into the kitchen. Sighing, I opened the door for her and spotted Uncle Earl in his reading chair.

"Hi," I said.

"Hi, yourself. Georgie wants you to call her as soon as you're up, but I recommend you have a bath and lunch before you open the floodgates."

"What do you mean, open the floodgates?"

"The phone's actually off the hook—people were calling to say they were glad you and Penny were home, but I didn't want the ringing phone to wake you. Once you use that phone to call Georgie, it will start all over again. I'm regretting installing the blasted thing."

I shook my head in bewilderment. "I don't understand small towns. You're right, though, a bath sounds wonderful.

They only had a shower at the sheriff's station, and I like having a choice."

I took my things into the bathroom and started the water running, but poked my head back out the bathroom door. "Uncle Earl, I hope this doesn't hurt your feelings, but I don't want to see a meatloaf sandwich or berry pie for a long while. Maybe never."

"Aren't those your favorites?"

"They were, but not since they came back up last night."

"Ah, gotcha. I feel the same way about peppermint schnapps. How about a grilled cheese for lunch, then?"

"That sounds better. Thanks for understanding."

Chapter Twenty-Seven

After a bath and lunch, I called Georgie. She sounded relieved to hear my voice.

"I was afraid you didn't want to talk to me. I told Peggy you were throwing up, and she's the one who insisted we tell Sheriff Nicholls."

"No, it's fine," I reassured her. "I'm glad to be home, so it came out all right in the end."

Georgie said, "I saw the letter. I'm sorry. I looked down on the floor and read some before I realized it was private." When I didn't respond, she added, "Do you want me to come over? Or you could come here."

"No offense, but I'm enjoying the peace and quiet. I think I'll putter around the garden today and maybe make sure Nap and Josie haven't forgotten all their training while I was gone. Uncle Earl has today off, so I won't be completely by myself. But let's get together tomorrow?"

Georgie agreed, and I played with the dogs a little before we left the house for the garden. Uncle Earl and I took turns rolling the full water tanks on the way, and then spent a few hours caring for the plants. He seemed to be waiting for me to talk about my breakdown yesterday, but speaking about it would make Nina's letter real. I wasn't ready to let go of that part of my life—or that part of me. I knew I would have to move on eventually, but I needed time to think about what my new future will look like.

So instead we harvested more squash, and fortunately Uncle Earl could use it at the diner, so we wouldn't have to be one of those neighbors who sneakily leaves them on porches. I groaned when I saw how much ground the Jerusalem artichokes had taken over again.

"No more fartichokes. If you cook those, I'm going on a hunger strike."

Uncle Earl laughed. "Next time I see Mr. Winters in the diner, I'll ask if he wants them for his hogs. Even if we dig out every one we find, they come back, so there will still be plenty for us this winter."

"Yeah, let's save them to eat when we're closed up in the house," I grumbled.

Uncle Earl put his hand in his other armpit and made a squeaking, blubbering fart noise that got me laughing. I put a hand to my mouth and tried to make the sound back at him, but I was laughing too hard.

"That's better," Uncle Earl said. "I know prison time can change a person, and for a minute I thought you'd turned sour. Or aged even more."

"No, not yet. I'm so jolly that I'm going to join the circus next. And Penny, too."

"Say hello to the elephants for me. Are you coming back to the house now?"

"I'll laze around in the shade for a little bit, but you can go."

Nap and Josie followed Uncle Earl and the empty water tanks, but then came back to the garden gate a few minutes later.

"I guess you missed us while we were in jail," I said, as I reached for Nap to give him a scritch. He leaned into my hand until Josie pounced on him and started a wrestling match. Penny and I retreated to our cool spot under the pumpkin leaves and watched the other two roughhouse. They finally settled down and found their own shade for a nap.

I dozed for a bit until Penny nudged me awake. I thought she just wanted attention, so I absently rubbed her belly. But Penny pulled away and stood on alert, her nose pointed at something, like she had done in the equipment yard. I stood and tried to see what Penny did, but the grass and weeds were so tall there could have been an entire herd of deer out there. Plus, there was a thick band of trees along the road, and even more along the river in the distance.

Just in case it was a chaseable critter, I fitted Penny's leash on her collar, but I didn't have leashes for Nap and Josie. I whistled them awake, and they happily followed Penny and me to the gate and across the street to the driveway. But once there, they joined Penny in focusing on something in the trees. Before I could grab them, they gave snarling barks and leaped into the overgrowth.

I had never heard them make this noise before: it was no playful bark, but a deep-throated one that said they meant business. I tried to call them back, but the dark hounds completely ignored me as they ran east. In the distance, I heard a car door slam and an engine roar to life. The barks got fainter like they were chasing the car, something they knew better than to do.

I flew up the drive and I breathlessly told Uncle Earl his dogs were up to something. He went out the front door and gave a piercing whistle which surely carried all the way to town, it was so loud. We waited and then saw Nap and Josie kicking up dust as they hit the driveway. The pair had big smiles on their faces, like they had won a race.

"I hope it wasn't a bear," Uncle Earl commented. "Every once in a while, one follows the river and ends up breaking into the diner's dumpster."

"But I'm sure I heard a car, and bears don't drive," I insisted. "Does Mr. Bindle have a car? Or Mrs. Ridgeway?"

"Mr. Bindle has an old pickup, but it makes an awful racket. I would have heard it and recognized it. You're not worried about him coming after you or Penny, are you?"

"I'm not sure if he's going to obey the county's decision, if the sheriff's report proves she's not a dangerous dog. He seems like the type to hold a grudge."

"You're not wrong, but the sheriff has made it clear he's not to bother you. We can let Bill know that Nap and Josie chased someone off, so they can send a car to check on things."

I dithered, not wanting to cause trouble for no reason. "Well, if they're going to be patrolling anyway, maybe they could come this way?"

Uncle Earl ruffled my sweaty hair and said, "I'll give him a call if it will make you feel better."

"Thanks. I'm going to get something to drink, and then I'll take the dogs out back and work on them coming when I call."

After spending half an hour working with the dogs, I called for Uncle Earl to come out and watch something. "I was teaching them this before I went in the clink, but I wasn't sure if they remembered."

Uncle Earl rolled his eyes. "The clink? Are you a gangster now?"

"Just watch." I stood with Nap in place and Josie a few feet behind him. "Leap, Josie!" I called.

Josie gathered her haunches and leaped at a diagonal, crossing over Nap's back as she traveled. Once she landed, Josie pushed in front of Nap. At another "Leap!" command, he jumped over his sister and they each repeated it a few more times without being told.

"Wow, you weren't kidding about joining the circus, were you?" Uncle Earl said. "That's pretty impressive."

But then Nap grabbed Josie's leg, and they were sparring instead, with Penny running around them and barking sternly.

I grinned, but shook my head. "They only do it a few times before it falls apart. I guess it's too tempting to play."

"Then make the training more like play, and they'll do anything you ask."

"That's good advice. I'm ready for a nap, though." At the sound of "nap," Nap perked up his ears and leaped over Josie one more time. When the humans applauded, Josie got jealous, and the two were brawling again. They only broke apart when Uncle Earl waved a long sock at them and lured them into the house with it. Penny and I climbed into bed for a nap, and fell asleep to the sound of Nap and Josie slaying the evil sock monster.

I felt more like myself by the time I headed to the Woods's the next day. Penny came along, of course, and promptly disappeared into the garden with Cami. Fae hugged me tightly, apologizing for not spending more time visiting when I was locked up.

"Are you feeling better now?" she asked. "I hope it wasn't something you ate, considering Earl and I were the ones feeding you?"

I turned red and my stomach clenched at the reminder of Nina's abandonment. I made an effort to smile, not wanting to let this setback get the best of me. I wasn't actually worse off now, just changing plans. "Yes, I'm better now."

Georgie dragged me away, saying, "We'll be in my room, but let us know when there's snacks and we'll be right down."

In her room, Georgie showed me all the pieces she'd been working on for the Fair. A menagerie of animals had joined the fox, including the driftwood otter family, a bumpy-barked toad, a tiger with wood-grain stripes, and a cat washing its face with one paw.

"I've never seen anything like these. I want them all!" I cried. "The galleries in San Francisco would be crazy not to sign you up for a show as soon as you come over the bridge."

"I'll make sure to have you write me a letter of reference," Georgie said with a blush. "Fidget keeps stealing the cat, so I won't be able to sell that one. It would break her heart."

"But you're selling the others? Do people place bids or what?" I unconsciously stroked the head of one of the otters.

"I mark them with prices or 'NFS' if they're not for sale. The first person to pay for it gets the carving, but they have to wait until the Fair ends to pick it up."

I would have to figure out some way to get there early on the first day, cash in hand, so I could get the otters for myself.

"Now, I want to see if I can figure out your card tricks." Georgie rubbed her hands together with glee.

We sat on the front porch and played a raucous game of blackjack, attracting Cami's attention. When she came over and asked to play, I shook my head.

"Absolutely not. I draw the line at turning both sisters into criminal masterminds."

Instead, Georgie and I joined Cami and Penny for a game of hide and seek in the garden. We were all dusty and sweaty in no time, and when we went to get drinks out of the hose, a water fight broke out. Screams and mud and water droplets were flying when Fae called to us from the porch.

"Everyone come inside, please." She sounded so serious that Georgie and I didn't protest; we rinsed off as much mud as we could and headed inside.

"Sorry, Mom, are we late for lunch?" Georgie handed towels to Cami and me.

"No, I need to talk to you and Bet." She turned to her younger daughter. "Cami, can you be a big girl and get changed into a clean dress? We're going to leave in a few minutes."

Cami frowned as she listened, but then nodded. "Penny too?"

"That's a good idea," Fae answered. "Take Penny, but dress yourself before you pick out a ribbon for her to wear on her collar, okay?"

After Cami ran upstairs, Penny in tow, Fae gestured for me and Georgie to sit down. I didn't know what was going on, but my heart was thumping as if it already knew it was something bad.

Fae didn't wait for questions. She just got down to business. "Bet, the sheriff called looking for you, and he wants you to come down to the station right away. He wouldn't tell me what it was about, but he asked your uncle to be there, too. You can get cleaned up a bit, and then I'll walk with you."

I stood on trembling legs, propping myself up with the table. "Is it about Penny? Are they trying to take her?"

Fae started to speak, and then exchanged a glance with Georgie before saying, "I truly don't know any more, but I think if it was good news, he would have told you over the phone. He didn't say to bring Penny, though, so it might be a good thing?"

But it might be a bad thing, too. What if someone came to take Penny while I was at the station? I sat hard in the chair, tears turning the room blurry. "No, no, no, no." I would have to run, whether or not I have the money. Or if I don't know yet where to run to.

Before I could get too worked up, Georgie wrapped her arms around my shoulders and said, "It's okay, we have a plan. Your uncle and my mom already talked about what to do."

I looked at Fae, who nodded encouragingly. "It's true. It might mean you'll be parted from Penny for a little bit, but she'd be safe. Do you want to hear more?"

I nodded and struggled to speak around the lump in my throat. "What's the plan?"

"Georgie knows the woods behind the house, inside and out. She's going to take some supplies, and Penny, and go hide out in a secret spot. She'll keep watch to see if it's safe to come back with her. If we need to, we can sneak Penny out of the area entirely, and then you can find her later. Is all of that okay with you? Keep in mind we don't have a lot of time to come up with something else."

I leaned my head on Georgie's shoulder, who had scooted her chair next to mine. "I don't really want to be apart from Penny. Can't I go hide with her and Georgie? We could follow the river around to Uncle Earl's house and get my clothes before I run."

Fae reached across the table for my hand. "I know it's scary, but I think you should trust our plan. Having you at the station will buy time for us to figure out what the county intends to do with Penny, if that's what this is about. This is your best chance."

"How do I know it will work?" My anguish was clear.

"Because we've done this before," Georgie said softly. "Mom and I planned our escape, and came here to Amber-fields. We're runaways, too."

Chapter Twenty-Eight

I stared at my friends, not sure I'd heard right. "What are you running from?"

Georgie went tense beside me as Fae answered, "Like you, it's more like a 'who' we were running away from. It's a long story, though, and I'll tell you as much as I can on the way to the station. But if you trust this plan, then Georgie should grab some things and go. And you'll want to say goodbye to Penny for now."

Fae and Georgie stood up, but I stayed planted in my chair while my thoughts raced. I didn't want to say goodbye to Penny, even temporarily, but it was better than Penny being gone permanently. I couldn't bear the thought that Penny would suffer for defending me. The shy dog had been so brave to bite her tormentor, so how could I not be brave too? I hadn't realized I'd need to make good so soon on the promise to myself to accept help, but now was the time to let my walls down, for Penny's sake.

"Okay, I'll trust you," I decided. "We'll try your plan. What do I need to do?"

Fae sent me to wash up and change into some of Georgie's clean clothes, while she packed food and blankets for Georgie and Penny. Cami still hadn't gotten dressed, so Georgie helped her fidgeting little sister look presentable. We all met again in the kitchen, much sooner than I was prepared for.

Penny sniffed the pack Georgie was holding and danced like she could smell the food in it. "I packed plenty of fried chicken livers so she'll go with me," Georgie confessed. "I might even share the salami."

I smiled weakly, then kneeled to hug Penny. My dog squirmed to reach my tears, and settled for sticking her tickly muzzle into my ear. I laughed in spite of myself and dragged Penny away so I could look her in the eyes.

"You go with Georgie, and don't give her any trouble. I'll see you soon, okay?" Penny whined softly, but she looked at Georgie as if she had understood what I said. Or maybe the fried chicken livers were still beckoning to her nose.

Fae came back in the room, wearing her hat and gloves, and took Cami's hand. "We need to go, Bet. If the sheriff has to come looking for you, he will be a lot less sympathetic."

I stood and reluctantly followed her to the door, but Penny was right at my heels. My voice shook a little as I said, "No, you're going with Georgie. Stay, Girl."

It took all of my courage not to look back, and Cami grabbing my hand didn't make me feel even a tiny bit better. "You said you were going to tell me about you running away?" I asked Fae as we turned onto the sidewalk.

Fae sighed. "I hope these little ears don't repeat this, but there's no helping it. First, you should know Fae Wood isn't my real name. None of us are a Wood, and Georgia had a different name when she was younger."

I was so flummoxed by this information that I could only ask, "Why would you pick such silly names, then? Don't they stand out?"

"The silliness is the best protection. Most folks couldn't imagine saddling themselves with names like these—they'd try to come up with something more distinguished, or more Hollywood sounding. But once they've had a laugh, they don't question it."

"Okay, so why are you hiding?"

"Since Earl has told me your stepfather is not exactly a law-abiding man, maybe you won't judge me to know when I was younger, I was a—I worked in a brothel. After some bad times, I was lucky enough to land with a madam who was like a mother to us. A mother who took two-thirds of our earnings, but it was better than the places I'd started out at by the docks."

Fae snuck a glance at me to see how I was taking this, and I nodded for her to continue.

"I worked my way up to being Ida's right hand, so when I fell pregnant, she didn't throw me out. I was happy with little Mildred and the family we'd built, with Grandma Ida and Grandpa Louis. Louis was our bouncer and he's the one who taught Georgie to carve."

I stumbled on the sidewalk for a moment. "You named Georgie Mildred?"

Fae chuckled. "It was my favorite aunt's name. We called her Baby Millie."

Her smile faded and I knew things didn't stay happy for Fae and Millie.

"Everything was fine until Louis had a stroke. He didn't pass right away, but he would have been in no shape to work if he recovered. Ida was close to him, so she decided to retire with Louis—only, she sold the brothel right out from under the rest of us girls. We could leave if we wanted, but the tiny sum she gave us was not enough to set up anywhere else. So, we stayed and took our chances with the new owners, but as a precaution I started dressing Millie in boys' clothes and called her Billy. She was a little younger than Cami at the time, so it wasn't a big change for her to learn. I've never been able to get Georgie back into dresses, alas.

"Anyway, my instincts were correct, because the new owner set up a mean old prune to run the place. She wasn't interested in my help, and I was treated like a new girl and given all the…less than ideal customers. When one of my old regulars offered me a way out, I took it and Millie and I didn't look back."

Fae waited until they'd crossed the street to take up the story again. "I'm going to skip ahead a little because we'll be at the station in no time. My man was a bootlegger who supposedly turned legit, but I think he and your stepfather would have a lot in common. He was still involved in all kinds of shady business. By the time I was pregnant with Cami, the sweet man who had rescued us showed his true colors and was beating me. I almost lost the baby and I'd had enough— I knocked him flat with a washboard and stole as much of his cash as I could find.

"I didn't know where to go, except to Ida's, who was now on her own since Louis had died. She didn't want me bringing trouble to her doorstep and wouldn't let me stay, but sent me to an old friend. This lady had set up something like an Underground Railroad for women and children escaping abuse, and she helped us get fake documents and start fresh somewhere else. We made a few stops along the way—Cami was born in Nevada—to cover our trail, and ended up settling in Amberfields. I don't own the house; it's part of the network and we stay there in return for helping others. Most of my canning goes to the group's food pantry."

I gave my brain a moment to catch up with that convoluted story. "So this Underground Railroad, it's how you're planning on getting Penny out of town?"

"Yes, it's not what it was meant for, but they're allowing it as a favor to me. We're almost there. Do you have any more questions?"

"I can save them for later. Right now, I'm more worried about what the sheriff is going to tell me." As we approached the steps to the station, I paused to gather myself. Good thing I hadn't eaten lunch, or I might throw up again. "Let's get this over with."

Fae opened the door and Cami trotted inside, with me reluctantly following behind her. The sheriff was waiting at the front desk to lead me to his office, but he asked Fae and Cami to wait in the lobby. I hugged them fiercely and went with him, spying Uncle Earl waiting outside Sheriff Nicholls's office. My uncle looked like he'd been kicked in the stomach, and if Sheriff Nicholls hadn't grabbed my hand, I would have made a run for it. I had to settle for sending a desperate look to Fae, who nodded with eyes wide in acknowledgement that the plan was still on.

Uncle Earl stepped towards me, but before he could say anything, a man popped out of the office and said, "There she is! There's my girl!"

It was Felix. He'd found me.

The sheriff still had ahold of my hand, and he winced as I squeezed his fingers in a death grip. I looked up at him like I was a little child again, and pleaded in a whisper, "Please don't make me go with him. Please, please, I won't be any trouble ever again."

Sheriff Nicholls looked genuinely sorrowful when he replied, "It's not up to me. Remember, I have to uphold the law."

Felix had walked over in the meantime, and heartily cried, "Where's a hug for your father, girl? I was so worried about you when I found you'd run away."

He waited in front of me with his arms open and a big, welcoming grin. But I had years of experience with that look in his eyes and I knew it meant I would pay later. Pay for making him come to fetch me, pay for making him look foolish by not playing along with his joyful reunion. And pay back the money I'd taken, likely with interest due. Well, if I was already in trouble...when the sheriff pried my hand from his so I could greet Felix, I instead ran to Uncle Earl and hid behind his bulk.

Felix laughed, but it rang hollow in the station. "Okay, Bet, I'm glad you got to know your uncle, but it's time to go home. We can stop and get your things on the way out of town, so say goodbye to Earl."

Uncle Earl didn't try to bring me out from behind him, so I felt brave enough to say, "I'm not going with you. I'm staying in Amberfields with Uncle Earl and my friends."

Felix shook his head. "Once you've been home for a while, we can talk about visiting, but you are coming with me. Now. I'm your father and I say so."

"You are not my father!" I yelled back. "You're just some crook who moved in with us. Mama would still be alive if it wasn't for you."

Felix stepped towards me, but the sheriff intervened. "Mr. Carter, why don't you give Bet a moment to calm down, so she can say a proper goodbye? Let's go to my office and talk about this."

I let Uncle Earl herd me into Sheriff Nicholls's office, but there wasn't enough room for Uncle Earl, Felix, and me— the small space wasn't meant for a crowd.

Sheriff Nicholls asked, "Earl, would you mind stepping back out? If you want, you can pull a chair over to the doorway and join the discussion."

That left me and Felix in chairs next to each other, and the sheriff didn't miss that I scooted my chair until I was out of arm's reach. Felix noticed too and his lips tightened before he forced himself to relax back into his seat.

"Sheriff, I appreciate you being tender to my little Lizabet, but remember, she's in the wrong here. She ran off while I was still grieving for her mother, leaving me to worry about her for weeks. If a friend hadn't shown me that newspaper article about her and a dog saving a child, I would still have no clue whether she was safe. I'm willing to overlook that Earl here has been harboring a runaway this whole time, but she belongs with her father."

"You're not my father," I grated.

Felix shook his head sadly. "I don't know why you insist on that farce. I've showed the sheriff your birth certificate and my name's right on there." He leaned over to show me a piece of paper and I snatched it from his hand.

There it was in black and white: under "Father," the name Felix Reg Carter was neatly typed. It had to be fake, but my name, my mother's name, my birth date, looked right. "This isn't real. He added that later."

Sheriff Nicholls sighed. "I don't think so, Bet. Your uncle confirmed it, too."

My head whipped around to stare at Uncle Earl.

"It's true," he said gently. "Your mother and Felix were together at the time of—at the right time for him to be your father. They separated for a while during the war, but he came back, as you know. As much as I wouldn't want it to be true, either, I'm afraid it is."

I shook my head violently. "No. I met him for the first time five years ago, plus there were lots of other men before him, so any one of them could be my father."

Felix laughed awkwardly. "What a thing to say about your mother! I warned you, didn't I Sheriff, that this girl lies as easily as breathing? Her mother and I did our best."

I huffed as he accused me of lying and then told such a whopper: Felix only ever did his worst. "No, you can't be my real father." I knew I sounded like a stubborn child, but it was the only thing I could cling to.

Sheriff Nicholls said, "I've told you I need to uphold the law, Bet, and in this case the law says you need to go with your father. It's up to him where you live, and he says you can't stay with your uncle. He's not even pressing charges against Earl, so you might try thanking your father."

"He's not any kind of father!" I stood and yelled at the top of my lungs. "My father wouldn't do those things to me!" Silence descended on the hot, stuffy office.

The sheriff narrowed his eyes and asked, "What things? What do you mean, Bet?"

Felix stood up huffily. "Here come more lies and stories, but we've indulged this little miss quite enough. We tried it your way, and now I'm exercising my right to take her home, if I have to drag her to my car. If you stand in my way, I'll take it up with your superiors."

"I want to know what she means, too, Sheriff." Uncle Earl's voice was firm. As his brother-in-law sputtered a protest, he stared him down and said, "When this girl came to me, she was worse than a wild dog for acting like she'd never known a kind word or soft hand. She's told me some, but I want to know why going with you scares her so much. It's Bet's right to tell us."

"I'm not wasting my time listening to farfetched—"

The sheriff held up a hand to cut off the fresh protest.

"If Bet wants to tell me something, then I want to listen," Sheriff Nicholls replied.

"I do want to tell," I said, avoiding looking at my father. "But I want Uncle Earl in here."

Uncle Earl pushed his way in, not caring when he forced Felix against the desk. My father's eyes communicated how sorry I would be when he got me alone.

The sheriff said, "Mr. Carter, if you don't mind taking the seat outside the door—and shut the door behind you, please."

He scoffed, but put on his hat and left, pulling the door shut. The sound of the chair scraping into position disturbed the now-silent office. After some encouragement, my words came pouring out.

Chapter Twenty-Nine

The sheriff took notes while I spoke, and Uncle Earl tried not to flinch as my grip on his fingers tightened. I focused on a dark stain on the wall behind the sheriff, so I wouldn't have to see either man's reaction. I didn't even tell the really awful stuff, not at first. I wished Penny was there to offer comfort, but it helped that Uncle Earl was at my side.

At one point, the sheriff asked me to pause so he could catch up with his notes. "Thank you, Bet. I think I have the details straight about you starting work at the club at a young age. Since it's a family business, that may not be illegal, but I'll look into whether your father endangered you by making you secretly communicate about the cards. Were you ever directly threatened because of your part in the racket?"

"Yes, I think because they were too afraid to threaten Felix directly. But, not everyone cared they were being cheated. I think Felix had a different arrangement with them."

The sheriff frowned. "They didn't care if they lost money? What kind of arrangement?"

I hesitated. "This started when I was little, too. These other men knew I was looking at their cards, because I sat in their laps. At first it was fine. They sometimes gave me candy or other treats, but...the way they breathed on me, the way they held onto me...I didn't like it. I told Felix I wouldn't do it anymore, and he said yes I would, or he'd do like they had asked and send me home with those men for a few nights. So I kept on sitting in their laps, but the men lost interest in me once I got older."

Uncle Earl made a small sound, like he was choking, and he cleared his throat before saying, "Lizabet, she knew about this?"

I nodded. "Felix got his way with nearly everything, by charm or by force. She told me she'd never let him hire me out like that. But then she got sick, and I knew she wouldn't be around to argue with Felix about anything."

The sheriff's scratching pen filled the gap of silence as he fleshed out his notes.

"All right, thank you, Bet. Have we covered what part others have played in your—in your troubles? Did anyone working in the clubs hurt you or make you take part in any other illegal activities?"

"Oh, there was plenty of things the law would be interested in, but Felix kept me out of most of it. I don't know if it will last if you're making me go with him, though."

"We'll come back to that, because I'm definitely interested in hearing more. As for me making you go with him, has Mr. Carter ever directly caused you harm? Other than the usual whipping or punishment?"

"I don't know, what's the normal amount to be whipped for stealing money for food because you haven't eaten in days?" I challenged. I genuinely wanted to know, but the sheriff frowned at my flash of defiance.

"Answer the question, please."

"He did beat us, Mama and I both, but that isn't what have nightmares about."

I didn't say anything else, but Uncle Earl squeezed my hand before saying, "Bet, it might make a difference in whether you stay with me or go. Your nightmares and fears are always worse at night. How about you start by telling us why? I know it's more than a child's fear of the dark."

I drew in a shaky breath. "I was afraid of the dark at first, when he locked me in the shed. It was cold in there, especially if I was aching from a beating, or it was sweltering during the summer. But it wasn't so scary after all, compared to what he'd do instead when I was bad."

My breathing changed as I continued. "He'd come into my room and wake me up to tell me all the things I'd done wrong that day. Anything from not greeting him with a cup of coffee when he got up in the morning, to me not washing my face before I came to work at the club—me not doing things, or doing bad things, was willfully making his life harder. Nevermind that he changed the rules whenever it suited him, so I never had a chance to get things right.

"Anyways, the whole time he was talking, he put his hand on me." I saw the sheriff and Uncle Earl exchange a glance, and added, "Not like that. He'd put his hand and arm across my belly, just below the ribs. He talked so calm, but all the while his arm was getting heavier. Every time I breathed out, he'd press down a little more, and I'd have less room to take in a breath. If I tried to move or struggle, he'd hold me down with the other hand. He still sounded mild as could be, but for me darkness was creeping around the edges of my eyes, and flashes of lights. He only did it long enough for me to pass out a few times—often enough to prove he could and would. The rest of the time, he only pressed on me until I begged him to stop. One time, I even peed myself."

I stopped talking, trying to even out my breathing, and the sheriff's pencil kept scratching. Uncle Earl wiped his eyes with his other hand and suddenly pulled me hard into a sideways hug. I let him squeeze me for a moment and then disengaged; it was too much contact after reliving those breathless nights.

A ringing phone from the bullpen caught the sheriff's attention, and he looked up from his papers, blinking like he'd forgotten where he was. He rubbed his eyes and stood, saying, "If you'll excuse me a moment, I think I'll move Mr. Carter into an interrogation room. Wait here so I can finish up my statement."

But when the sheriff opened the door, the chair outside it was empty. Sheriff Nicholls glanced back at me and my uncle, before shutting the door behind him. I stood and shamelessly cracked the door open so I could see and hear what was happening.

"Deputy, where is Mr. Carter? Is he in the restroom?"

"No, sir," answered Deputy Ramirez. "He went out for a smoke just a moment ago."

With an exclamation of frustration, the sheriff went out front to look for him, but came back alone. The thunderous look he directed at his deputy had the younger man stammering, "Did I do something wrong, sir? No one told me he couldn't leave the building. Was he a suspect? I thought he was here to claim his daughter."

Sheriff Nicholls rubbed his neck. "You're right. I didn't give you orders to hold him. Do you think he heard what was said in my office?"

"Well, probably. I don't think the door was shut all the way, and I saw him with his head angled that way—I didn't think anything of it, since you'd had Earl sitting outside before. I just thought you'd had them switch places. After a while, he stood up and said he was going for a smoke. It wasn't too long before you came looking for him."

"He's gone now, and so is his car. My office door was cracked when I went to open it. I'll need you to—" the sheriff broke off when he glanced at his office and saw me and Uncle Earl peering out. He threw his hands out in disgust. "Okay, so nobody respects a closed door here."

Caught in the act, Uncle Earl and I joined Sheriff Nicholls and Deputy Ramirez near the front counter.

"Do you think he pulled a runner?" Uncle Earl asked.

"If he heard what Bet said and decided things could easily go against him, he may have decided to cut his losses."

"Does that mean he's given me up?" I asked. "I can stay here with Uncle Earl?"

"I don't have anything in writing to that effect, so it's not clear-cut. Why don't you wait in the kitchen where it's a little more comfortable and let me do some paperwork? I want to put out a bulletin that he's a person of interest."

Fae had been listening in, and now she stood and approached the other side of the counter. "If Earl and Bet are going to be here a while, do you mind if I run home and grab something for them to eat?"

"Go ahead, no reason for you to be here," the sheriff grumbled.

"I'm here for Bet and Earl, our friends," she said gently.

The words seemed to deflate the sheriff's annoyance. "So you are. Bringing some food while we sort things out is a good idea, thank you."

"Earl, can I have the car keys? I can be there and back quicker."

Uncle Earl fished the keys out of his pocket and handed them over. I hadn't even had a chance to feel relieved this wasn't about Penny. I wasn't sure whether we should keep our plans in place—would I be joining Penny on the run, after all? Fae seemed to be waiting for some kind of signal, too.

"Sheriff, did you hear from the county about Penny?" I asked.

"What?" He scratched his head. "Oh, yes, they say no further action is necessary. I was going to call you this afternoon, and then this thing with Mr. Carter showing up derailed me. Mr. Bindle knows if he continues to harass you and your dog, he'll be facing charges."

"I'll see you back here in half an hour then," Fae said.

While she was gone, the sheriff got busy with issuing a bulletin with Felix's description. Uncle Earl and I played cards in the kitchen until the sheriff came looking for me again.

"Bet, would you mind giving me the details of Felix's club, and anywhere else he might try to hide out?"

The list of my father's questionable businesses was longer than the sheriff expected, and after we finished, he stared at it in consternation. "I thought I was an excellent judge of character, but I had no idea the man was involved in things like this. I might need to get the feds involved, since it sounds like he's working across state lines. He's a regular crime boss."

Uncle Earl huffed. "I can attest to that. When I tried to see Lizabet before Bet was born, he had some of his cronies beat me up and warn me not to come back. My shoulder still aches from where they broke my collarbone."

Sheriff Nicholls shook his head. "Bet, I'm sorry I didn't listen when you were trying to communicate how afraid of him you were. It was very brave of you to keep speaking up until I heard you."

I nodded to acknowledge his apology, but I didn't go so as far as to tell him it was okay. "So, what now?" I asked. "Can he try to take me to Sacramento with him?"

"Legally, he's established he's your father. But that doesn't do a bit of good if he's abandoned you now, or if he's going to be facing charges for this list of crimes. By tonight, police and sheriff departments in the area will be on the lookout for him. I have every faith they'll catch him, and I wouldn't be surprised if his businesses get visited by some formidable lawmen."

"So Bet can stay with me?" Uncle Earl asked, and this time it was him squeezing my hand too hard. I squeezed his right back.

"You're her closest living relative, so yes. Congratulations, you're a parent. We'll need to fill out some paperwork, but we can do it after Bet has rested. You're free to go home."

Uncle Earl opened the door to leave, but I didn't follow him right away.

"I'm worried about Felix," I said. "I think it might have been him who was hanging around near the house the other day. Nap and Josie may have surprised him once, but he'll come better prepared next time."

The sheriff bit his lip as he thought about what I said. "You may be right. I'll send a deputy in a patrol car to sit outside your place. Once I have more news on his whereabouts, I'll be sure to call."

"Is that enough to keep us safe?" I asked. I genuinely didn't know when it came to Felix and something he wanted. "He's capable of hurting a deputy. I wouldn't send Deputy Ramirez."

The sheriff's lips twitched. "I'll send a more experienced deputy. Other than a patrol car outside your house, I'm not sure what we can offer. I can call the feds and see if they can put you in protective custody. A safehouse may not be as luxurious or as lax as your time in my cell, though."

I did not want to get back in that cell, so I looked to Uncle Earl for his opinion. "Sheriff, do you mind if Bet and I use your office for a private talk?" he asked.

"Go ahead. I still need to make some calls."

Once Uncle Earl and I were in Sheriff Nicholl's office, we made sure the door fully shut before speaking.

"Just say the word, and we can pick up the dogs and be out of town before dark," Uncle Earl said.

I wasn't expecting that. "Isn't your whole life here in Amberfields, though? You'd give it all up for me?"

"Of course I would. I'm not going to make the same mistake I did before, when I left you with him and Lizabet. Fae told you we were already set up to get Penny to safety, didn't she? I was already packing our things, too. And that was even before we knew Felix was in the mix."

I let the warmth of his words spread through me before I answered. "Yes, Fae told me her friends could help me and Penny, but she didn't say anything about you coming, too. I wasn't sure if going away meant I'd never see you again."

He grinned. "Not a chance. You're stuck with me. What do you want to do? Start over somewhere else, or stay here? You decide."

I sank into a chair while I thought. Every instinct told me to run, but I had already tried it and my stepfather—my father—had found me anyway. Was it because I had stuck around too long? If I hadn't, I wouldn't have Uncle Earl and the Woods on my side. Uncle Earl also had people who looked out for him here in Amberfields. Would my chances really be any better in a strange town, with strangers who might not care about us? Would I be looking over my shoulder for as long as Felix was free?

That was no way to live, and I had had enough of Felix ruling my life, even from afar. I wanted to have exciting dreams, and to run around with Georgie and the dogs, and to prank Uncle Earl, and...I just wanted.

"I'm staying." I threw my arms around Uncle Earl and knew I had made the right decision.

When Fae pulled the car up to the curb in front of the station, with Georgie, Cami, and Penny in the back seat, I waved. "Hey, Mildred! Can we have a ride home?"

Georgie stared at me in astonishment before turning it into a glare. "You're more of a Mildred than I am! I'm going to call you that from now on."

Of course, Cami picked up on how much Georgie objected to the name Mildred and chanted it all the way home to our house. Penny barked along like a metronome, making me laugh until I cried.

Epilogue

October 1953
Amberfields

I paused in my work to wipe my sleeve across my eyes as the bleach fumes made them water. The mop made a steady slapping sound as I swabbed the far corners of the last kennel for today, and the overgrown puppy in the pen next door tried to catch the mop strings as they went by.

I laughed at him and put on a stern tone as I said, "You don't want that. You wouldn't like the taste. Although, you did manage to pull a hose in there yesterday and chew that up, so you're not exactly a food critic."

Hammie, a Great Dane here to get his ears cropped, grinned at me like he remembered the destroyed hose with pride. I'd spent some time yesterday assembling all the pieces of it to make sure he hadn't swallowed any, so I didn't think it was nearly as funny as he did. Nonetheless, I stopped to ruffle Hammie's soft, floppy ears one more time before they transformed into stiff towers of tape later to-day. I didn't agree with cropping ears, but then this wasn't my dog. Decisions like this were the only thing I didn't like about working for Doc Marsh.

After one last pat on the puppy's head, I rinsed the mop and stowed it in the supply closet. I pulled off my smock, leaving me in my jeans and a checked shirt. Since school started, I'd switched to afternoon shifts instead of cleaning in the mornings, so at least I didn't have to sit at my desk with slobber (or worse) on my shoes. With a quick comb of my hair, I was ready to head out.

As I passed Doc Marsh's office, he called, "Are you leaving, Bet? Don't forget to grab some of those frames on the way out so you can switch out the photos."

"I remember," I said. "There's a dog show this weekend in Placerville, so I should come home with new shots."

He nodded and went back to his paperwork, leaving me to continue to the lobby. Penny heard the opening door and popped her head up from behind the front desk, ready to leave, too.

"See you later, girls," the receptionist said with a kiss for Penny.

Penny's nose poked me on the back of the knee as I paused at the wall of picture frames. After I'd started working here, Doc Marsh had asked me to create a rotating gallery of my photos in the lobby. Some people even came in to look at them when they didn't have an appointment. In pride of place was the one of Cami, the dogs, and Georgie, with its second-place ribbon from the 1953 Yuba County Fair. The picture of Georgie and the fox carving had won first place, and I kept it at home.

With my arms full of frames, it was a good thing that Penny would stick by me so I could let her leash drag. It was only a few doors down to the camera shop to drop off the load to deal with later, and then I picked up Penny's leash and we ran to the Woods's yellow house. We went there every day after school since Felix was still on the loose, and then we went home with Uncle Earl when he got off work.

The smell of apples and cinnamon hit us as soon as we came through the front gate, so Fae must have baked a pie or canned some applesauce.

"Mildred, we're here!" I hollered, and waited for Georgie's squawk of indignation at the name.

Instead, Fae poked her head out of the kitchen and said, "We're in here, Bet. We have something to tell you."

Uncle Earl was at the table, too, with a serious-looking Georgie. My smile fell away, and I asked, "Do I need to be sitting down for this? It feels like déjà vu of when the sheriff sent for me before."

"You might wanna sit," Uncle Earl said as he pulled out the chair next to him. "It's a bad news, good news, kind of situation."

"Lay it on me." Penny put her paws on my lap once I sat down, as if she sensed how worried I was.

"Sheriff Nicholls called me to say he just got back from Las Vegas. The Vegas police called him in response to the bulletin he put out on Felix."

"So, they found my father. Hopefully, he's locked up in Nevada."

"Actually, he's in the morgue. Sheriff Nicholls went to Vegas to identify the body, so you wouldn't have to."

I blinked as I absorbed this. "So, the bad news is that Felix is dead, and the good news is that Felix is dead?"

"Yes, because it means I can adopt you officially," Uncle Earl said, but he looked worried about how flat my voice sounded.

"Plus, now you don't have to worry about him coming after you anymore," Georgie put in.

"No, it's good news all around," I said with a whoop that startled Penny. "I'm glad that part of my life is over. What happened to him?"

"He tried to cheat at the wrong card game, apparently. The other players didn't take too kindly to it. Fortunately, they left his face alone so he could be identified."

I shuddered, and I might even possibly have some tears later for how Felix never had to explain himself in court. Never had to face up to how he'd tried to destroy my spirit. But he didn't succeed, and I had better people in my life now. Friends and family who I could count on, and who only expected good things from me.

I gave a grateful sigh and asked, "Georgie, do you want to be my assistant again at the dog show this weekend? Or did you already sign up for a craft fair?"

The others took their cue from me and soon we were all fork-deep in slabs of apple pie, laughing and chattering. Making plans now that we knew for sure I could stay.

ABOUT THE AUTHOR

Angelica R. Jackson, in keeping with her scattered Gemini nature, has published articles on gardening, natural history, web design, travel, hiking, and local history. Other interests include pets, reading, green living, and cooking for food allergies (the latter not necessarily by choice, but she's come to terms with it).

She's also been involved with capturing the restoration efforts for Preston Castle (formerly the Preston School of Industry) in photographs and can sometimes be found haunting its hallways.

She shares a home in California's Gold Country with a husband, a Miniature Pinscher/Nibblonian mix, and far too many books (if that's even possible). She is the author of the award-winning Faerie Crossed young adult urban fantasy series, and her photos are collected in Capturing The Castle: Images of Preston Castle (2006-2016).

ACKNOWLEDGEMENTS

Many thanks to my critique group, The Gold Spinners: Nancy Herman, Erika Mailman, Betty Sederquist, and Christina Mercer. We are each other's anchors through everything life throws at us.

Kelley York of Sleepy Fox Studio once again gathered my somewhat-incoherent directions into a stunning book cover. Thanks for making Bet and Penny look so good.

My editor this time around was M.L. Hamilton of Black Cat Editing, and she provided excellent notes in a very tight timeframe, so extra thanks go to her.

And it's cliché to say, "last but not least," but it is so appropriate that I'm using it anyway:

Last but not least, thanks to Tim for showing me what real love is like.